I0784435

Richard R. Becker

50 STATES

A collection of short short stories

Copywrite, Ink.

For Griffin and Jenna
Write your own stories.

50 STATES

Richard R. Becker

BROKEN PEOPLE

Idaho 2003

When Jonathan Cole accidentally ran over his six-year-old boy with the carbine harvester, it was the worst day of his life — one that was quickly followed by a procession of runners-up for this honor in rapid succession.

There was the divorce. There was the custody battle over their three surviving girls. There was the loss of 980 acres, two-thirds of his original farm, to buy out what the court decreed to his wife as alimony. There were the hundreds of days he would come home to an empty house, each of them part of his penance to reflect on all that he lost.

The most difficult days were in November after all the winter wheat was planted. Once sown, the crop would go through cold acclimation to survive winter and mature for a spring harvest. This year, planting had gotten off to a late start because of an unexpected rainy season, one that Jonathan knew would likely delay harvesting next year. But as long as frost didn't plague the fields before the plants flowered, the yield and head quality wouldn't be much different from the year before.

Knowing that, Jonathan had started to think of the late planting as a blessing. It meant fewer idle days looking for things to do in an effort to ward off what had become a seasonal depression.

Even today, he found himself looking for something to do. So he spent a good portion of it walking the property's fence line with a crowbar in hand and an assortment of tools hanging off a well-worn construction belt, stopping here and there to bang in a nail or tighten an unraveling piece of wire.

With the better part of the day behind him, he walked toward the house. There was still an hour before dinner — he had concocted a slow-cook chicken chili recipe before leaving early in the day — so Jonathan stopped at the front porch to look back upon the low hanging sun. It wouldn't be long before the clouds would flush and turn crimson, a sight he had never grown tired of when he had someone to share it with.

Life was different when he had a family. His wife always referred to him as her rock, strong and determined. His four children loved him because he was funny, often bursting through the door singing the Mighty Mouse song that he was home to save the day. He considered himself lucky, not at all overwhelmed by the kind of large debts that many family farms had faced over the years, some of them succumbing to pressure and selling out to larger operations. Or worse, as in the case of one Jacob Peters, added to an uptick in farmer suicides over four decades.

Despite his personal misfortune, Jonathan wasn't susceptible to either. While his farm was no longer profitable enough to buy back the acres he lost, he couldn't see himself doing anything different. As for suicide, it wasn't viable as a Christian, even if he had stopped going to church to avoid the quiet discomfort that seemed to follow him like a personal storm with queries of how he was getting along or if he wanted to talk. He would never burden his girls or their future children with such a deeply haunted legacy.

So he suffered alone, as safe from prying eyes as possible. Nobody came around anymore, not after he sent the last funeral casserole dish back without even a spoonful taken from its ceramic and tinfoil-topped shell. Nobody came around anymore, except today.

What started as a small dust plume on the horizon quickly took shape as a silver Outback racing down the road that led to his front door. He walked down to meet the driver as she circled around and rolled down the window.

"You lost?" he asked, tilting his tall frame to get a better look.

"There's been an accident," she said, dismissing his question. "On the highway, about a mile from your property."

"Did you call it in?"

"No, I mean yes, but there's two people — a woman and a boy — trapped in the car," she said. "I don't think they can wait."

"All right," Jonathan said. "Let me get my keys, and I'll follow you back."

"I don't think there's any time to spare," she insisted. "I'll take you. Get in."

"All right," he said, opening the door and climbing into the passenger seat.

As soon as he was in, she stepped on the gas and headed toward the highway. The fasten safety belt warning rose up and broke the awkward silence of two strangers sitting side by side.

He reached back, pulled the seatbelt forward, and clicked it in place.

"It was terrible," she said. "The car that was hit was in front of me, slowing and pulling off along the side of the road. I slowed down with it until it made an abrupt U-turn, accelerating and expecting to be in the clear since I had slowed. They never saw the truck behind me, also gunning the gas to get around me. Then it struck them, sending the car spinning, glass shattering, and something — their dog — flying out the back window."

Jonathan noticed a faint column of black smoke rising up as they cleared the ridge that separated his farm from the highway. She had made the right decision to go for additional help after making the emergency call.

"After the collision, there was nothing. The whole world had gone unnaturally silent, no sound at all until I rolled down the window," she said, seeing her memory of the accident superimposed on the road in front of her. "I could hear her after that. The lady who was driving the white car started wailing in uneven, pain-fueled sobs."

"Any sign of a fire?" Jonathan asked, considering the smoke as they approached.

"Not when I left," she said with a sob. "Just broken people everywhere. Three in the car. Two in the truck. The man in the car crawled out of a window to check their dog, then he collapsed on the side of the road. The other two are trapped. The woman who was the passenger in the truck seemed to be in shock or something, and her husband, the driver, was unconscious. I didn't know what to do. I called, but you know how it is. It could be a half-hour out here."

"You did the right thing," he said. "I'll figure it."

As they pulled up, he assessed the scene. The truck rested at an awkward angle across the southbound lane, the cab hanging over the soft shoulder. The driver's side door was open; the older man who was driving still leaned into the airbag that had knocked him unconscious. The broken front grill foreshadowed the damage done to the smaller, sportier white sedan.

It had spun completely around, perhaps several times, and now sat askew in the northbound lane with a trail of debris in its wake. Everything was as she had said, frozen in a horrid aftermath of an accident, except for a growing trail of smoke rising up from somewhere toward the back of the vehicle. Freeing the two trapped in the car would have to be his priority.

"What's your name?"

"Jessica," she said.

"Nice to meet you, Jessica. See how the man is doing," Jonathan said, motioning to the car's passenger who was sitting quietly, drawing in slow, steady breaths and stroking the fur of the family's unmoving dog. "I'll work on getting them out."

He circled the car, checking the door handles. None of them worked, apparently damaged in the collision. Peering in at the woman through the passenger side window, he could see where he needed to start. Her left foot was pinned by the twisted interior. He would have to free her in order to reach the boy, who was struggling against the safety belt and angle of the encroaching driver's seat.

He moved over to the driver's door, pushing the crowbar into the seam that divided the door from the front quarter panel, hoping to release some of the pressure off her foot. As he did, she began to wail again, pleading with him to leave her alone and free her boy first, who was now complaining that the back seat was growing hotter. Ignoring her, he worked his way down one side and then inserted the crowbar in between the two doors, directly adjacent to the lock. He pushed, snapping the lock and giving himself just enough room nudge the door open one inch at a time.

When he managed a large enough opening, he climbed into the cab to reach her broken foot, removing the jagged edges of plastic and metal that pinned it. Once clear, he maneuvered her through the opening, and handed her off into the waiting arms of those who had stopped to lend more help and direct traffic.

When she was out, Jonathan climbed into the driver's seat and worked his way over the center console between the front seats. He was young, maybe six years old, red specks of blood sprinkled across his face where the glass shards had cut him. He was crying, pulling desperately at the frozen safety belt. The back seat was warm, smoke creeping into the cab.

Jonathan started to choke, the acrid smell of burning rubber, plastic, and engine oils rolling into the cab making his eyes water. The boy was crying, breathing in the toxic mixture, and then erupting into deep coughs.

"Hey, hush now," he said, seeing his own boy laying in the field and covered in blood, trapped in the blades of the carbine. "I'm going to get you out. You're going to be all right."

As he cut at the safety belt, he could feel the growing heat of the fire from somewhere behind the back window, a red glow and muffled crackling noise that bore down on him and the boy. Jonathan knew that the chance of an explosion was slim, but there would be a point when the gases and oils would ignite and fire would engulf the car.

He cut through the belt and pulled the kid toward him, but the boy only cried out. His knee was still stuck between the back seat and the driver's seat. Jonathan began working his knife on the back seat, patiently cutting the fabric in an attempt to create more space between to free the boy's leg and ignoring the growing heat inside the cab.

When a section of the seat fell away, he pulled at the boy's leg at the knee and slid out, giving him just enough room to pick up the kid, twist around, and pass him out the door. Once the boy was clear, Jonathan had to work himself out of the cab, climbing out head-first as someone yelled at him to get out. As he pushed past the door, kicking to free his foot from the wreckage, the back seat erupted with flames.

He stumbled away from the heat, cradling his left arm. It had been burned while freeing the boy. Even before he heard the sirens in the distance, Jessica had come to him with something cold to drape over his arm.

"You're a hero." She smiled at him.

"I'm no hero," he said. "I'm as broken as the rest of them."

"We're all broken, Jonathan," she said. "But some of us push past the pain of it so others don't have to feel our hurt."

Her words left him speechless, his thoughts slipping away toward the boy he couldn't save — his own son all those years ago. These people would never have to know the pain of losing a son like he had.

Hours later, after Jonathan was treated for second-degree burns and Jessica had given her statements, she asked him to join her for a drink before taking him home. Surprising himself, Jonathan agreed, allowing the pain of his past to burn away with the remnants of the white sedan even if his grief for having lost a son would never fade away. He agreed because of the way she smiled at him. It was the first one given to him freely in more than five years.

THE LAKE HOUSE

Connecticut 2005

The light was reflecting off the water and into the lake house while he chopped scallions on the kitchen counter. They were having a light lunch, mussels and fettuccine.

His grandmother, Stella, was boiling the mussels, frowning at the few that wouldn't open. She looked good for her age. Her blonde hair was catching the light of the sun. She dyed it but wore it in a way that some might guess it was natural.

"I hate it when they don't open," she said. "It seems like such a waste."

"Sometimes they're fine," he said. "Don't throw them out until we check them."

"No? I always thought it meant they were dead."

He smiled, first at her, and then out the window at his wife and daughter. They were playing hide-and-seek among the shrubs and trees that framed the clearing down to the water. It was a perfect summer day, with just enough of a breeze to cool the air.

"How's the family?" she asked, following his eye line while moving from the mussels to the pasta.

"Look at them." He nodded in their direction.

"That's not what I meant, exactly," she said. "Are things better?"

"I forgave her if that's what you mean," he said. "What else can I do?"

She nodded and fished out a strand of fettuccine, breaking a tiny piece off the end.

"Here, taste this and tell me if it's done," she said and popped it into his mouth.

"Wow," he laughed. "You knew that wasn't done."

"Kind of like I know you aren't done making amends," she said.

His smile fell away and he pressed his lips together. He didn't say anything, deciding to scrape the scallions into a bowl instead.

"Do you see the lawn chairs out there?" she surrendered.

"The ones with the gray stain?" he said. "Beautiful. Where did you find them?"

She beamed.

"I didn't find them. I refinished them."

"I'm impressed," he said, recovering his composure with a change of subject.

"It was quite a process," she said. "I didn't know the first thing about refinishing furniture, but now I know quite a bit."

"Really?"

"You have to remove all old damage and finish first," she continued. "And then you have to care for whatever you find underneath with mineral spirits and maybe a little sandpaper."

"Did it take a long time?" he asked.

"Of course it did. I wanted to get it right," she said. "Then I applied the stain and some clear coat to help protect it from any future problems. You know, the stuff that put it in such a miserable condition to begin with."

He checked the mussels that she set aside and tossed those that looked good together with the pasta. They would eat it alongside some greens the four of them had picked from the garden earlier that morning — a first-time experience for his daughter.

"There is one thing to remember when you refinish lawn furniture," she said, putting a finger to her lips as his wife and daughter made their way to the French doors. "Just because it will never be the same as when it is new, doesn't mean you can't make it better with a little elbow grease and tender loving care."

"Hey," his wife said as they came in through the door. "What are you two talking about?"

Their daughter ran up and hugged his grandmother before she could answer. Maddy was holding a collection of daisies in her hands. Stella could tell they needed immediate attention and water.

"These are just beautiful," she said. "Thank you so much, dear."

"You're welcome," said Maddy. "Are we going to eat what we picked from the garden?"

"Absolutely," she said.

"Stella was just telling me how she salvaged that furniture outside," he said, lifting the two bowls off their work area and setting them down gently on a counter-high kitchen table. "And we're done."

"Oh, good for you, Stella," she said.

"Yes, I was just about to tell him the most important part," Stella said, placing her hands on his daughter's shoulders and guiding her to the table. "I wanted to save both chairs with the side table. But if that wasn't possible, I would have settled for one chair and the side table."

As she helped Maddy into the chair, he suddenly understood. She may have refinished the furniture, but she wasn't talking about it right now.

"You did a great job," his wife agreed. "But weren't you afraid it wouldn't turn out?"

"Don't be silly," she laughed. "You can always find new furniture."

After lunch, they spent the rest of the afternoon together, with Maddy showing him a secret path along the breakwater and through the reeds. They were happy. So much so, he couldn't remember a time they had been happier together. It starts with sandpaper, he thought. Then you go with the grain, or you don't.

DEAD ENDS

Utah 1992

She hung the cigarette he had lit for her out the window of the Pontiac Sunbird, the car handling the desert highway nicely at 65 mph. Steady as she goes. Liam lit his own, sitting back in the seat and putting a foot up on the dash.

The air blowing into the cabin was hot, but neither of them cared. The ride was smooth, and the drive back to St. George was long enough that his head started drifting along with Pink Floyd's "Momentary Lapse of Reason." Her car always surprised him on the open road.

His only mental reference to Pontiac was the dark blue Grand Prix his grandfather drove in the '70s, back when everybody drove them until GM hurt the brand in the '80s. His parents had been more practical, favoring compact cars like a Vega, an Omni, and even a Gremlin. He couldn't imagine rumbling through the desert in any of those.

Somehow the Sunbird had saved some of the brand's stigma, and he could see why every time they took a trip. GM had made the car for road trips, and he and Evelyn had taken plenty together, long hours exploring the American west, which was not what her dad had in mind when he bought it seven years ago as a college commuter.

"You're riding that centerline an awful lot, Ev," he said. "Want me to drive?"

"No, I'm fine," Evelyn lied. "It's the music. Floyd makes me sleepy."

"Ah, what do you want then?" he asked. "Sing-alongs with Paula Abdul — Opposites Attract. You be the damsel, and I'll be the skat cat?"

"Very funny," she laughed. "Maybe we should just get off the highway for a while."

He put his foot down and untucked the map he had inserted between his seat and the center console. They hadn't seen anything for several miles, so he was sure there had to be a turnoff, side road, or easement access somewhere up ahead. A break would do them both some good.

"What's that ahead?" she asked, pushing the map down so he could see.

"I don't know," he said, flipping it back up. "It's not on the map."

"Awesome," she said, tossing the cigarette out the window. "Let's take it!"

Her declaration gave him a feeling of déjà vu, which he mostly attributed to a flashback from last year when they had cut across Death Valley along poorly marked back roads better left forgotten. The thought of it still made him queasy, that chronic nag every time they crested a summit not knowing if the road would fall off the edge of a cliff. Or the contrast, that strange and oppressive loneliness that came upon him in the middle of an expansive valley when the only lifeline to civilization was the thin, well-worn tread on the tires.

The back end of the Sunbird fishtailed as it hit gravel, throwing up a cloud of dust and bringing him back to the present. She laughed as she took the turn too fast and he thrust the open map down into his lap, ripping it along the centerfold. Then she steered in the direction of the slide, slowed slightly, and sped up again.

The highway fell behind them, like a ship losing sight of its harbor while heading out to sea, an ocean of deep beige with tufts of green sage in place of white caps. The road rolled along, gravel giving way to two ruts as they approached the opening of a distant fence line. There was no gate, only a cattle grate and the remnant of what was probably a no trespassing sign.

"What do you think?" he asked.

"I think it's an adventure," she said.

He asked her if she still thought so when they passed another sign a mile in, and then again when they passed a newer sign about a half-mile beyond that one. It wasn't until they came upon an old tire with the words "Keep Out" written in orange fluorescent paint that she seemed slightly deterred. Just beyond the tire, about three hundred yards ahead, a newer gate with a larger yellow sign sat before them — type too small to make out. It was flanked by a smaller black, red, and white sign that screamed DANGER.

"What do you think it says?" she asked after stopping the car near the tire.

"I can't read it clearly," he said. "But I know what this one says."

He was looking out the passenger-side window at a smaller sign below the tire.

"Trespassers will be shot," he said flatly.

"Think we should turn around?"

"Yeah," he said.

"I saw a place we can stop a ways back," she said.

She backed up the Sunbird and haphazardly negotiated the turn on the narrow road, clipping the shoulder and adjusting the car forward and backward and forward again. Liam imagined the car slipping on the soft sand and into the wash on the left. It would be almost impossible for him to push the vehicle out on his own, prompting him to count how many fingers on the map he would have to walk to find help if something like that happened.

"Maybe we should head back to the highway."

She looked at him and frowned. Then she smiled again, brushing off his reservation.

"You're funny," Evelyn said.

"It's a feeling," he said. "There's no welcome mat out around here."

"Since when has that stopped us?" she asked. "Come on. I'll make it worth your while."

She had him there. They had taken road trips all over the west, finding everything from petroglyphs to ghost towns. He never felt entirely comfortable with their explorations, especially those that felt less like eco-escapism and more like an adrenaline fix while staring down into the inky blackness of a mine shaft that could swallow up a small bus.

But that was part of the package, wasn't it? Evelyn was the spontaneous counterpoint to his structured routine. She did what she wanted. He followed along, knowing that risk-aversion threatened to hold him back more than anything she could dream up.

So that's what they did. They pulled over to the shoulder of the road and walked down into the wash, where the grayish-green sage had burst into a ribbon of deeper green brush with tiny yellow flowers. She squealed as she slid down the embankment, encouraging him to hurry as she discovered a knot of shade trees that they could rest under and a small stream that still remained from the previous week's downpours.

"Isn't it beautiful?" she said. "Lay the blanket down there."

He did as she told him, relaxing slightly as the warmth of the sun touched his shoulders. They wouldn't be there long — just long enough to shake off the feeling of having sat in a car for too long. He laid down on the blanket, put his head back, and crossed his feet. She joined him, folding into him rather than lying down next to him.

"Know what I want?" she teased and bit his lip.

"I have an idea," he said, putting his hand on her waist, just above her hip, as she sat up on him.

All his anxieties floated away with the wisps of white clouds that framed her face. They traded places as she tugged his shirt out of his pants. She welcomed his weight as she adjusted her body to the soft sediment of the embankment. They were alone.

Except they weren't. Somewhere between panting kisses, Evelyn said "ouch" and pushed him off her.

"Am I hurting you?" he asked, rolling aside.

"No, something bit me," she said. "Ouch ... ouch."

"What?" he asked, trying to understand.

"Yes, ouch," she said, looking down. "These ants. They're everywhere."

He helped her up as she swatted her legs, making a pat-pat-pat sound as she did. Her pats were joined by a slow clap, two men standing above them. Rugged silhouettes on the ridge.

Liam thought they were ranch hands at first, with the taller of the two men wearing a cowboy hat. But then he didn't feel so sure. Even with the sun behind them, he could make out a mix of denim jeans and military cammies, tan and brown. One held a rifle, but it looked lighter than the M16s he had seen on television. Survivalists?

"What do we have here?" asked the man with the hat.

"Trespassers," answered the other.

"Look, it's okay," Evelyn offered, taking a step forward despite Liam placing a hand on her shoulder. "We didn't know. We can go."

"It was marked." He came at her. "Two, three, four times. We even watched you circle back after coming up on the gate."

"She's right. We're sorry," Liam said. "We'll get out of here."

"It's not so simple, son," he said. "It's not so simple."

"What?"

"She was bit, right?" he asked. "Were you bit, too?"

"No," he said, frowning.

"Well, we'll have to test you all the same," he said. "You wandered into the wrong restricted area. Come on up, and we'll square this away."

As he moved away from the ridge, Evelyn gave Liam a look of disapproval. She motioned behind them, suggesting they make a run. Liam grimaced, shaking his head.

She turned to run on her own, but Liam grabbed her wrist.

This wasn't the time or place for her risk-taking nature, he thought. It was all just some sort of misunderstanding. Follow the rules, and they'll let us go.

Evelyn relaxed her hand and then yanked, a trick she learned when she was five years old and disinterested in being led around by her nanny. She took two steps away from him, abandoning him, until the man called out, prodding them to climb up again.

They acquiesced like two school children passing notes in class and began to work their way back up the embankment with Liam retrieving the blanket. Evelyn was sore at him, sulking.

The second man had prepared two tests on the back of a military-styled Jeep, two rectangular strips and syringes. Liam stepped up, hoping his action would persuade Evelyn to follow along for a change, but she was looking at the needle and shaking her head.

It was clear the man had done it before. The needle prick was quick, clean, and relatively painless. There was a tiny pinch to draw some blood, which was quickly placed in a small cup on one end of the rectangle. The man looked at it with interest.

"He's clear," the man said before turning to Evelyn with a smile. "Step on up, darling."

Evelyn hesitated, looking at Liam for help. He nodded.

"I don't think I can do this," she said.

"You don't have a choice," said the man with the hat, pushing her forward. "Come on, already."

"Hey, you don't have to do that," Liam said.

"Sit down, sheeple," the man said, nudging her forward while turning to Liam.

"Hey," he protested, searching. "You haven't even shown us any identification."

The man smiled and reached for his back pocket. But rather than producing a wallet, he reached for his sidearm when it came back around. Liam found himself staring into the barrel of a Beretta, and sat down alongside the Jeep.

"Game time is over," he said. "You're one test away, so let's go. It's getting late."

Evelyn flinched when the second man administered the test, a small drop of blood placed in the receptacle. The man looked at it with the same scrutinizing interest and then shook his head.

"What?" she said.

"Positive," he said.

"What do you mean positive?" she asked, her face distorted. "What does that mean?"

"I'm sorry," said the man with the cowboy hat before he shot her.

The sound of it jolted Liam into a standing position and he involuntarily reached out for her falling body. He was too far away, but the man blocked him all the same as Liam roared in anguish, his voice lost to the emptiness.

"You killed her!" he cried. "I can't believe you killed her!"

"She was already dead," he said. "And you, we don't know yet. You might be too."

"What are you talking about?"

"The pathogen spreads with close contact," he said. "So we'll take you back, quarantine you for 48 hours, and then try to sort this mess."

"None of this makes any sense," Liam said. "She wasn't sick."

"Oh, she was sick," he said. "Those ants down there? They're just like you two, taking chances and ignoring fences. Now get in the back of the Jeep before I restrain you."

Liam obliged slowly, still reeling from shock and asking himself how any of it could have happened. How could they have been so stupid in the first place? And why hadn't he let her run when they had the chance?

"Bill," the cowboy-hat man said to the other. "I'll keep an eye on him if you want to call it in. We need a contamination clean-up crew out here."

When the call was finished, the Jeep lurched off the shoulder and toward the gate that had originally convinced them to turn around. As the Jeep approached, Liam could see the sign now. It read: "No Trespassing by order of the Centers for Disease Control and Prevention. Controlled Area.

Biosecurity Measures Enforced," with the balance of the text outlining the code and authorizing the use of deadly force.

Liam stared at the words until they blurred with tears. He put his head down and squeezed his eyes shut. When he opened them again, they focused on the cowboy-hat man's holstered sidearm and the safety strap left undone.

THE BLUE DOOR

California 2019

She decided she didn't love him anymore just before opening the door. His suits. His smile. His smell.

They had all lost their luster over time. No, she didn't love him anymore — not in the way she did when they first kissed over highballs, laughing at how they were the only two of their friends to show up at the wrong bar; not in the way she did, looking down at him on bended knee, accepting the princess-cut diamond in their first apartment; not when she had opened her eyes in the hospital, waking up in a panic after a maintenance van sideswiped her white Camry on the way home from work.

The admission left her in a free fall. It was exhilarating and frightening to let all those moments go, to give up a safety net that would never catch her again, to watch the hundreds of snapshots they had used to build a house of cards come tumbling down. It will break her heart all over again to tell him, she knew. So with the turn of the key with a green plastic motel tag, she settled on tomorrow. Her lover had waited long enough.

THE BEST LIFE

Arkansas 2019

Mason sat in front of his computer as he sometimes did after his wife went to sleep. The house was always quiet now, an empty nest with two kids away at college.

He enjoyed the quiet, which was only interrupted in these late-night hours by the soft plunking of his fingers on the keyboard as he spent an hour or two looking up old flames on Facebook. He had been doing it for a few months now, and it always surprised him how easily he could chase down the digital breadcrumbs they left behind.

The first few he had looked up had been easy. The Internet was rife with high school and college alumni sites. He found everyone who attended his high school and neighboring ones. Everyone's yearbook was scanned and indexed. A membership made it even easier to pinpoint them, but Mason preferred to skip the subscription and perform a few creative word combinations across various search engines and social media sites.

He had to be creative because most women left their maiden names behind. When they did, he had to remember little things about them like what kind of interests they had, their favorite books or movies, or even where they were born. Then it was just a matter of plugging in different search terms.

When that didn't work, he sometimes searched for their more easily found friends and checked for connections.

He seldom contacted them once he found them. He was content to peek into their not-so-private lives and get a glimpse of what might have been. Did they look happy or sad? Genuine or fake? Heavy or fit? Did they have kids? What did their kids look like? What kind of guy did they marry? How big was their home? Did they take care of it? Could Mason compete? Did he even want to?

One of the old flames he was having the hardest time finding had also burned the brightest. What made the search so challenging was that he hadn't known Carol Cabrini from school or college. They only met one summer because of a part-time job he had picked up at a grocery chain to help pay for college. They didn't work at the same location. They built a rapport calling each other's respective stores to transfer products and produce when supplies ran low or surpluses couldn't be managed.

"Hey, Carol," he said.

"Hey, Mason," she said.

"Do you have those candy hearts leftover from Valentine's Day?" he asked.

"Necco hearts? You can't be serious." She giggled.

"Yeah, I'm looking for a specific one," he said. "It says 'Date Me.'"

"Oh my," she said, flushing on the other end of the phone. "So corny."

"You prefer something more subtle, I dunno, 'Hi Chick.'" He laughed. "Or 'Sup Cool.'"

"I think you're missing some letters. It's supposed to say 'Super Cool,'" she said. "Anyway, you're insane, I have an inventory, and you know I'm married."

"Yeah, he's not invited," Mason said. "Think about it and call me back. I don't care if you say no. I just want to hear your voice again."

He did. He had fallen for this girl based on nothing more than the sound of her voice and their daily banter. Sure, he knew she was attractive because everyone said so, but he always liked to think that her looks wouldn't have mattered anyway. At best, they were soulmates. At worst, she made working a Wednesday shift all the more enjoyable because there wasn't as much to do except call each other up.

It was harmless fun until it wasn't. Their phone romance took a serious turn when the two of them happened to attend a birthday party for the district manager. The pool was colder than he expected so he had decided to warm up in the Jacuzzi.

He didn't even know she was sitting across from him until one of the managers made introductions. He'll never forget her smile when they made the connection, nor would he forget how his heart leapt when all these weeks of anticipation ended with an unplanned confirmation. Yes, they shared a physical attraction. Then it leapt again, when she reached across the hot tub with her foot to find his.

The next few months felt as improbable then as finding her again now. Mason was sure the hiccup must be in his method. Maybe she had not only left her first husband and remarried, but left a second or third husband as well.

Then it struck him like a lightning bolt. He typed in her first name, her ex-husband's name, her son's name, and Little Rock. The return surprised him. The obituary was three results down. It belonged to her sixteen-year-old son. Robert Fischer died in a motorcycle accident, and he was survived by his father, Samuel Fischer, and his mother, Carol Crossman.

There wasn't much more, but he vacuumed up all the little bits he could find with bookmarks. There was her current residence with a picture. There was her second husband's Facebook page. They were divorced. There was her abandoned Facebook page with her last post being a weatherman meme that forecasted "Sunny today, Breakdown tomorrow." A handful of people had responded with hearts, laughing smiles, and a few comments that he glossed over — except for one.

"We're praying for you to get through this."

Get through what? The post was two years old, but the funeral for her son was almost two decades ago. He couldn't tell much more from the post. Some people take to social networks and some people do not. Her profile didn't even have a picture of herself. It was a Necco heart. "Miss You."

"Me?" he whispered.

He took a deep meditative breath and closed the window, but left a second window open. It was her second ex-husband's Facebook page. He was a construction worker. He had a daughter in college. Mason could tell Carol was the girl's mother. They looked so much alike. So he started scrolling down the page, timing his mouse to the continuous refresh. He knew it would be there.

It took some time, but he found it. There was a single picture of Carol at the counter of a breakfast nook. She was a phantom of her former self, which Mason always defined as her high school picture, one he kept hidden away in an old shoebox.

This version of her looked liked someone he never knew. She looked tired. Her eyes were heavy, the sparkle of her younger years lost. Her face was expressionless, drawn down from the smile he once knew into an unfamiliar but well-cut frown. Her skin had a yellowish cast. Time had not been kind.

"I'm so sorry," Mason said out loud again before he skipped.

Skipping, as he had come to call it, was something quite extraordinary. It was the reason he started looking up old girlfriends, employers, and places from the past.

The first time he skipped was a few days after he had regained consciousness from a head trauma. He had been shot, a bullet grazing the right side of his forehead.

While the bullet didn't do much damage, the force of it had knocked him off balance. He crashed into the convenience store's shelving and banged his head on the floor. Lights out.

During recovery, they had shown him the surveillance video. He was outside pumping gas when two men entered the local Food Mart about two blocks from his house, drawing guns as they crashed through the front doors. Adrenaline coursed through his body, seeing it a second time and then a third and a fourth and a dozen.

Mason left his car, the nozzle of the gas hose hanging from the filler inlet, and rushed into the store after them. He didn't know why he did it, but he did. He didn't have a gun or knife or weapon. He just had this crazy idea that his presence would discourage them. It didn't.

He entered the convenience store, startled the assailants, and the one closest to the door fired without warning. Lights out. From what he was told and later witnessed on the surveillance video playback, Mason didn't prevent the robbery but he did disrupt it. The clerk escaped to the back room, the shooter panicked, and the two criminals left with only half the money in the till.

Watching the video over and over, Mason couldn't help but ask himself what would have happened if he hadn't had entered the store. And that's when it happened for the first time. He skipped.

He could see it clearly. The entire experience played out again. Only this time, Mason didn't go into the store. He stood there, watched them rob the store, shoot the clerk, and remove their masks while exiting. When they saw him standing there, slack-jawed and stupid, the one who had been farthest away from the front door in real life proved to be the better shot. Lights out.

It wasn't a grazing shot. He was dead.

He winced. His eyes welled up. He wanted to scream but found he had no voice. He tried to tell himself it was his imagination or even a concussion-induced hallucination. But deep down, he knew it wasn't anything of the sort. It happened this way, somewhere, sometime — a glimpse of the road not taken — an alternative reality that left him dead and bloody with the gas pump trigger lock quietly disengaging on its own.

There were other skips too. There was the time Mason tackled the closest robber, only to be shot by the other. There was the time he tried to flee the station in his car but was struck by a tractor-trailer while turning onto the street. There was the time a bullet ripped through the gas hose and ignited the pump. He would never forget the heat of it or the sweet smell of gasoline before a sickening stench of charcoal.

In the days that followed, Mason discovered this strange ability wasn't limited to the gas station robbery. He could skip across hundreds of major decisions he had made, tracing down different experiences, some of them feeling suspiciously more real than his memory. In some of those instances, especially those that led to an untimely death, it felt as if his alternate self had somehow folded into this easier existence.

This is how he felt looking at Carol's picture on the computer screen. He felt the familiar tug when he closed his eyes. Instead of coming back to the apartment clubhouse and abruptly breaking everything off with him, she spent the night as they had originally planned. The two of them made love, folded up into each other's arms, and fell asleep.

What really happened that night was sharply painful. Instead of coming back to make love to him, she said it was the last time they would see each other. At first, she said she was breaking it off with him because she didn't want to hold him back from going to school. But when he wouldn't accept her self-sacrifice, she said she was breaking it off for her son. It was non-negotiable.

"Never call me again," she said.

Except now he knew better. Her decision was disastrous. Her son was dead.

Had she stayed, things would have ended better for her — everything he hoped and feared. Their future together seemed bright. There would have been tequila bellybutton shots late at night and lazy, late Sunday breakfasts. There would have been moonlit walks around the lake where he went to college. There would have been football games with her son hoisted upon his shoulders. There would have been a small apartment where whatever they lacked in money was made up with by laughter.

"So why not that life?" He peered deeper, following the thread further along.

But the further he went down this less-traveled road, the more he understood. His memories of this alternative thread began to grow darker, drifting into heated arguments, drunken fights, and drug addictions. It ended with his overdose. He was dead by 34. It ended with a car accident. He was dead by 28. It ended in a suicide. He was dead by 32. The choices he would have made had they stayed together hardly mattered. His candle would have been snuffed out early and his life left unfulfilled. Lights out.

Mason turned off the computer. He felt a familiar emptiness as every new dead end crashed into him, leaving only the sad, dull eyes of a woman he once loved haunting him in the darkness. He knew she was haunted.

"Miss you too," he said to no one.

He climbed into bed a few minutes later. His wife was sleeping on her side, facing away from him. He faced the same way, and tucked a pillow between his head and shoulder. This is it, he thought. The best life.

SHINE ON YOU CRAZY DIAMONDS

Michigan 1975

Other than the overgrown lawn, most passersby would say the old two-story home in the middle of Lafayette Street looked like any other uninhabited house that dotted Detroit's west side. But to anyone who lived in our neighborhood, the Diamond house was different. You could tell by the way people would pick up their pace as they passed it, averting their eyes from the house's dark and absent windows.

The house was called the Diamond house after its original owners, the Diamonds. The Diamonds had moved into the home during the early 1900s before Detroit annexed Delrey. Originally, the family was in favor of the annexation because it promised a boon for their furniture business. But then they were against it as progress proved to mean less profit for them and more chemical plants and factories along the river.

As years passed and their children became young adults, the Diamonds grew increasingly uneasy by how many of their neighbors moved away from the encroaching industrial area and into larger homes in newer developments. And then their children moved out. First, their daughter, Effie, married. Then their son, Harold, despite being the older of the two siblings, found his own place.

Harold still spent plenty of time at the house, though. Since he never married and their father had made him a partner in the family business, it was wasn't unusual for the young man to stay over on the weekends, especially in the months following an accident that took Effie's life.

As the story goes — or at least the three of us boys thought it went before we snuck into the derelict house ourselves — it was on one of those weekend visits when Harold shot his dad dead. From that day on, the consensus was the house was haunted, mostly confirmed by the steady procession of owners who never stayed in the wake of some personal tragedy or the scores of unexplained happenings when the property was empty.

It was strange. Growing up on the same street as the Diamond house was interesting but never enough to lure us inside. We mostly ignored the old house despite all the gossip and ghost stories. But all that changed in June of 1975 when Pink Floyd played their concept album *Wish You Were Here* at Olympia Stadium.

They opened the show with "Sheep" and "Dogs" before blowing our minds with "Shine On You Crazy Diamond (Parts I-V)" — an epic, otherworldly track that rolled along for more than thirteen minutes. Then they cut back to shorter songs off their setlist before returning to "(Parts VI-IX)," another twelve minutes. The band once said their bodies were there when they recorded it, but their minds and feelings were somewhere else.

Our minds and feelings were elsewhere too. We were outside the Diamond house, looking up and peering into the windows of a place that had haunted our childhoods.

I'm not sure if the idea belonged to me or my friend, Yuri, but we were in deep by the time the leaves were changing from deep greens to splendid reds, oranges, and yellows. The three of us were going to break into the Diamond house under the cover of Devil's Night and find out who, or what was shining inside.

We might not have waited four months to work up our nerve had we known breaking in would be the easy part. The back door was unlocked, and we walked right inside.

"Are you sure about this stuff, Yuri?" I asked him.

"Yes, Steven, no problem. I've read my grandmother's books," said Yuri. "It goes back a long way ... this idea that there are spaces between the sky and the earth, between good and evil. But don't call me Yuri anymore, okay. Call me Mike."

"That's so stupid," David chuckled. 'We've known you since third grade. Now you want us to call you Mike?"

"Yuri was my Russian-Polish name," Yuri said, matter-of-factly. "Mike will be my American name."

"The name doesn't matter. You're still a Polack to me," David mused. "Hey, hear about the Polish firing squad?"

"Come on, man," I said. "I don't even know why we brought you."

"Bummer for you," he said to me before finishing his joke. "They all stood in a circle!"

That's when Yuri drew a circle of his own. He drew it around us and asked us to settle in.

"This is a circle of protection," he said. "Whatever happens, we stay in the circle."

"Spooky," David beamed before seeing my expression. "All right. I'll behave."

We sat down, crossing our legs, and facing each other like the three points of a triangle. In the center of the circle, Yuri placed three candles on a circular mirror, lighting each with a match before waving it out and setting it aside. We joined hands.

"Okay, first, I want you all to relax and breathe slowly," Yuri told us. "And then I want you to stare at the flame until it feels like you can't keep your eyes open anymore."

I remember trying to look at the candles, but I was no good. My eyes kept drifting off into the darkness. I hadn't really taken any of it in before: the peeling wallpaper, the demonic graffiti, the water damage and debris on the wood floor. I was second-guessing the whole thing because the place just wasn't safe.

"I call on any spirits in this house with the whole of our existence," Yuri whispered. "I pronounce my intentions to thee, come forth and seek me, and equal we will be."

It all happened fast, or what I thought was fast. At first, David was chuckling through tightly closed lips. I was going to ask him if he hit something before we came over, even though we had all agreed not to, but he stopped before I did. We all stopped.

The flames that were casting a soft, flickering glow over the room sputtered and jumped. Then they dimmed, taking on the bluish hue of a smaller flame. The room felt darker. The smell of sulfur from the original match came back.

"Someone's here," Yuri said. "I can feel it."

I could feel it too. There was electricity working its way up my back. The hair on my neck was standing up. And then I could feel David squeezing my hand.

There was something moving beside me, a shine barely visible in the corner of my eye. The air felt heavy. The darkest shadows in the far corners of the room pressed in on us.

I nearly jumped a foot the first time I heard it. A thump. It came from the rooms above us — like someone dropping the corner of a bed or heavy dresser.

"I don't think we're alone," I blurted out. "And I don't mean spirits."

"What do you mean?" David said.

"We didn't check the house for squatters."

"I don't think it's squatters," Yuri offered.

Thump.

"Nope," exclaimed David, quickly standing up. "I'm not doing this. I'm out."

"What?"

"Spooks are one thing," David said. "A Michigan Manson family is another."

"There's no such thing," Yuri said.

"I don't care," he said, shaking his head and retreating toward the door.

"Oh, great," I told him. "You broke the circle."

In the second it took for David to cross it, something changed. Yuri's back jerked, and his head lolled on his shoulders. He exhaled and began muttering in a foreign language. Russian or Polish? I didn't know. I'd never heard it before. I've never heard it again.

"Yuri?" I called to him.

The third thump was unnerving because it sounded closer, at the top of the stairs. I looked over at David. He was standing by the door, torn between looking at the stairwell or keeping his eyes locked on Yuri.

"This is messed up," David said. "I'm sorry."

And that was it. David was gone, leaving me and Yuri sitting alone in the broken circle. The muttering had stopped, but it was replaced by an eerily unmoving trance as if Yuri was looking through me with only the white of his eyes. He wasn't breathing.

Another thump.

"Yuri, you have to wake up!" I screamed at him. "You've got to wake up!"

I didn't know what to do, so I slapped him. I hit him as hard as I could, and then he gasped for air as if he was breaking the surface of water. He was disoriented, but I didn't care. I pulled him to his feet and shouted that we had to go.

The thumps were coming down the stairs. They were slow but gaining momentum. I didn't know what it was because I was too busy dragging Yuri along. It wasn't until I was outside that I looked back. All I saw was the den aglow with a reddish-orange light as the abandoned candles tipped over. The house was on fire.

Yuri was looking at the house too, but not deep inside through the back door. He was looking up at the upstairs window. And for the first time since he insisted there weren't any squatters, he spoke.

"I think there's someone in there," he said.

"Yeah," I said. "Something that is none of our business."

"No, someone else, Steven," Yuri said. "Someone's in trouble."

And that was it. He didn't say anything else. He just turned from me and ran back into the house. We never saw him again. Nobody ever saw him again.

It took hours before the firefighters arrived. There had been dozens of fires across Detroit that night. And all I remember after the roof collapsed was sitting on the lawn with David watching the neighbors rally in an effort to keep the fire from jumping houses.

"What happens when they don't have a home?" David asked.

"They shine on," I said.

WET

Washington 1971

Dennis and Michelle sat on the soft gray sofa across from the television and watched a wave of red-shirted teachers lap against the sidewalk in front of their school, Washougal High. Most of them carried the red 'On Strike' signs deployed at the start of the strike, but homemade signs had been added to the mix in the second week.

How can you put students first if you put teachers last?
I love my kids.
We teach. We care. Be fair.

The sight of it had been a shock during the first few days. It seemed like every teacher and administrator in the world had gone on strike in southwest Washington, ending school for more than 78,000 students before the new semester could even start. But now everything was starting to feel like a new normal, seeing their most spirited teachers wear red instead of the orange-and-black school colors. Go Panthers!

"There's Ms. Hawkins again," Michelle said, pointing to the screen.

"Yeah, I wonder if she is going to cry this time," said Dennis.

"That's why they talk to her. She makes for good television," she said, lifting her leg off his lap and standing up. "Hey, I'm going to take a shower. You don't mind, do you?"

"No, go ahead."

"Okay," she said with a shrug. "If you want a drink or something, help yourself."

"Thanks," he said.

Dennis didn't know how most students were channeling their pent up excitement and anxiety for the first day of school that didn't happen, but he had found some unexpected solace with Michelle. Until a few days ago, she wasn't anybody he talked to or ever really noticed before. Now, he had shared the better part of this elongated summer break with her.

The happy accident started on the second day of the strike. Both of them had wandered over to Washougal High. Dennis went to show support for his English teacher, Mrs. Wright, and Michelle because she often gravitated toward crisis and confrontation — not as a participant but as a casual observer. Except this time, she ignited the conflict.

Dennis had brought Mrs. Wright and her coworkers some coffee and donuts on the morning of the second day and ended up staying longer than expected as his teacher told him why their twenty-five percent salary increase was justified. He learned about the pay gap between Washington teachers and other educated workers, the failings of overcrowded classrooms, and the cost of housing, which was very high in Washington.

Dennis didn't need to be convinced. He knew Mrs. Wright was one of the good ones. In a show of solidarity, he stayed on and picked up one of the red 'On Strike' signs as well. He wasn't the only one. While the community didn't want the schools to remain closed, they were supportive of teachers in general, if not the demands they made.

There were also those, however, who didn't support the demands, knowing somebody would have to pay for any salary increases, including fixed-income property owners. A handful of them had shown up to stage a counter-protest on the northwest corner opposite the school and about a half-block away from Dennis. His group wasn't part of the dispute, but he could see it escalating rapidly as Mr. Donohue, a civics teacher and self-proclaimed life-long liberal since the impeachment of "Tricky Dick" Richard Nixon, started taunting the pensioners and patriarchs on the other side of the street.

Dennis couldn't hear what they were saying from where he was standing, but their hand gestures and proximity conveyed the mounting tension. If somebody didn't do something soon, two septuagenarians were sure to meet each other in the street and relive some long-forgotten playground brawl.

The "somebody" turned out to be Michelle. Just before Donohue and another older gent wearing a Veteran of Foreign Wars hat could roll up their sleeves, Michelle materialized out of the counter-strike group with a Big Gulp. She grabbed Donohue by the belt buckle and dumped the entire contents of her Sierra Mist down his pants to the delight of the crowds on both sides.

"Cool off, already," Michelle told him.

As the sickly cold liquid spilled down his legs, Donohue immediately stiffened, his arms and legs drawn up toward his body. Dennis couldn't help but chuckle as he likened Donohue to a pencil, his pointed black shoes serving as the tip, and his receding hairline resembling an eraser. The entirety of it was comical until Donohue had regained just enough of his composure to grab Michelle's offending arm.

"Oh dear, is that Michelle Hendricks?" Mrs. Wright asked. "You're going to have to save her, Dennis."

Dennis didn't know why Mrs. Wright had asked him to step in on her behalf at that moment, but he didn't hesitate. He ran over and said the first thing that came to mind.

"I'll hold her for you, Mr. Donohue," he said. "Why don't you go get cleaned up."

Mr. Donohue shot Mrs. Wright a look for affirmation and released the girl. As soon as he turned away, Dennis and Michelle shuffled into the counter-strike ensemble and broke into a two-block run in case Donohue had noticed their departure.

"Can you believe that creep?" Michelle asked, panting and laughing.

"Yeah, what was all that about?" asked Dennis.

"You don't know?" Michelle grinned, brushing stay hairs behind her ears. "Donohue is a real creeper. He tried to rub Jenny Talbot's shoulders last year, play footsies with Maria Garza, and who knows how many feels he copped in line. 'Whoops, sorry, Ms. Wilson. Clumsy me, Ms. Miller. My pardon, Ms. Huang.'"

"Did he really touch Tina Huang?" Dennis smirked, seeing Michelle for the first time.

"I couldn't possibly make this up," she laughed. "The man has no shame. So thanks ... like, for saving me."

He let her gratitude hang in the air for a minute before acknowledging it. Then she mentioned how close she lived to the school and offered him a drink. He didn't have anything else to do so he accepted. They walked to her house and spent the afternoon talking about prose, poetry, and life at Washougal High. Before he knew it, that first afternoon drifted into spending every day with Michelle Hendricks, their separate social circles temporarily shrinking away to include only two people.

As it turned out, Michelle had much more in common with Dennis than he ever could have guessed. He only knew her as the girl who wore her hair unkempt, eyeliner heavy, clothes layered and lumpy, including an unneeded well-worn black leather jacket as soon as the temperature dipped below 60. She, like him, had a fondness for writing — one of Mrs. Wright's "other" favorite students from another class period. Michelle had even confided in her about Donohue's inappropriate actions, which they planned to address as soon as school resumed.

But Donohue, despite being the catalyst that brought them together, was long forgotten along with everyone else when Michelle slipped him a four-line poem. The sticky note, addressed to him, said what her trembling lips could not.

I wish there was a way
to make you see
just how much I want you
to make love to me

Dennis turned off the television and walked over to the fireplace decorated with family pictures. Growing up, Michelle looked like any other American girl — eyes wide with the wonder of it. It wasn't until sometime around middle school that something changed. As her father phased out of the pictures, so too did the upturned corners of her smile and sparkle in her eyes. She became the Michelle he never noticed at school, stained by sadness and bundled in clothes.

"I have something to share with you," Michelle said from behind him.

He didn't immediately turn around to hide a flush of embarrassment. He had been tracing the contours of Michelle's eighth-grade picture with his finger when she came in, so he carefully and purposefully placed it back on the mantle. When he did turn around, she wasn't standing at the back of the room anymore. She came up on his right and pulled a vinyl record from the cubby of an entertainment nook carved into the wall next to the fireplace.

"Just because I wear leather doesn't mean everything is rock or punk," she said. "Listen to the lyrics with me. These words are as much of me as anything I write."

He looked at her as she placed the record on an old-style turntable. Her hair was still damp, lightly dried but somehow tamed by the water at the same time. All of her usual layers were gone. She had traded in her jeans and baggy sweatshirts look for short shorts and a half-shirt cut high above her navel. She draped a towel over one shoulder. His heart raced.

Dennis didn't recognize the woman on the cover of the album, but he could see she was wet too. Her hair framed a face filled with longing and contemplation; her blue eyes fixed on whoever was looking at her. Her voice broke through the gentle instrumental.

He couldn't say her liked the vocals, but he understood the lyrics. She was singing about the wetness of rain and how it washes away the pains that everyone endures along the way in life. Then the singer drew comparisons to other things. Kisses and tears are wet, too — an invitation to start anew together.

As the warmth of the vinyl filled the room, Michelle had come over to him. He turned. They were facing each other; her head tilted back. He bent to kiss her and found eager lips waiting for him. They had kissed before, but never with such intimacy as they did right now.

They were both shaking as they embraced, gently pressing into each other. Then they were falling, searching for the couch to catch them. He laid back, and she was on top of him, giving Dennis his first glimpse. She wasn't wearing anything else but the clothes he could see, his hands racing alongside her body and under the shirt.

"Stop, just stop," she said, withdrawing.

He looked at her. She was shaking, no longer in anticipation but fear.

"Did I do something wrong?" he asked, reaching out for her hand.

"It's not you. It's me," she said, pulling her hands up into her chest and out of reach.

"I'm sorry," he said, not believing her. "If I was moving too fast..."

"It was my idea," she snapped at him. "All right? You didn't do anything."

He conceded — it was her idea. All of it. The lazy afternoon at her home while her parents were away. She had been erasing the space between them when they watched television, small touches evolving into curious cuddles. She was the one who changed into what she was wearing now, leaving little to the imagination and suggesting the prelude to an invitation — one he didn't act on but was led to take.

"Can I ask you something?" She broke the silence.

"Of course," he said.

"Why didn't you follow me into the shower?"

"What?"

"You could have, you know," she said. "I wanted you to."

"I was moving too slow?" He considered it, head spinning in confusion.

"Yes, no." She was working it out. "I don't know."

Dennis sat back and looked at her, wanting to hold her but unwilling to risk the unexpected divide between them. Her head was down and she was pouting. Her sudden sullenness, arms crossed and damp hair spilling down to hide her face, begged for space and comfort at the same time.

"After my father died, my uncle Robert stayed with us for awhile," she said suddenly, adding a heaviness to the room that wasn't there before. "He was here to, you know, help my mom sort things out. It worked, mostly. He stayed with us for over a month."

Dennis didn't say anything. He was too busy trying to process it, asking himself how he could have missed the fact that her father wasn't in the pictures for a reason.

"There was this one time," she continued. "The reality of never having my father in my life again became so overwhelming that I was losing it, like, really losing it. I started crying, not just crying, wailing hysterically, and Robert came to my rescue, wrapping me up into his arms and telling me I was going to be all right. I believed him, almost feeling like my dad was hugging me through him. Except he didn't stop there. He started kissing me. So I tried to pull away, but his arms only tightened around me. And then ... and then ... and then ..."

She trailed off, shuddering with the memory of it. Dennis could only look at her and consider the words. He didn't have any experience dealing with anything like this. It was a subject they talked about in school once, but no one he knew had ever gone through anything like it. They seemed like stories: modern fairy tales and boogie men.

"I'm so sorry," he finally said, not knowing what else to say.

"I'm the one who should be sorry," she said. "You showed me that I could trust again, and I ruined it by trying to give you what he took from me."

"Michelle," he said, trying to force a smile. "I mean, I'm attracted to you, but I was hoping we had something deeper."

"I know," she said. "I'm sorry. I still have a lot of things to work out. Just know how much these past few days meant to me, Dennis. I'll always love you."

She leaned over and they hugged, but without any of their earlier passion. In the blink of an eye, they had somehow resigned themselves to be friends, and for some reason, he knew this was all they would ever be, whether he wanted something more or not.

"Look, I should probably go home," he said. "Unless you need me to stay."

"No, I think I need some time alone."

"Okay," he said. "Hey, it sounds like the strike is almost over, so I'll see you at school?"

"Yeah, sure. At school."

Dennis said goodbye and headed home, trying to make sense of everything, even if nothing made sense. In the days that followed, the strike ended and classes resumed. He anxiously looked for Michelle in the classes and hallways for the first few days, until learning she was no longer enrolled at Washougal High and Mr. Donohue had been quietly dismissed.

When the weekend rolled around, Dennis rode his bike over to her house. There was nothing to greet him except a bright red for sale sign posted on the lawn.

PRIVATE CONVERSATIONS

Colorado 2020

The first time I heard voices, I was walking out of the barbershop with a brand new cut. The voices didn't say anything. They just laughed a little, a chorus of young girls whispering in the cool blue light of winter.

I turned around when I heard them and, seeing no one, I laughed at myself and picked up my step. I wanted to catch the next MallRide bus down to the bookstore, which was clear on the other end of what we call a mall in Denver.

If you've never been, you need to know that the 16th Street Mall isn't a mall at all, but a mile-and-a-quarter-long stretch of store-lined streets in downtown Denver. All the buses down 16th Street are free to ride, and sometimes I ride them all day when I don't have anything better to do, hopping out to take a selfie or two next to one of the art pieces tucked along the alleys.

It was too cold to do that today, especially after a haircut. You never want to wear a hat after a cut, or you'll be picking hair out of it for weeks. It's bad enough fishing little bits of damp hair out of your ears afterward. Hats make it all the worse, so I kept it in my coat pocket.

The bus wasn't packed because most people were still shopped out after Christmas, but I decided to stand anyway, grabbing onto one of those straps that hang down from the rails on either side and bracing myself for all the little starts and stops the driver would make from one end to the other.

"How are you going to tell her?" A voice said behind me.

"Shut up, she might hear you," another voice answered.

I turned around, expecting to see no one, but I was wrong. There were two girls sitting behind me, talking quietly and occasionally motioning toward an older woman across the aisle. The older woman was reading a book, apparently ignoring them in her role as a silent chaperone.

I'd seen it before. There were always two or more girls who spent the day shopping together with whichever of their parents drew the short straw. As the loser, it was their job to give the girls as much space as possible while shadowing them at the same time and protecting them from any weirdos.

Normally, I wouldn't think much about it, but the girl with the pink hat and powder blue puffer jacket was clearly agitated by the prodding of her friend. I felt especially bad for her because she would have been cute without the frown spreading across her face.

"But I thought you only did it one time with David," said the duller of the two.

"It only takes one time, stupid," she said.

When it registered what they were talking about, I turned my back to them again so they couldn't see my face flush and pretend not to hear them. It was awkward, listening to two girls who could have just as easily been playing with Barbie dolls talk about the pressures of having a baby. I was glad to see my stop was coming up because I couldn't take it anymore.

"Excuse me," I said to the woman. "Is that your daughter in the pink hat and blue puffer jacket?"

"Yes, yes it is," she said, obviously perplexed by my question.

"Well, I think you should know," I said, all of them looking at me now.

"Yes, know what?"

"This is my stop," I said, watching her withdraw from me as if I was some nut job. "And your daughter, she's pregnant. Have a nice day now."

I gave her a big grin and a two-finger salute before spinning around and exiting the bus. If there was any reaction after I left, I didn't hear it. The door of the bus went whoosh-whoosh, and I started laughing. It's not that I thought what I did was funny. It was more of a nervous tension-releasing laugh that rose and fell when I heard those giggling voices again.

I wouldn't say I liked the idea of someone watching me, so I put my head down and entered the bookstore to lose myself for a few hours. It was easy to do inside this indie-owned treasure chest. You could find any book imaginable walking around the moss-green carpet maze of bookshelves, leather-backed chairs, end tables, and reading nooks.

Scattered here and there among the books were staff recommendation cards. Most of their recommendations stuck to the books, but if you read deeply and carefully enough, you could pull out little bits of who they are and what's important to them.

Cindy was one of my favorites in prose and in person. She was a blonde twenty-something college student who was always looking for something purposeful and powerful. I'd read all of her recommendation cards, and one day I thought I might even take one of those books home to read.

"Be careful what you wish for," someone said from behind the metaphysics titles.

I raced around to the other side to see who it was, but no one was there. I backed out of the space and turned around, looking for a familiar face, but there wasn't any. Cindy wasn't working today, and most of the staff looked like newbies. I didn't know any of them very well.

I was a pretty good judge of when to leave the bookstore, usually before someone noticed me placing little bits of papers in the books I browsed, bookmarking for future visits. I used to dog ear the pages but decided it wasn't the right thing to do. Somebody might want to buy these books.

I headed up the stairs toward the main entrance and backed out into the cold air. My ears felt better. I was still scooping out stands of stray hair, but at least the wetness had worn off. I almost turned around to go back inside, and then I decided against it when I heard that voice again.

"I don't want it to end like this," it said to me.

I turned around, expecting to stand face to face with nothing, but I was wrong. A man was looking at me and mumbling something about ending a relationship. He had these thick eyebrows and wore a flannel jacket. He wasn't wearing a hat, which surprised me because he was starting to bald. He would become a future Friar Tuck cut contender unless, who knows, he opted for a hairpiece.

"Are you talking to me?" I said, embarrassed for him.

"I really can't live without you," he said. There was even a little tear in his eye.

"Hey man, I don't even know you," I said.

That's when I noticed he wasn't looking at me as much as he was looking through me. I could see the AirPods in his ears when he turned his head as I waved my hands in front of his face in a sort of "is anybody in there" gesture.

You would think that he would have moved on after that, but he didn't. He kept on with whomever he was talking to, becoming more and more upset as he paced back and forth at my bus stop. It terrified me, the idea that I would have to listen to him go on and on once we boarded the bus. It was too much.

He had an affair, or maybe it was the person he was talking to who had the affair. It was really hard to get all the details beyond the overwhelming fact that this guy was a suicide risk. He kept pacing back and forth, smiling when he grasped some beautiful memory he had shared with his girlfriend or wife, then breaking down again into sobs that he might never see her again, then spinning sideways in anger because a phone call wasn't the right way to end it all.

He was so engrossed in his conversation that he didn't seem to care that I was staring at him. He wouldn't lay off even as another couple started walking toward us. He ignored them like he was ignoring me, and then moved in front of me when he saw the bus coming. He wanted a better pick of seats.

"If that's the way you feel, I might as well step off in front of this bus," he said.

That's when I pushed him.

I didn't even push him all that hard, just enough so when his right foot slipped off the curb, the rest of his body sort of toppled over in front of the bus. The driver tried to stop, but the road was wet and he couldn't brake fast enough. A lady in the front row of the bus screamed loud enough that I could hear her, the bus driver grimaced as if he was about to take a punch, and there was a hollow thunk as the bus took the man a few more feet down 16th Street. I had never seen anything like it.

When the police arrived, I told them how I tried to stop him from jumping in front of the bus — a story that the couple corroborated because that's what it looked like from their angle. He talked about stepping in front of the bus, and I reached out to stop him but wasn't fast enough.

"Too bad," I said. "I could have been a hero."

Those whispers I heard earlier in the day thought so too. They kept on the whole time.

A BEAUTIFUL DAY

Pennsylvania 1990

When the paramedics loaded Ellen Williamson into the back of the ambulance, she was wearing her bright yellow terry cloth bathrobe and orange faux fur slippers — an ensemble her granddaughter Ellie Mae used to say made her look like Big Bird.

"Gran," Ellie would say. "When you twist curlers in your hair, you look just like Big Bird."

"You hold your tongue, Ellie Mae," Ellen would smile back. "Or you'll be talking to Oscar the Grouch for the rest of the day!"

Then the two of them would laugh and laugh, toss themselves onto the couch, and scan the channels for their favorite Sunday programs. They seldom surfed long, usually settling in on something like Sesame Street, The Electric Company, and especially Fred Rogers since he was a local boy. Besides, it was also fun to sing along: "It's a beautiful day in the neighborhood ... it's a beautiful day for a neighbor ..."

Except today wasn't such a beautiful day in their neighborhood. It came on as a hot flash that made Ellen feel sweaty enough to check the thermostat. She was used to this kind of feeling from time to time, but it didn't pass this time. It clung to her like a weight, pressing down on her chest.

"You okay, Gran?" Ellie Mae asked.

"I'm fine, little girl," she said. "Must have been something I ate this morning. I'll be fine. Just let me catch my breath."

"Sit down, Gran."

"Oh, honey." She gasped as she tried for the couch but crumbled into the chair because it was closer. "I think I need you to call 9-1-1. Can you do that for me? And maybe you should call your mother too."

By the time the ambulance arrived, the pressure on her chest had grown from a loadstone into an anvil. The pain from it radiated up into her shoulder, and down into her left arm.

"You're having a heart attack, Ms. Williamson," explained the taller of the two medics when they arrived.

"I'm having more than that, dear boy," said Ellen. "My time has come."

"Now, don't talk like that." He smiled. "Your granddaughter did real good calling us, and we got here early enough. And see this carrot top next to me? Nobody's a better driver."

"Is that so?" she said, looking up and over to the redhead with his thin freckled lips pressed together in a line.

"Just be glad he's driving." He winked, smiled again, and then whispered. "... his bedside manner isn't all that."

"And Ellie?" Ellen said, looking around but not seeing her granddaughter.

"Oh, your neighbor volunteered to stay until her mom makes it. There's nothing to worry about. My name is Roger, by the way."

"That's good," she considered. "Nice to meet you."

"Now, I'm going to spray something under your tongue," Roger said. "And your blood oxygen seems a little low, so we're going to give you some air."

"All right," she said. "It's going to be a beautiful day."

"Hey Rog, less nice-nice and more rock-n-roll," said his partner, shaking his head at the darkening sky. "I don't like her ST segment at all."

"We're ready," said Roger as he laid her back. "Let's go."

The doors shut, and Ellen could hear the young redhead climb in on the driver's side of the ambulance. Roger put a gentle hand on her shoulder. She knew it was meant to comfort her, telling her to lay back and relax.

"Don't forget to sound the siren so heaven knows I'm coming," she said.

"Now, don't talk like that," he reassured her.

"Why? You aren't a believer?"

"It's not that," he said. "I just think heaven might have to wait a few years for you."

She sighed, too tired to argue. The pressure was already leaving her, replaced by something else. She immediately felt lighter. It was almost as if giving up on some things had lightened her load, making it easier to climb that stairway. So instead of concentrating on the dull ache of pain that remained, Ellen tried to imagine everything she considered important.

Her collection of angels came first to mind. Those would go to Ellie Mae. They were one of the reasons her granddaughter always volunteered to dust during her Sunday visits. Ellen would pretend to doze on the couch, and Ellie Mae would gently lift, polish, admire, and set the figures back in their curio cabinet. Her favorite was a brunette angel with long wavy hair, eyebrows raised in admiration, lifting a tiny blue star into the sky as if she was offering it to heaven.

"Angels have wings because they take themselves lightly, little girl," she reminded Ellie Mae.

Her neighbor, Margaret, would no doubt look after her calico cat. It would be an easy adjustment. Calypso had already claimed her neighbor's back patio as a retreat, where there always seemed to be an accidental saucer of milk left out or a Greenies cat treat. In recent months, the joke of the neighborhood was that Margaret was secretly trying to lure Calypso away, as if borrowing Ellen's cat somehow required less responsibility than getting her own.

"Cats love without penalties," she whispered to Margaret. "It's about time you felt it too."

Her Dodge Omni would go to her son. He helped her pick it off the lot new just a few years back. Ellen could still remember laughing when her son told her what the "GLH" stood for. "Goes like hell," he smirked. He meant it too. It might have been modeled after a subcompact, but the Shelby version was fitted with a 175-hp 2.2 turbocharged four-cylinder.

"Goes like heaven," she corrected her son. "Goes like heaven."

"Pardon me?" asked Roger, bringing her back for a moment, but only a moment before she swept further away.

Her sister probably needed the car more than her son, but she also knew Esther shouldn't be driving around. It was a wonder how she managed to get a renewal every four years as it was, given it was common knowledge that she couldn't read the street signs anymore — even with prescription glasses. No, Esther would have to settle on all those family albums, piles of black and white photos and faces. There were so many that a few of them were now referred to as "folks with familiar family resemblances" since nobody knew their names.

"We're more than a collection of our memories, Esther. We're stewards of memories that came before us," said Ellen with a chuckle. "Try not to forget."

She had decided a long time ago that she and her late husband's wedding rings would not be given to anyone in the family. They would go to charity. She may have loved her husband once upon a time, but he later proved to be nothing but a drunkard and a louse. Donating the rings to charity would mean there was at least one thing he worked for that would do some good in the world. She was sure nothing else ever did.

"You didn't turn out like you did because of him," she once told her son. "You turned out like you did in spite of him."

So she let the rings go. And along with them, she suddenly felt herself letting go of the anger she held for her husband too. It was the first time in her life that she realized her memory of him was easily the heaviest thing she owned and the one thing she clung onto the tightest. She wondered why she had chosen to hang onto so much resentment for so long, but then decided it didn't matter. The more she shed, the lighter she felt.

"I'm going to push some saline into you because your blood pressure is dropping," Roger said. "Still nothing to worry about."

"If you say so, but I know better." She smiled faintly.

"We're pulling in now," he urged, patting her shoulder. "You'll be fine."

"Just tell your friend up front to give the siren just one little whoop whoop," she said. "It's time to let heaven know I'm coming."

"I'll see what I can do," he said, hoping to humor her as he climbed into the front cab.

"Let's make the most of it," she said after him.

A few seconds later, she heard the siren give out an unnecessary wail, and she smiled. She was lighter than air. It was time to let go.

By the time Roger and Aiden worked their way around to open the back doors, Ellen Williamson was gone. All she took with her was her love for family and friends, life experiences, and a sense of purpose fulfilled. There was no body. All that remained of her was a yellow terry cloth bathrobe and two orange faux fur slippers.

The two young men looked at each other, disbelievingly, and shut the doors. There were no words to explain it. But it was as she had said. It was a beautiful day.

GOOD NEIGHBORS

Nevada 2019

"**H**ey," I said. "Good morning."

The neighbor shrugged.

"Get a good offer?" I tried again with a smile, gesturing toward the red-white-and-blue for sale sign by Signature Real Estate.

"Two years," he said, shaking his head. "We've lived here for two years."

It was my turn to shrug.

"I think that is the most you've ever said to me." He shook his head.

"Nice to meet you, then," I said, extending my hand.

"It's a little late for introductions, don't you think?"

"If you say so," I said.

"Two years," he said again, repeating the incantation. "How do you explain that?"

"I dunno," I said, remembering. "You know, the people before you, those neighbors, they were a family of four. German immigrants. I initially suspected they were German because of their accents, but then their mother confirmed it by baking us some wonderful lemon cookies. They weren't uniform, but they were perfectly crisp on the outside and tender on the inside.

The frosting was the best, which is why I always meant to ask for the recipe. She made them as a 'thank you' for the homemade brownies I gave them when they first moved in.

My daughter used to play with their two boys all the time. She even went over to celebrate their birthdays. She especially loved the one when they rented a bouncy house. It was good fun.

I thought we were getting to be pretty close as far as neighbors go. Then one morning, after they hosted a big rollicking party, the mother came over and pounded on our door. She didn't have cookies this time. She had a crushed note in her hand.

'You could have told us we were being too loud last night,' she lectured me. 'You didn't have to sneak over and leave a note on the door.'

We never wrote the note. She didn't believe us. We never spoke again.

They put the house on the market a few months later. It was very unexpected. One week, we heard his motorcycle roaring up the driveway like always. The next week, it never roared up again. He caught her. They were getting a divorce. Marriages don't always work around here.

The owner before those neighbors was divorced too. He was an older Brazilian man with a big black-and-gray mustache. He used to care for his mother. They lived here, on and off, the longest. They sold the house because his mother said she couldn't climb stairs anymore.

The reason I say they lived here, on and off, is because he had bought a second house. He lived there for several years instead of this one. The first person who rented the house from him was his son. He had a family of his own.

We never really connected with them because their two children, a boy and girl, spent one entire afternoon throwing rocks in our pool. Little ones. Big ones. It took about three hours to clean them out. It wasn't a big deal, but we let them know so it wouldn't happen again. The family apologized. We accepted, but they never seemed to recover from the embarrassment.

The son's mother-in-law lived with them. She's one of the reasons you had so many problems with pigeons. She used to feed them. The other reason, of course, is that the German family installed solar panels. You need pigeon guards if you install those on a house. They never did.

When the son couldn't afford to pay his dad the mortgage for about six months, he decided to skip out and get a place of his own. The owner tried to sell the house to recoup his losses, but it didn't work out. So, he hired a management company to rent it out again. The management company rented it but didn't screen the tenants. They lived in the house for about two years. They used to hang their clothes on a line in the back and barbecue almost every night because they never paid their utilities.

One day, the tenant decided he wanted natural gas after all and spliced into the line to steal it. I guess it was the final straw for the owner because they were evicted a week later. In retaliation, they broke in through these beautiful French doors the owner had installed and stole all the appliances. The owner always seemed irritated that we weren't home when it happened. It's also why your home only has one back door. They stuccoed up the damage.

Eventually, the owner sold his second house for a loss during the recession and then moved back. He lived here about two years before selling it outright. We got along and always said hello. We didn't have much in common, but they were nice enough.

He wasn't the original owner, though. The original owners were a couple with a troubled child. The kid used to sit on the front lawn wearing a football helmet and cut the grass with a pair of scissors. She said it was autism, but he also seemed deathly afraid of his father. His father was an accountant who was recovering from brain surgery. We knew this because his wife was a gossip, and that was the first thing she told us when we moved in. We also knew because she once ran over to our house just to see what the UPS truck brought.

When we didn't reciprocate with neighborly news or entertain her prying eyes, she took to complaining about some sagebrush in our back yard. That was before we installed a pool. It seems her husband was allergic to sage, among other things, which is why I thought Nevada was an odd choice for them. They said they only moved here because their sister lived down the street. They never saw each other. When they moved, they moved to Florida."

The neighbor shrugged. "Why are you telling me this?"

"You asked why this was our longest conversation," I said.

"What do all their problems have to do with anything?"

"Their problems have to do with everything. This city isn't like other cities. It's a transient town with transient people. We live in neighborhoods that resemble office cubicles, big-box structures with red tile roofs, and yards that are partitioned by cinderblock walls. Most friends are made where you congregate outside your home, not around your neighborhood, because most people move every two years or five, on the outside. Then they pack up their belongings and take all their friends with them."

"So?"

"What do you want me to say? You moved in during a busy couple weeks for us, so I didn't have time to bake you brownies. After the fourth week, it almost seemed too late, especially after my wife was cold-shouldered because your mother-in-law blocked our driveway," I said. "So we decided to leave you to be who you were, who you are, and who you will be, as they say. It worked. You've lived here for two years, and I don't know any of your problems."

"What do you mean?"

"You were good neighbors," I said, hand outstretched again. "My name's Paul, by the way."

"Francisco."

"Nice to have known you." I headed back inside with the mail.

He stood on the sidewalk, considering for a moment. Then I saw him nod knowingly before packing up the last of his belongings. We were good neighbors too.

THE QALLUPILLUK

Alaska 1982

Timothy saw him as a savage hunter. Kallik would gaze out at the ocean from the frozen shoreline and take aim with an old Lee Enfield rifle. One shot was all it took.

Then, the old man would sling his rifle across his back and cast out a grappling claw. The seal was hooked, and the rope pulled hand over hand until the animal was ashore.

Seal was a gamey and fishy dark meat that Yupiks and Inuits mostly ate raw. Timothy was told the fresher the meat, the more it tasted like the sea. He didn't agree. He could eat it with them, not wanting to be troublesome, but it wasn't something he would ever enjoy.

The Yupik people were resourceful. They combed the beach for frozen fish, launched small boats to capture driftwood, and occasionally brought home a sea bird instead of a seal. The loon, unlike the seal or most fish, was cooked over an iron stove.

"Have you found what you are looking for yet, Timothy?" asked Kallik as he bagged the seal.

"I don't know," said Timothy. "You've taught me so much already."

"I'm not asking about what you learned. I'm asking what you found," said Kallik.

"What do you mean?" asked Timothy.

"You know what I mean," he said. "When you first came to us, we took you in because I dreamed of you two years ago. But now, now it is time to make a choice."

"Choose between what?"

"Do you remember the story I told you about the owl and the squirrel?" asked Kallik.

Timothy did. Kallik had told him about an owl that had tried to catch a squirrel eating some berries, and the owl swooped down to block the squirrel's retreat into its den.

"I am going to eat very well," said the owl. "A nice fat squirrel."

At the sight of an owl, most squirrels would try to run away and be caught. But this squirrel said he had a better idea than being eaten.

"I heard you are the best dancer in all the north," the squirrel begged. "Won't you dance for me?"

The owl was very pleased by the request. So he began to dance, hopping from one foot to the next, fanning his feathers and flapping his wings. Encouraged by the squirrel and delighted by the attention, his moves became grander, twirls became wider, and hops higher into the air.

"Higher, higher," said the squirrel.

So the owl jumped higher. And just when the owl was at the highest point of his most acrobatic move, the squirrel jumped down into the den. The owl had lost his lunch.

"You are like the owl," said Kallik. "You are dancing between two worlds. The longer you dance between them aimlessly, the more you will lose."

Timothy didn't understand. He felt more like the squirrel.

When he ran away from home months ago, he had found work on a salmon trawler. It seemed fine at first, but then the crew grew more abusive the longer they stayed out at sea. The captain called it hazing. The bruises suggested bullying. His apprenticeship became indentured.

"Who are you going to tell?" the captain asked him once. "You're a runaway. Suck it up."

He did for a while. And when it became unbearable, Timothy did the unthinkable.

The captain had kicked the engine into high gear during one catch and attracted a pod of nearby whales. As all eyes turned to the encroaching whales, Timothy noticed a small skin boat closing in on the whales from the shore.

The whales didn't notice the small boat. Like the trawler crew, all their attention was on the fish. The approaching skin boat was silent, too; any noise was drowned out by the hum of the engines and slapping of whale flukes against the water.

The harpoon man at the front of the boat thrust the barbed end deep into the whale, near its blowhole. It had struck home, allowing the Eskimos to release a buoy that was tethered to the harpoon. Then they moved off as the whale thrashed about in the water. The hunt would be over in minutes.

Timothy took it as an opportunity to escape. He jumped into the icy and turbulent water, chased only by a chorus of their shouts: "Man overboard! Man overboard!"

The captain reduced the throttle of the trawler by half, considering whether to risk the rest of the catch or circle back. But when he saw Timothy swimming toward the skin boat instead of the trawler, he gunned the engine and left his deckhand behind.

The Eskimos, who Timothy later learned were called the Yupik, picked him out of the Arctic water a few minutes later. He was cold and frozen, risking hypothermia after being immersed in the unforgiving ocean. They took him home.

This small tribe of Yupik followed a chaotic mix of traditional and modern lifestyles — some attempting to follow the ways of their ancestors and some embracing a semblance of western culture after the government intervened. They had been organized into a corporation and awarded a small grant to help them transition from subsistence to commerce about ten years earlier. The plan wasn't working.

Kallik's family was one of those that preferred tradition. And since everyone suspected the crew might come looking for the boy, Kallik took him deeper into the wilderness.

"Your turn," Kallik said, handing Timothy the rifle.

"What?"

"You've watched enough, Timothy," said Kallik. "Time to do more than dance."

He pointed out to sea at a small dark shape on the water. It appeared and disappeared under the waves. Timothy squeezed the trigger and missed. His second shot missed as well.

Kallik laughed, gently reaching for the rifle.

But Kallik stopped laughing when he heard his grandson scream. They had left him to fish an ice hole while Kallik showed Timothy how to shoot.

"Qallupilluk! Qallupilluk!" screamed young Yaqulpak again, calling out the name of a mythic monster.

The two of them raced up the snow-dusted ridge, with Kallik in the lead and Timothy following close behind with the rifle. But upon clearing the small ridge, Kallik twisted his ankle on the frozen pocked earth and Timothy had to save the boy on his own.

He couldn't believe his eyes when he saw it. A towering figure dressed as an eider duck was picking the boy up, wrestling him with large claws, and attempting to thrust him into a large pouch. Its face was inhuman, poorly defined under long clumps of stringy hair — a creature that the tribe had warned him about.

Timothy raised the rifle, aiming high and hoping not to hit the boy.

"Timothy!" Kallik called out in protest. "No!"

There was no more time. He fired. The shot hit the Qallupilluk in the head. The hulking figure flew back and dropped the boy. Blood splatted the ice and the snow.

The boy immediately ran to his grandfather, who had worked his way up into a standing position to test the ankle. Timothy kept the rifle trained on the creature.

The three of them approached it cautiously. And as they grew closer, Timothy let out a gasp.

"Did you know him?" asked Kallik.

"He's one of the trawler's crew," said Timothy. "I thought …"

Kallik put out a hand and touched Timothy's shoulder before taking the rifle.

"It will be all right," Kallik said. "You saved Yaqulpak's life. The ice around the hole was cracking. Too much weight in one location."

"He grabbed me, *apa'urluq*," said the boy. "He grabbed me from behind."

They stared at the body for several long minutes. The inhuman face was merely a ski mask. The claws were oversized gloves. The eider duck coat was likely borrowed from a trading post.

Without saying a word, Kallik rolled the body into the fishing hole. The body slipped under the ice and disappeared. All that remained was the smear of blood.

"There is more to the story of the owl and the squirrel, Timothy," said Kallik.

Timothy said nothing.

"When it dove into the den, the owl managed to catch the squirrel's tail with a talon," he said.

"'Come on out,' offered the owl. 'I will give you the tail back.'

"'No,' said the squirrel. 'You could have had a fat squirrel, but now all you have is a furry tail.'

The owl waited and waited for the squirrel to come out for the tail. But the squirrel would not come out. So, finally, the owl flew away, tired and very hungry.'"

"What does it mean?" asked Timothy.

"It means I will take you to Point Hope," said Kallik. "Then we find you a way home."

Kallik and his grandson fed the dogs a few small strips of seal before packing the sled. The journey to Point Hope along the high ridges of ice that pushed up from the shore wouldn't be as easy as a trip back to the canvas igloo where they had spent the last week, or the old man's main house several weeks before that, but Timothy was ready.

"Have you found what you are looking for now, Timothy?" Kallik asked.

"I found that courage comes from standing your ground," he said. "Not running away."

"For all of man's toils, nothing changes except the man," said Kallik. "The earth, all of this, remains forever."

Then Kallik urged the dogs on, riding the sleigh with his grandson to keep weight off his ankle, leaving the crewman's snowmobile behind. Timothy ran alongside them. He wanted to go home.

THE CHAIN

Iowa 2016

When the detective opened the cell door, her eyes instinctively drifted to the cardboard pizza box. She could smell the hot freshness: baked crust, melted cheese, basil, and grease. It reminded her how hungry she was, her stomach in knots after missing breakfast and lunch.

"I thought you could use something," the detective said, holding out the box. "I brought you a soda pop too. Coke's okay, right? I can get water instead if you want."

She didn't look at him, just reached for the box. He pulled it back slightly, and she withdrew, never looking up. She knew what it meant. It wasn't a free transaction.

"Do you mind if we talk, Ms. Sharp?" he asked.

She shrugged, and he held it out again. She hesitantly reached for it a second time, and he let her have it.

"It's a new place — maybe the best in town," he said, crossing his arms. "It's also the closest to the station, just on the other side of the river."

She ignored the small talk and opened the box. It wasn't the typical twenty-minutes-or-less variety. The mozzarella and Margherita sauce swirled together in broad, uneven strokes. The charred hand-tossed crust framed bits of basil, pepperoni, and onion.

She hated onions but took a bite anyway. It was hotter than she expected but not hot enough to burn the roof of her mouth.

He handed her the Coke, and she took a sip through the straw, drowning a mouthful of half-chewed pizza just so that she could take another bite.

"I know you asked for an attorney," he said. "But I think you would be more comfortable with the table in the interrogation room. What do you say?"

She was chewing her third bite greedily and didn't say anything. She didn't have to. She folded the box lid over the pizza instead and slowly stood up with it, grabbing the drink in her free hand.

"Good," he said. "Who knows? Maybe we can get some Maid-Rite sandwiches in here tomorrow."

She didn't want to like him, but she liked him. The other detective, Detective Wallace, was heavyset, old and crusty. He pressed her earlier with a hard heard-it-all attitude, which is why she had asked for an attorney. This one was different.

Detective Hotchkin was in his mid-30s with a handsome face, square jaw, dimples, and a broad smile that made his eyes squint every time he flashed it. Aside from a receding hairline, he was just the kind of guy she would have hooked up with when she was ten years younger.

She swept the hair out of her face, suddenly feeling self-conscious about her appearance and the sweat that seemed to form on her skin with every lost hour. She was unfamiliar with it, having never been in trouble with the law before. She guessed it must be desperation.

"So," she said, setting her dinner on the table. "You're the good cop?"

"If you want to think of it that way," he said. "But mostly, I'm just trying to figure out why you did it. I mean, we all know you did it. The question is: why did you do it?"

She took another bite and thought about it while she chewed. She had been thinking about it all day: Billy Everson pulling over in front of her worn-out Volkswagen Golf on the side of the road. He had been on his way to work, taking the same route he took every day.

"I was the third of four children, detective," she said. "Did you know that? The other middle child was a boy, the only boy, which my father never appreciated. Fewer boys meant fewer farmhands, but I made up for it in other ways. I never fussed much as a baby and tended to keep to myself as a toddler. I was more like my mother as I got older, more likely to quietly do my chores and curl up with a book instead of hunt feral cats, tip cows, or empty red party cups full of cheap beer like my siblings."

Billy had looked back at her in the side mirror before turning on his flashers, assessing her not as helpless but as in need of help. She had already taken the back driver's side tire off and set it down near an open trunk. All that was left to do was take out the spare, put it on, and tighten it down. It wouldn't take long.

"You know what I mean? I was the kid who took the middle seat. I was the one who gave up my brown bag lunch when somebody stole my brother's lunch money. I was the one who ran interference any time our father was angry so none of them ever had to feel the sting of a switch," she said, tracing an old wound on the side of her leg.

"When my English teacher told me how I could make up a grade for the test he lost, I opted to take it all over again. When my older sister was married, I didn't tell her how her new husband copped a feel at the reception. When I met the man who would later become my husband, I dropped out of college to waitress and support his career."

Billy had greeted her with an all-too-familiar good morning smile and offered to lend her a hand. She almost waved him off and told him not to be late for work. If he insisted, she could always call him out for being a chauvinist pig. She knew how to change a tire. What forty-something widow didn't know how to change a tire in Iowa? She thought about saying all sorts of things until she decided to quietly accept his help.

"A few years after we were married, I pretended not to know my husband was cheating on me. I just settled in and told myself he would come around because I was pregnant," she said. "I just wanted to be the peacemaker, you know? Seven months later, our beautiful baby daughter Addie was born. I was right. He never cheated again."

Billy then put the spare in place and tightened the lug nuts. She let him hand her the tire iron and take down the jack. She let him go on about her daughter Addie and how she was going to make an honest man out of him yet. She nodded and smiled.

"Addie is a lot like me," Amy said. "I never had to scold her or tell her what to do. She just drifted, always going along with whatever came her way. It was easy because we always had her dad to lean on. He was our rock, you know? That's what made it so hard when Kevin was killed in a hit-and-run. Neither of us knew how to roll with the loss. We had a hard time letting go, especially Addie, but then we did, I guess."

Billy didn't notice anything out of the ordinary until he lifted the tire she had taken off. He even commented while carrying it around to the trunk. "Isn't that funny," he said. "I don't see anything wrong with it."

"That's who we are. Addie and I are both calm and rational, always thinking before we speak, always absorbing whatever comes our way," she continued. "Even when some animal took advantage of her in the upstairs bedroom of a party last week, she wanted to let it go. 'Let it go, Mom,' she told me. 'It's my fault. I was drunk.'"

When Billy set the tire in the trunk, she let out a grunt. She brought the tire iron down on the back of his head. He let go of the tire, his hands springing to the injury as he reflexively turned around. She hit him again in the forehead. He took a step back, looking out with a blank expression of uncomprehending confusion before he fell forward to take the third blow.

"'No, sweetie,' I told her. 'It's my fault,'" Amy said. "'I don't want you to grow up and weather everything that comes your way as I did. Sometimes you have to stand up, draw a line in the sand, and say enough is enough.'"

She looked down at Billy for a minute, hands trembling at the sight of him lying there on the embankment. She stared at him for what seemed like minutes, wondering if there was any way to save him or take it back. But then she relented, dropped the tire iron next to the wheel, slammed the trunk shut, and drove away, leaving his Challenger a car length away from his lifeless body.

"So you're saying that's what happened?" the detective asked, a note of empathy in his voice. "Billy Everson assaulted your daughter Addie last weekend?"

"No, I'm not saying that," she said, wiping at tears with both hands. "All I'm saying is I broke a chain, and she'll be better for it."

She slid the pizza away because she couldn't look at it any longer. The sight of the red sauce was making her queasy. Resignation had stolen most of her life; guilt wasn't going to steal the rest of it.

THE STRAW

Virginia 2012

A light breeze warded off some early summer humidity as the seven of us cleared the tree line and walked out onto the overlook. We were high up, maybe eighty or a hundred feet from the deep blue of the New River. The quartz, sandstone, and shale outcropping sat above the gorge like an ancient throne, reinforcing the illusion that we were the masters and all of nature our subjects.

Somehow it fits with being a Hokie. Virginia Tech was all about re-imagining education and technology, bending the world for the better to serve our communities. At least that is what they told us in class.

Matt whistled in reverence. It was the first time he had ever come up with us to the cliffs. He wasn't the only newbie. Darrin, Calvin, and I seldom brought girls along on outdoor excursions. We had made an exception today, making our trip to the cliffs as a carryover from the night before.

Darrin had led the way up, which made sense because he was the odd man out. Andrea, Jesse, and Megan had already paired off with the rest of us. I had brought up the rear with Megan, trying to steal a few seconds to talk about last night.

She said I was exaggerating and didn't want to talk about it. I maintained that seeing your girlfriend kiss your best friend

— for what timed out to be two minutes and felt like an eternity — wasn't an exaggeration. That was the game, she insisted.

The game. Padiddle was a holdover game from high school, an upgraded version of spin the bottle. Anytime someone saw a car with a burnt-out headlight, they would call it out. Padiddle!

In some places, people played for points. In other places, they exchanged punches. Since our sophomore year in high school, the same year Darrin earned his driver's license and we started double-dating, we played for kisses.

Whoever called out padiddle first would be able to kiss the girl of his choice or the guy of her choice. A padoodle, which was a car with a burnt-out taillight, was worth two kisses. Pigdiddles and pigdoodles, which covered police vehicles, were worth fifteen minutes and all night, respectively.

It was pretty simple when we double-dated. Everybody picked their dates, as if any of us needed another excuse to lock lips. When we weren't dating, we always gave the girl the option of rejecting any kiss with a slap or slapping the guy of their choice instead of kissing them. It was all good fun, silly, and juvenile — something you'd expect to outgrow after high school, but Darrin insisted it continue on when we decided to attend the same college. His car. His rules.

Last night, the five us crammed into Darrin's father-financed four-seat Shelby GT500. Calvin, Jesse, and I sat in the back. Usually, I rode shotgun but wanted to be a gentleman and put Megan up front.

We were supposed to go to Naughty Scotties, which is this crazy three-story colonial with a waterpark and bar. Not really. Naughty Scotties is a prank that turned into something unexpected, but suffice to say that sometimes the best place to party is a college apartment house with a kiddie pool and keg set up in the back.

Darrin had another idea. He wanted to turn a short ride to Scotties into a road trip to Roanoke because Schooners had a decent live music lineup for that Friday night. Calvin threw up his hands because the place sometimes packed an older crowd and he wasn't looking forward to riding around with Andrea sitting half on his lap and half on the back seat divider. But then I went along with it to be a pal. If nothing else, the food was good.

I wouldn't have been so agreeable had I known how things were going to play out. Not ten minutes into the ride, Darrin spotted a truck with a burnt-out headlight and yelled out.

"Padiddle!"

"What?" I asked, lifting my head off the small triangular window in the back. "I didn't know we were playing."

"Come on, Drew." He laughed. "We're always playing."

"Padiddle? What's that?" Megan asked with a nervous, curious laugh.

So Darrin explained the rules to her. She acted like it was the funniest thing she had ever heard, coming from Tennessee. She was probably right. She couldn't get over that we still played a high school game in college. I couldn't get over it either. His car. His rules.

"Oh look, I see one too," she laughed. "Padiddle! Now what?"

"You pick the guy you want to kiss," Darrin said.

"Well, you didn't pick," she pointed out. "Who did you pick?"

"Oh, I was going to pick you," he said, as if it was the most casual thing in the world.

"Then I'll pick you too!" she exclaimed, caught up in the stupidness of it, leaning over to kiss his cheek.

"No, not while I'm driving," he said. "Let's wait until we get there."

"Really?" I protested. "You're doing this?"

"If it's going to make you uncomfortable, I'll take it back," Darrin said.

"Oh come now, Andrew," Megan said. "It's just a game."

"It's fine," I said, wondering why she didn't pick me. "Whatever."

That seemed to settle it for the front seat, even if Calvin and Andrea felt the heat rising off my face. The dynamic had changed. Darrin was making a play for my girlfriend and I was ten inches too far back to do anything about it. It wasn't the first time. He had a habit of making plays for girls I dated.

I always told myself that the last time would be the last time, but it never really was. Somehow I always twisted it into being more about the girl than my friend. Some girls gravitated toward the guy with the better car or, in my case, the guy with any car at all.

The next thirty minutes felt like forever, eclipsed only by the amount of time they kissed before we entered the bar. He had gotten out of the car, opened her door, and helped her out.

Before I could even pull on the seat release, he said it was time to pay up.

He gave her a peck on the lips, and then she pulled him into her. She could have given him a little slap for my sake, but I was the one she slapped. She kissed him — a long, wet, opened-mouth kiss, tongues dancing across teeth, and ending with Darrin biting her lip. And then, they kissed again.

"Hey now," I said, pulling myself out of the car. "That's enough, already."

"It's just a game, Drew," Megan said, rolling her eyes at me.

Then we all went inside and pretended like nothing happened. Pretended was the operative word. I sulked for most of the evening. There were a few times Megan and I held hands, but I couldn't bring myself to kiss her. I was too busy sizing people up for a fight, but there were no takers at Schooners. They were an older, tamer crowd, and I was more likely to get arrested than blow off some steam.

I took shotgun on the way home, leaving Andrea and Megan to share one of the back seats like I should have done from the start. I didn't say anything the whole way, claiming to have drunk one IPA too many. There was some truth to it.

But that didn't stop Darrin from talking. He told the girls that Matt, Calvin, and I were going to check out a new cliff-jumping spot. He said they should come too. If they said yes, he'd tell Matt to bring Jesse and added that there would be two cars and more leg room. They made it clear they wouldn't be jumping off any cliffs, but wanted to come all the same. A little sun in all the right places would do her good, Megan said.

True to her word, Megan wore a pink spaghetti-strapped tunic over a white two-piece with teal and yellow flowers. When we left, she hugged her blue-striped terry cloth towel like a teddy bear, conveying a shyness I hadn't seen before and I didn't know whether I should believe. She was stunning.

The other girls were wearing swimsuits too, but were more sensibly dressed for the short hike to the overlook. The contrast between them convinced me that maybe last night's stupidity was only a game. Megan was still my girlfriend, after all — my naive and naturally sexy girlfriend.

"Earth to Andrew," Calvin said, waving a hand in front of my face.

"Yeah?" I said.

"Do you want to climb down the trail with me and find our route back up?" he asked.

"No, it's cool. I can see it from here," I said, pointing down and along a small path in the sandstone.

"If you say so," Calvin said, somewhat unconvinced. "Just make sure someone other than Matt goes first. I'd hate to see him stranded down there on his jump."

"Yeah, sure," I said, looking around. "Hey, have you seen Megan?"

"Sure, she was helping Darrin with something," he said, pointing to the bushes.

I don't know if I expected to see them making sandwiches when I followed the trail over to where Calvin had pointed or what, but I wasn't prepared for what I saw. They were standing there, with the northern Blue Ridge Highlands as their backdrop, facing each other. His hands were on her shoulders. She was smiling.

"Well, this is awkward," I said. "I was looking to see if you were ready to jump."

"Ah, Drew," he said. "It's not what you think."

"Yeah, whatever," I said, and rejoined the rest of the group. "I'll go first."

"Don't you guys usually go down and check the depth of the water?" Matt asked.

"It'll be fine," I said, wanting my bravado to make up for not owning a car.

I could hear them behind me as I peeled off my shirt and ran toward the cliff. They were laughing and screaming — that crazy mix of fear, anticipation, excitement, and disbelief that made jumping so addictive. I jumped, up and out to avoid the sides, tucking my legs up when I was momentarily airborne and then straightening them as the water rushed up toward me — my arms flapped in little circles like a featherless bird the entire way down, gravity pulling me to the lucid water.

They cheered me as I hit the water. When I surfaced through a million tiny bubbles, they applauded. I raised my hand in the air to show them I was all good, thumbs up and everything. What I didn't want them to see was that I had grazed a shallow outcropping on my left, skinning my leg from thigh to knee. It wasn't bad, but I immediately considered how lucky I was not to land on it.

Shallow outcroppings like these are why so many quarries have no trespassing signs, warning people that there have been multiple bone fractures and even a few deaths. In some places along the New River, being caught was a Class 1 misdemeanor.

"That was awesome!" Darrin called down. "How was it?"

"It was awesome!" I echoed.

"I'm next, buddy," he said.

"Cool," I said. "Just stay to the right on the way down. There's an outcropping I didn't see earlier."

His entire jump was almost exactly like mine, right up to the end. He had tucked his legs and then straightened them out. He had flapped his featherless wings. He had laughed and screamed with the others all the way down. It was higher than any jump we had ever taken and the most exhilarating.

The only thing different about his jump was the end. Instead of a splash, there was the thump of a meat tenderizer hitting a roast. There were jagged snaps, dry noodles giving way when they are slowly broken.

Matt was the third person to jump, but not for the thrill. It was obligatory as a premed student. He was coming to help me as I was already trying to hold Darrin's head above the water.

"I can't believe this," Matt said. "I thought you said the outcropping was to the right."

"Yes, my right," I said.

He looked at me for a second and squinted, tasting my words and finding them unpalatable.

"Call 911!"

He reached under Darrin and laced his hands with me, creating a makeshift human swing before gently guiding him to the side of the cliff where we both could stand. Matt suggested we keep his head above water, but not move him to land. The buoyancy would support some of his weight, he said. We waited there, not saying anything, until the paramedics arrived.

Along with two broken ankles and a fractured fibula, Darrin damaged three discs in his lower back. The prognosis for long-term paralysis wasn't clear. I never asked Megan out again but she came to visit once, bringing Darrin a card and some flowers.

"You know what he told me on the cliff that day?" she asked. "He said it didn't mean anything. I said it didn't mean anything to me, either. Then he said he was sorry."

"I know he's sorry," I said. "We're not even friends anymore."

She didn't know what else to say so I sent her away. When she was gone, I threw the card and flowers away. He had plenty already.

LEFTOVERS

Wyoming 2020

Rachel Wyman poured two mismatched cups of coffee, one for her grandmother and one for herself, from the easy-pour spout of an old stainless steel percolator. She knew the coffee pot all too well growing up on the ranch, mostly how much she hated cleaning out the removable filter basket and perk tube.

"I can't believe you still have this old thing." She laughed, setting the cup down on the rectangular picnic table that was framed by two long benches worn smooth by use. "You could use an upgrade."

"Why would I do that?" Mabel asked. "No apologies. It still makes the best coffee."

The smell was strong. The warmth of it eased away the morning chill outside the window framing the rustic morning nook. Seeing her grandmother hunched there in her flannel robe over a yellow cup with a backdrop of rolling plains brought back memories. But it still felt so incomplete.

There should be three cups on the table, with her grandfather's being the largest and set down by the wide-mouthed ashtray he used to tap out the spent ashes of his cherry pipe tobacco. Back then, her cup would have been filled with hot chocolate instead of coffee, and the smell of bacon and eggs would somehow push back against her grandfather's always larger-than-life presence of pine, coffee, and smoke.

"He's really gone, isn't he?" Rachel asked absently, not meaning it to be a question as much as a disbelieving statement of fact.

"Yes, I suppose he is," Mabel said so the question didn't linger with the rest.

They hadn't talked about any of them yet, but those unanswered questions loomed like a shadow over the tedium of funeral arrangements. The biggest one left unanswered was what would become of the ranch, if not now then when Mabel eventually joined Clayton "CJ" Wyman in the great big open above.

Mabel was more than capable of running the ranch for a few more years, maybe even a decade. But, sooner or later, she would have to surrender it. And unless Rachel stood up to claim it, there weren't likely to be any takers. Neither one of her aunts, Lydia and Marjorie, would even stay overnight and, frankly, Rachel was surprised they let their boys — three between the two of them — spend the last few nights here.

Rachel supposed things would have been different had CJ not outlived her parents. For all her anger, her mom Jettie always loved the ranch and knew how to work it. But that wasn't meant to be.

On September 11, 2001, her parents had been waiting for the observation deck of the World Trade Center's South Tower to open. They were on the 103rd floor in her uncle's office.

The observation deck never opened. And any chance they would come home disappeared in a cloud of fire, smoke, and concrete. Rachel was only three years old at the time, and her two-week stay in one of the east rooms of the ranch turned into permanent accommodations.

She was too young to understand what had happened, but it became terrifying as she grew older and the news media hit the replay button on the film footage every year. She never wanted to look but couldn't turn away — wondering what floor were they on when it all came tumbling down, or if one or two of the unidentified specks in free fall had been them.

"Have you thought about what you are going to say today?" Mabel asked.

Rachel winced. She was still struggling with the responsibility, especially because so much of it would fall on her shoulders. Mabel would be too shaken to talk. Lydia and Marjorie would scratch the obligatory surface. Between their husbands, Andrew was more likely to say something than Dale, but neither would be memorable.

That's not to say there would be a shortage of things said. CJ Wyman had family and friends from all over. He was a prominent beacon for a fifth-generation ranch family that had set down roots in Wyoming after drifting across the country from Wisconsin via South Dakota, leaving small pockets of their German-English stock along the way.

It was her great-grandfather Earl Wyman who originally picked Wyoming to stake his claim and build a soddy — a house built of not much more than sod, without air conditioning, heat, or running water. Later, he made a home for what became a large family of five boys, always stressing the importance of paying it forward to the next generation.

"Work hard, and don't worry about going broke. I've been broke twice and still turned it around better than where I started," said Earl, always fond of passing along something paraphrased from his dad. He had plenty of stories to tell, CJ always said, mostly of lean times and tragedies. The family had weathered both the Great Depression and World War II admirably, which left them with a sizable government bailout loan and a banner emblazoned with four Gold Stars.

This, more than any other reason, is why CJ took over the Y-Knot Ranch when Earl died. He was the only one sent to Europe instead of the Pacific, and the only one to come back. He was a decorated war hero of two wars, served his community on various cattle boards and county commissions, and earned the rank of lieutenant in the volunteer county fire department. He did so much that Rachel could never keep up with it all.

"It is today, you remember," Mabel said. "His funeral is today."

"What do you want me to do?" Rachel shot back. "Should I recite the story they printed in the *Tribune-Eagle*?"

"Come on, Rachel," Mabel said. "He loved you."

"Too much, maybe," she huffed, shuddering as she said it.

She had just turned 13 when he sent her to fetch some baling wire for a broken bit of fence, only to come up behind her in the old barn. She remembered thinking how ridiculous it was for him to follow, especially after she had protested being sent on a barn errand in a sundress.

She was just about to turn around and tell him that it was a fool thing to ask if he was going to rummage around for it anyway, when he gently covered her mouth. Then he pushed his head between her jawline and shoulder, breathing in the shampoo she used to wash her hair. It startled her at first, but she didn't flinch or pull away, half expecting him to tickle her or lift her off the small ladder so she wouldn't ruin her dress.

Instead of doing either, he hooked his elbow over her shoulder, squeezed her to his body, and pushed her up against the ladder. She felt the weight of him, his free hand moving down with urgency. She heard the buckle of his belt falling away, and an uncomfortable pressure as his grip on her tightened. When he shifted his weight again, his hand fell away from her mouth. He was confident she wouldn't protest.

"Did you hear that," she whispered instead. "Grandma's calling me."

He didn't say anything. His grip just tightened — his panting slow and even.

"Did you hear her?" She asked again, louder as she craned her neck to the barn doors. "Yes, Grandma! I'm coming! I'm coming!"

He let her go, and she ran out of the barn. Her hair was tangled, framing a face flushed in confusion as she tried to comprehend what had happened. What had she done?

They didn't go to the store as planned. Her grandfather mended the fence and kept his distance for the rest of the day. She mostly stayed in her room, expecting a visit from her grandmother that never came. What happened didn't even come up until six months later, and only after Rachel had taken to wearing two layers of clothes.

"You thinking about that day?" Mabel asked, pursing her lips in an exhale like she used to do before she quit smoking.

"Not just that day," Rachel said, taking a drink of coffee before grimly adding the truth. "All the days."

"All the days?" Mabel asked, shaking her head. "It wasn't like that with you. It was one time and nothing happened, not really."

"I don't know," Rachel said. "Memories are funny things. Maybe I remember that day so I don't remember all the other days like that day."

Rachel walked to the window and looked outside as if to reach out and grasp one of the conflicted feelings that swirled around her head. The worst of them was guilt. Guilt for not talking to her grandmother sooner after it happened. Guilt for whatever she had done to trigger him.

When she did finally tell Mabel, everything fell into place. All of the unnoticed mysteries of her life suddenly came into focus, questions that she had never thought to ask. Why did her grandmother sleep in the room next to her instead of with her grandfather? Why was bath night always on the same day as her grandfather's bowling night? Why could she hear some woman laughing upstairs anytime she and Mabel played "motel" in the downstairs family room?

Until that day, she always thought the ranch house was haunted. Maybe it was haunted in a way, but not by the disembodied laughter of a long-forgotten housekeeper.

"Something happened to him in the wars," Mabel said, emphasizing the 's' in wars. "He wasn't always that way, you know. And, he eventually left it behind. You might've even had something to do with it."

"Small comfort," Rachel said.

"Come on now, Rachel," said Mabel. "There's no use backpedaling to ground you've already tread. It's not like you two didn't get close again."

"Yeah, maybe I pretended," she said. "I'm a good pretender."

"So that's it?"

"Maybe I'm pretending right now."

"How so?" Mabel asked, surprised by the statement.

"Maybe I'm pretending it's all right that you never warned me," she snapped.

"I didn't think I had to," she said. "You were always more boy than girl anyway."

"Oh, was that the plan — keep me in flannel and overalls?" she said, her voice rising. "Keep my hair short and my elbows rough?"

"You'll wake the boys." Mabel hushed her with a hand gesture.

Rachel hadn't realized it, but she had started pacing the kitchen in tiny circles. She felt like she was climbing out of her skin, needing to go somewhere to do something. She needed to escape somewhere where the air was easier to breathe.

"Did you ever ask yourself what you're really mad about?" Mabel said, standing up.

"What is that supposed to mean?" Rachel asked.

"Are you mad about that one day, or are you mad he's gone?"

Rachel felt her knees buckle. She put a hand out on the table to steady herself and set the coffee down again. She squeezed her eyes shut to act as a levee, but it was too late. The tears came a few at a time and then streaked her cheeks.

Mabel put her arms around Rachel, embracing the girl she had raised as her youngest. She looked more like her father, except for the eyes and nose. Those belonged to her mother, Jettie, unquestionably the toughest and most adventurous of Mabel's three daughters.

"They're just leftovers, honey," Mabel said, soothing her granddaughter. "Here now, look at me."

Rachel regained some of her composure. Mabel pulled back to see her eyes.

"When we lose someone, they're all gone except for the leftovers, whatever we carry around in our hearts and minds," said Mabel. "Don't misunderstand me. What happened with you is hard to understand and harder to forgive. So hard, I know I never will, not completely. But leftovers, you decide what to keep and what to throw away."

"I'm trying, Grandma," Rachel said. "I really am."

"We all do things in life that detract from great accomplishments or make us fall short of lofty goals," she said. "It's hard enough without the weight of someone else's shortcomings too. He did so much for you, Rachel. I hope you keep the best of him."

"Okay," she said, taking a deep breath and noticing two of the boys standing there for the first time.

"Is this a bad time?" asked Michael, who was the older of the two.

"No, no," said Mabel. "We were just talking about breakfast. You boys want to keep it simple and have bacon and eggs?"

"You know what? I'm all in for some new memories instead," Rachel said with a final sniffle. "Let's make French toast together."

"Grandpa hated French toast." Michael shrugged.

"Yes," said Rachel. "Yes, he did."

SPINNING WHEEL

Florida 1969

For the first time in months, Luke felt good. He had turned in his final project for art class — an oil painting that extrapolated and expanded upon the stylings of post-impressionist artist Paul Gauguin. The work would lock in another A since he enrolled in college as a fine arts major. It was easy. Everyone knew he had more talent than his junior college art instructor. Some even mused he should be teaching instead.

But that was it. Art was his last class for the semester, and he was walking to the parking lot. Summer had arrived. The weather was near perfect. It was a balmy 92 degrees, but there was a gentle breeze that kept his shirt from sticking to his skin.

His father's '63 red sports coupe was waiting for him. He had been borrowing it all semester after abandoning his own car clear across the country in California almost seven months ago.

He wasn't worried about it. The aging Volkswagen Beetle was in good hands with his longtime friend, mentor, and former art teacher Ray Ritchie. After driving it from Columbus to Los Angeles, no one was sure it would make the trip to Orlando. No one was sure he was in any shape to drive, either, so his parents had sent him a one-way plane ticket, not to his apartment in Ohio, but to their home outside Orlando.

He was a wreck when they met him at the gate, disoriented and uncertain, but much better than the night he called up Ray before he made the cross-country trip ten months earlier. He could still remember calling Ray like it was yesterday.

"Hey, Ray," he had said, cradling the phone with his shoulder and holding a kitchen knife in his left hand.

"Luke? What a great surprise. How are you?" Ray said. "How's the baby?"

"She left me, Ray," Luke said. "She took the baby and left. She wants a divorce."

"Oh, I'm sorry to hear that," Ray said flatly, absorbing before lifting his voice an octave. "It must be a lot to process. You okay?"

"I just don't know," Luke said, choking back the tears and considering the knife.

"Well, what are you going to do about it?" asked Ray.

"Nothing. She went to her parents," he said. "So I'm alone. My family is gone. My parents are gone. You're gone. Most of my friends are gone. Everybody's moved on from this place except me and all this hurt, all this suffering."

"What about Wayne?" Ray asked. "Have you talked to him lately?"

"He's up north somewhere. Minnesota, I think," Luke guessed.

"Oh, I see. And what are you doing right now?" Ray asked. "Any dark thoughts?"

"I'm standing here in a kitchen with a knife," said Luke. "I'm thinking maybe I'm done with it. I'm just done. I just wanted to call and thank you … and say goodbye."

"No, no, no," said Ray. "I have a better idea. Put the knife down and tell me how much money you have in your pocket right now. I need to know."

"What? All right," he said, putting the knife down and reaching for his wallet. "About $42."

"Good, good enough," said Ray. "Now listen, I want you to forget about the knife. Just leave it. Turn off any lights in your apartment, lock up, get in your car, and come see me. Don't even pack anything. Okay. Drive all night. Don't even stop, except for gas and if you feel like you have to sleep somewhere."

"Okay," Luke said. "I can do that."

"Great! Do it right now," Ray said. "And if you get into trouble or run out of money, give me a call. It should take you about two days. Okay? I'm hanging up now. Leave now."

"Okay, Ray," Luke said. "I'll come. I'm coming right now."

And he did. He locked up the apartment, left everything behind, and drove from Columbus to Los Angeles, stopping only once at a motel outside Amarillo, Texas. He lived with Ray for about three months, making pottery and helping run shows until his parents phoned in early December. That's when everyone decided that maintaining wasn't the same thing as getting better, so he accepted the offer of flying out to Florida for Christmas.

When he did get home, his parents were more accepting than they had ever been in his life. He went to therapy, enrolled in the junior college, and met a girl — one who said she would accept his child with open arms. That was especially important to him after receiving the first of several letters in the new year.

His soon-to-be ex-wife wasn't even raising their child. She had left him with her parents, of all people. It's not that her mother was so bad, although she was a bit on the controlling side; her father was downright frightening. His wife had told him stories that he couldn't believe — horrible stories that he wished he never knew. The very idea that she would leave their child with that man cut him to the core.

It also confirmed something he started to suspect almost immediately after starting therapy. He may have been suffering from chronic manic depression, not all that uncommon among artists, but his wife was a crazy maker. She felt trapped in their teenage marriage just like he did, but she had set out to make sure he failed right along with her — and their son, for that matter. She wanted to be free and live her life. They had no place in it, and if they were in it, holding her back, they would pay. They paid.

Luke unlocked the car and slipped behind the wheel. He looked over at the passenger seat where he had left his overnight bag. It was time to make things right.

With school out of the way, he was going to drive up to Columbus and get his son. He had already planned the trip. He would arrive late at night, stay at a motel, pick up his son in the morning, and drive back. It would be a long drive, almost fifteen hours, but nothing as challenging as when he drove out to see his teacher Ray in California.

He turned the ignition, and the radio came on. The number two song, Spinning Wheel by Blood, Sweat & Tears, was playing and he smiled. The words were almost too perfect.

He had no money. He had no home. His troubles had spun out of control and he was left all alone to face them.

What goes up must come down, he thought, but maybe he wasn't coming down. Maybe he was spinning his way back up. Everything was coming together. This was it. If he wasn't sure, he could turn right and head home. If he was sure, and he was sure, he would turn left.

There wasn't another thought. He turned left onto Spessard Holland Parkway and stepped on the accelerator. He would certainly make better time in this painted pony than he ever did driving his in-need-of-paint-job punch buggy to California. He laughed.

Then he turned up the radio and started singing along with the band. Someone was waiting for him, and it was his son — the boy he named Ray after his art teacher. And Ray, like his art teacher and himself, was destined to be a great artist too, if Luke had anything to say about it.

Of course, all that assumed the '62 Pontiac Catalina in front of him would turn down a side road or otherwise get out of the way. It wasn't the car as much as the driver. She was an older woman, hair done up in curlers with a scarf over them. She reminded him of the driver he had to pass in Arizona when he was heading toward California, except he was in a different state of mind at the time.

When he was driving across Arizona, he was slowed up by a woman driving an older New Yorker Town & Country Wagon. He wasn't sure how fast she was driving, but it felt like twenty-five miles per hour, so eventually, he decided to pass. As he did, he pulled up right alongside her and gave her a long look, taking his eyes off the road as he did it.

The curlers were so tight on her head that he sure they were pulling a few wrinkles out of her face. He got a good look, seeing how hunched over the wheel she was, eyes squinted and knuckles white. Then she turned to look at him, revealing a scowl that held a cigarette between two thin lips. Her hands never left the wheel, but she looked at him as if she were wagging one of those long bony fingers right at him. Shame on you. Shame on you for having a baby while still in high school. It was unnerving.

When he looked back to the road in front of him, he saw a truck coming straight at him. He had waited too long to pass. He could hear the truck's horn blaring as it started to slow but not fast enough. Then Luke thought about speeding up to pass until the woman, inexplicably, began to speed up too.

For a split second, he almost wanted to let the accident play out. Maybe that is how he would go, another accidental casualty on America's highways. But then he did the only thing he could do. He veered to the left and onto the oncoming lane's shoulder and out of the way. The Beetle spun out into the desert, nobody was harmed, and it put some distance between him and the shaming slowpoke once he got back on the road.

The near-miss was his first step toward recovery. When he finally turned back onto that Arizona highway, he realized things were bad, but he didn't want to die. It was also one of the first stories he told Ray when he arrived at his teacher's modest studio home.

He considered telling his son a similar story, minus the near miss part, when Ray got older as he started to pass the Catalina. There was plenty of room to pass, especially with all the power of his dad's coupe. While it wasn't nearly as light as his Bug, there was plenty under the hood. It had a small block V-8.

As he passed, he glanced into the window of the car and was startled with recognition. The woman in the Catalina could have been the sister of the woman he tried to pass in Arizona. She flipped him off with her eyes: Shame on you. And when he turned his head to the road in from of him, he saw a truck coming out of nowhere. At first, he stepped on the gas, expecting to pass her easily. But just like in Arizona, the woman sped up and he knew he wasn't going to make it.

As if recalling muscle memory from that fated near-miss, Luke veered toward the shoulder of the oncoming lane. Except unlike the dry open desert, there was no real shoulder framing the lakes and swamps of Florida. The coupe tagged a cypress tree.

In the seconds after the fatal crash, there was only one question on Luke's mind as he watched an out-of-place front wheel spin around and around above a shattered windshield. Would anybody believe he wanted to live?

VERTIGO

New Mexico 1955

Heights made him feel dizzy, so he jumped.

His only regrets on the way down were the people below. He didn't mean to ruin their day.

THE DOMINO

Missouri 1962

When Merri Belle Booker called out from her kitchen for someone to answer the front door, everyone in the household knew it was already too late. Someone was in trouble.

"Now who's in the front room being foolish," she said, thundering out of the kitchen with a wooden spoon in her hand. "You hear the front door, don't you?"

Elijah supposed he and his younger brother Percy did hear the front door. They had just chosen to ignore it, their attention rapt by an unsteady tower of dominoes.

"Yes, ma'am," said Elijah, looking up with wide eyes.

"Ya, 'am," Percy chimed in, but only after his brother poked him.

"Well," she said, "somebody going to answer it?"

She drew out the last few words, lacing them with angry sarcasm. It was like an early warning siren that sometimes sounded in nearby Wavery or Coniford. A tornado was coming and you better get out of the way.

"But Momma," Elijah pleaded, one hand still steadying the base. "We don't want the tower to fall."

It was the wrong answer. Elijah knew it before he said it, but it came out anyway.

Merri Belle took two giant steps, impossibly big for her size, and suddenly appeared beside them. Percy, in an equally miraculously fast motion, slid under the table, leaving Elijah trapped with both hands steadying their monstrous creation.

Then it happened. The wooden spoon, still damp with whatever concoction she had stirred together for supper, cut through the center of the tower and knocked it down.

"There. Now you boys don't have no worries," she said. "Get the damned door."

Elijah sulked over to the door and opened it, looking back toward his mother. He didn't know who was standing in the doorway, but his mother looked surprised.

"Percy, go get your father," she said. "Mr. Benayoun. Good afternoon."

"Good afternoon, Merri Belle," he said, holding his hat in his hand.

Elijah turned and looked up at the man. Nehemiah Benayoun owned the supermarket in Coniford where his father worked, stocking shelves and doing odd jobs. Mr. Benayoun had always been kind to their father, employing him despite being convicted for violating curfew on more than one occasion.

He was a short, lean man with a prominent beard that stood out against his white shirt, which Elijah guessed was impossibly hot for late spring. He couldn't imagine how hot it would be in the summer or why anyone would wear two hats — a small circular one under the broad-rimmed black one in his hands.

Elijah didn't welcome Mr. Benayoun into their home as much as he backed away from the door, giving a wide enough berth so the man could do what he wanted. Mr. Benayoun could come in or not.

"Mister Benayoun?" asked his father from the hall. "Something wrong, sir?"

"Duane," Nehemiah acknowledged. "Sorry to bother you at home."

"No bother," his father said, perplexed by the unexpected visit. "Is there a problem at the store?"

"No, no," Nehemiah said, searching for the words. "Duane, do you know anything about the ruckus that happened at the mill today?"

Duane looked down, lips pressed tight.

"It's all right if you do," Nehemiah said.

"I wasn't even there, Mister Benayoun," he said. "So, all I've gots is hearsay."

"Go on," Nehemiah encouraged.

"There were about a dozen boys involved," Duane said. "Old man Crawford was going to cut their pay again and things got out of hand. They didn't mean nothing by it, but they deserve a fair pay like any man."

"So then what happened?" asked Nehemiah.

"Everybody knows that," he said, looking up. "The sheriff came and sent everybody home. He said go home, stay home, and it would all be sorted. He said to tell everybody, all you folk living by the river, stay home until it's sorted."

Nehemiah nodded. A grave expression shadowed his face.

"Duane," he exhaled. "I don't want to be an alarmist, but I want you and your family to leave with me right now. Don't pack. We'll just tell as many of your neighbors as possible and head into the woods."

"Makes no sense," Duane said. "I didn't do anything, but I could get in trouble if I leave. You know I've already been in trouble."

"Who's leaving?" Merri Belle said, coming back out from the kitchen again. "I have supper on, so I don't know anything about a fool thing like that."

They were all in the front room now: Duane, Merri Belle, Elijah, Percy, Monique, and Shandra. They crowded around Nehemiah as if he were about to deliver a Baptist sermon despite being Jewish.

"The sheriff isn't coming back to question anyone," he said. "They are coming back with enough men to run you all off."

"Who's they?" asked Duane.

Nehemiah shrugged. "Men."

"Come on now," Merri Belle said. "You're scaring the children."

"Pack some things, but pack light," said Duane. "Merri Belle, leave the stew, but pack the cornbread and, I don't know, sandwiches or something we can stick in a poke."

Elijah and his brother and sisters stood there, looking up at their father for direction.

"Go on, now." He shooed them before turning back to Nehemiah. "We have to tell the others."

"We will, we will," the storekeeper said. "Get your family in order first."

Packing a few things each didn't take long, a privilege of being poor. All of them still felt uncertain about following this man who had never come to their home before, but they followed him out of the four-room shack all the same. It didn't take long for others who called the riverside shanty town home to wonder why the Bookers were leaving.

"Duane, what do you think you're doing?" asked Terrance as he crossed the trampled dirt path that had become a street. "You know what the sheriff said. He said: Stay home."

"Well, I had nothing to do with what happened at the mill," said Duane. "So we don't need to be here when he comes. You shouldn't be here, either."

"That makes no sense," said Terrance. "You'll get us all in trouble."

"He's telling the truth," said Nehemiah. "The sheriff isn't coming here to sort out what happened today. He's coming to evict you all."

"Evict us?" Madelle Smith said from the back of the growing flock.

A chorus of disbelief followed her question.

"We don't have much time," said Duane. "Take as little as you can and we'll leave right now."

"Where would we go?" someone asked, prompting an inquisitive hum from the crowd.

"I don't believe it," said Madelle. "Is anybody here ready to move on?"

"I agree with Maddy," said Terrance over the hum of discontent. "The sheriff says stay home, and you stay home."

"Haven't you gotten in enough trouble for breaking curfew before, Duane?" Madelle added. "You'll get fined, or worse."

"There is no time," shouted Nehemiah. "Your very lives may be in danger."

Elijah shuddered at the urgency of it. Mr. Benayoun was desperate for them to leave, pinching his fingers together to emphasize his haunted plea. Everyone fell silent as Elijah's brother and sisters pressed in closer together.

"There is no time," he whispered.

"Yvonne." Madelle broke the silence, looking down at her daughter, who had come over for a better view. "Go on home and shut the door. All you all should do the same. Go on. Go on home and tend to your suppers."

The small crowd immediately began to disperse with her words, all of them wandering back to their shacks and shanties. Their murmurs faded as clusters of ten split into quieter groups of four or two. All that remained were a few stragglers who took one last peek before shutting their doors behind them and a few folks who lived further out, casting a confused glance back at the Bookers.

"Maddy." Duane shook his head. "Don't do this."

"You both should be ashamed of yourselves, scaring everyone like that," she said, wagging a heavy finger at them. "You'll go home, too, if youse knows what's good for you."

Nehemiah raised his own finger to say something, but Duane staved him off by placing a hand on his shoulder. No words would change any minds today, Duane seemed to say.

The seven of them started toward one end of the small shanty town, an eerily silent trek broken only by the occasional door being shut or the creak of a floorboard. It had become a virtual ghost town except for the smells of fragrant stews or grilling meat.

As they passed the last house, Elijah looked up to see one of his friends standing in an open doorway. He raised a cautious hand to Trevon, but the boy's mother came up behind and swept him inside.

They were a mere twenty yards outside of town when they heard horses approaching from the other end of town. It came upon them as an unexpected thunder under a cloudless twilight. Nehemiah quickly led them all off the road and into the woods, where they crouched down in a tangle of bushes and broken trees.

There were maybe a dozen riders that crashed into town, three riding straight in the direction Elijah and his family had fled. They dismounted and turned around, two drawing revolvers and one unslinging a rifle from his back. At the other end, groups of three men went door to door, breaking in and entering homes.

"They're not even hiding their faces," said Elijah, who had taken refuge next to the storekeeper.

Nehemiah looked at him with sad eyes, gave a knowing nod to the boy's parents, and then pushed Elijah's head into the soft ground. He resisted at first but then held still as gunfire rang out. People were screaming. The men said they were only looking for weapons, but every action or inaction was interpreted as lawlessness.

The smoke came next. There was a blend of smells, sweet and musty plumes, passing over them. There was something else, an awful, acrid odor not all that unfamiliar from a barbecue but with a heavy metallic flavor.

Elijah pushed his head up when he heard his mother's muffled sobs, but Nehemiah held firm. There were louder heaving sobs in the distance, a chorus that shrank with each successive shot after shot — each of them with a different, deafening retort.

"That's the end of it," one of the men said. "Burn it all."

As the fire grew in the ferocity and the presence of the men — those devils — fell away, Nehemiah eased himself off the boy. The flames were growing hot, wood crackling, and smoke drifting in their direction, leaving nothing to see except the glowing frame of the shanty town's southernmost home.

"Come on," Duane said. "Let's go."

The seven of them headed in the opposite direction of the men, cutting deep into the woods until their father led them to a game trail. They stopped in a small clearing and discussed breaking away from the river and turning south toward Marshall. Nehemiah would journey with them there but then head home.

"How did you know?" Elijah asked.

Nehemiah didn't say a word at first. He rolled up a sleeve of his shirt and let the boy trace a line of numbers that had been tattooed on his arm. Elijah didn't know what they meant, but he could see by the man's face that they told a painful story.

"Thank you," Elijah said.

"Don't thank me," said Nehemiah. "Someday, you will be me."

Elijah broke off a piece of cornbread and gave it to the older man. Nehemiah accepted it and then gave him $40 for Duane. Elijah understood. His father wouldn't accept it, but they would need it to get on their feet again.

THE INTERVIEW

New York 2017

There was a certain lecherous reputation associated with the West Village gastropub, enough so that he slipped in behind the potted plants that framed the doorway, but it wasn't his choice. Cynthia Rothman, Esq., one of the newest partners at Martin & Morgan, had called him the night before and said this is where to meet for lunch.

He knew what that meant. They weren't just meeting for lunch, but rather "the lunch" that would put him in the final three to become an associate of a top New York law firm. It would be a dream come true, especially after an emotional hiring process that frequently left him in a state of ambiguity. It had been that way since the start. Despite being sought after by other firms as an attractive candidate, his first choice — Martin & Morgan — had acknowledged his application and then all but ghosted him.

He stepped inside and onto a hardwood plank floor, weathered and worn, and took in the eclectic mix of pictures and artifacts that decorated the brick walls. The seating was also embellished, booths adorned in a red plaid, and bar stools with colorful animal prints — zebras, cheetahs, and tigers. The customers were similarly mixed, dressed in anything and everything, ranging from casual to business attire. But it was the servers wearing black jeans and shirts, more than anything, that made him feel overdressed.

The hostess smiled at him with a knowing, inquisitive nod. He smiled back, momentarily unsure of what he should do. He had arrived before Ms. Rothman, giving him a choice between waiting at the entrance or securing the seats.

"Two for lunch," he said, deciding it would come across more proactive than assumptive.

"Oh, Ms. Rothman, so good to see you," the hostess said, looking over his shoulder. "I'll be right with you."

"No worries, darling, this young man is with me," she said. "William, good to see you. I see you were confident in getting seats. Very good."

He smiled, about to add a point to his "win" column until she took it away.

"Except, we already have a table upstairs," she said. "It's one of the reasons I picked this place. There are nooks and crannies all over. They no doubt lend something to the allegations of groping employees, but they also ensure we can eat someplace quiet and out of the way."

"Of course," William said. "Thank you for inviting me."

"You earned it," she said, waving him on. "Follow me."

He did, following her through a labyrinth of tables, chairs, and patrons. She was dressed smart, wearing a well-tailored dark blue pantsuit with a double-breasted Cady blazer. He guessed Altuzarra by the cut, but could see her wearing pencil skirts and hip-length jackets in warmer weather. He also noticed how young she looked, with only a single streak of gray that her stylist probably added to make people think twice. She didn't want anyone to confuse age with brains.

They sat in an unassuming booth away from the rest of the customers.

"You did very well with the assignment," she considered. "One of the best. You might have even won the case, had it been real, with the work you put together."

"Thank you," he said. "I put some real effort into the research."

"Did you?" she said. "I suppose you did. I was wondering if you thought the assignment was too easy, but I can see that it wasn't."

"Oh," he said, considering how he might roll his answer back. "I only meant I spent considerable time researching my initial theory. I could see the problem right away."

"Relax, William." She laughed. "This isn't that kind of lunch. The next interview, the one we save for the 34th Street office, is where the rest of the partners will make you jump through hoops and defend how much billable time is too much for the client or too little for the firm. This isn't about that."

"What's this about, then?" he asked, seeing the waitress coming toward them out of the corner of his eye and realizing he hadn't even glanced at the menu.

"It's a compatibility lunch," Cynthia said. "It's my job to see if you would be a good fit."

He glanced down at the menu, considering what that meant. She ordered the sheep's milk ricotta gnudi; he ordered a chargrilled burger with Roquefort cheese, medium.

"Bold choice," she said. "Most people wouldn't order a sandwich during an interview."

"Should I reconsider?" he asked, remembering he had to be on point and consider details like only salting his food after tasting it.

"Do you want to reconsider it?" she laughed. "Do you really think what you order is part of a test?"

"I'd like to think it isn't," he said before confessing, "but I'm starting to feel a bit paranoid."

She told him to pretend the little things — like when he arrived, if he asked for a table, what he wore, whether he followed the hostess or her, what kind of lunch he ordered, the cost comparison between her meal and his, whether he drinks with a straw or not — didn't matter. What was important, she said, was what he thought made the firm successful, how he saw himself fitting into that culture, and which shared values and competencies would give him an advantage over the other two candidates.

As he answered her questions, he felt his confidence rising and then soaring. It wasn't long before the conversation turned from pointed questions to small talk. He could picture himself working with her.

"The Bibb salad," said their server, setting a bowl in front of her, and then a plate in front of him. "And here you are, the best burger in New York City."

"Wait," he said, first looking at her order and then his own. "This isn't right."

"Sir?"

"I'm pretty sure she ordered the ricotta gnudi," he said as he watched burgundy juices from his own burger seeping into the bun. "And there is no way this burger is cooked medium."

"Oh, I'm so sorry," said the server, flushed. "I'm pretty sure I put it in as medium rare."

"Medium," he corrected again.

"You know, I'm all right with the salad," Cynthia said. "The gnudi would be too heavy anyway, and this looks great."

"Are you sure? Because I have to send mine back." He frowned at the red meat. "The beef must be very fatty if this is medium rare."

"I'll take it back," the server said. "I'm sure it was my fault."

"Obviously," he said. "You didn't even get her order right."

"I'm sorry that happened, William," Cynthia said as soon as the server left. "They're normally very good here. We have an account with them."

"Oh no, I should have told her to leave the fries so we can both start," he said. "I just hope you don't mind that I sent mine back."

"Not at all." She picked at her salad. "You know what you want."

He did, and he could tell she respected his decision by the way she reinforced everything he said. Even when he shared how he handled an especially uncomfortable situation at college, she told him it was a great answer and how she could see him climbing to the top of the list. At one point, she even confided in him that he was the only candidate being recruited out of college, which was an opportunity for Martin & Morgan to mold him. He was nodding enthusiastically when his burger came back.

"Seriously?" he asked, looking at the crushed bun and reassembled burger.

The server didn't flinch, but her face said it all. Her eyebrows were raised, her smile broken by an expectant apology on her lips. She knew he wouldn't be happy.

"The chef said he put in on the grill for another minute, but anything more would ruin it," she pleaded. "I didn't want to bring it out, but he made me."

"This is ridiculously stupid," he said, looking to Cynthia. "Have you ever seen anything so incompetent?"

"No, never," she mused. "Can I steal one of your fries before you send it back?"

"That's a good idea," he told the server. "I'll keep the fries, and maybe bring me a pork rillette instead."

"I am sorry," she said.

"You should be," he added, watching her sulk away.

"Wow, William." Cynthia smiled. "I think you made her cry."

"Yeah, I suppose I did," he said, regaining his calm. "But this place has enough trouble without incompetence. I hope you tip her appropriately."

"Oh, I intend to," Cynthia said, looking away.

The rest of the lunch went on without incident. The two of them chatted about where he grew up, what his favorite subjects were in school, and what his interests were outside of study. Toward the end, he was even starting to wonder if she was interested in him more than as an associate.

"This has been a pleasure," he said. "Well, except the ... you know."

"It was a pleasure meeting you too, William," she said, standing up before he could.

"So when do you think I'll receive a call for the final interview?"

"Oh, I'm so sorry," she said. "This is our final interview. I'm not moving you forward."

The words hit him like a punch. His face flushed as he tried to backtrack and figure out what changed in the course of their lunch — in the course of the last few minutes.

"You don't know, do you?" Cynthia smiled. "I'm the one who put the orders in wrong, William."

"What?"

"I always put the orders in wrong," she said. "I need to know, or I should say Martin & Morgan need to know, that whatever associate we hire can hold up under pressure. Don't get me wrong. I admire your tenacity and need to get things right. Sending an undercooked burger back is expected. But she didn't deserve the rest of it."

He looked up at her, dumbly.

"Look, you're a good kid. Top of your class. We were interested, and maybe we will be again in a few years," she said. "The truth, though, you're not mature enough for a firm like ours. We look sharp, but we also roll up our sleeves and work together with respect. Again, it was nice to meet you, William. Now, go do the right thing and apologize to Jennifer on the way out."

It took a few minutes for him to recover after she left, but he did exactly what she asked. He found the server, apologized, and caught a cab back to his hotel. It was going to be a long day tomorrow. Two other firms were interested, though neither was as prestigious as Martin & Morgan.

THE STRANGER

South Dakota 1982

When the Schroeders first bought the historic building in downtown Sioux Falls from Kinney Shoes in 1963, Bill Schroeder had a familiar gleam in his eyes. It was one Rosie had seen a few times before — when he asked her out on their first date, when he bent down on one knee to propose, and when they bought their first home.

The sparkle said "Buckle up. The bank papers are signed, and the keys to the front door are in our hands. Great things are about to happen."

He was sure of it, and would happily outline his six ingredients for success to anyone who asked. The first three were good coffee, his mother-in-law's cherry pie recipe, and his wife's larger-than-life smile. The second three were location, location, and location.

He was right about all of it, especially the location. Rosie's Diner attracted an eclectic crowd. Located just west of the Big Sioux Falls River and south of 10th Street, which also did double duty as Highway 42, the diner attracted a steady mix of regulars, tourists, and passersby for fifteen years. Then the worst happened.

Somewhere between the service counter and luncheonette, with a cherry pie in one hand and a coffee refill in the other, Rosie's legendary smile twisted downward on the left-hand side. Her eyes went vacant and five random words tumbled out of her mouth.

"Dinner isn't done, hun. Ding," she muttered, right before dropping the plate and crashing forward into the counter with the coffee.

When Bill laid Rosie to rest a week later, he buried his love for the diner along with her. Every day he opened it after the funeral was a reminder of all he had lost. Rosie was gone forever, and maybe Rosie's Diner was too.

While the regulars were sympathetic despite the dreariness for a few months, they eventually started peeling away for friendlier pastures. By the time those months became years, Rosie's was barely getting by on the sporadic ebb and flow of road-weary travelers who were too tired or too hurried to drive any deeper than a half-block into town. Location, location, location was all he had left.

It wasn't exactly true, but that's how he felt. The truth was that Rosie's would have dried up entirely if it hadn't been for his big-hearted cook, Kaycee Spooner, and the always level-headed waitress-turned-manager, Wilma Nivens. They had become the diner's life support system despite being unable to duplicate Rosie's coffee, pie, or smile.

"So, as I was saying to Kaycee," Wilma continued, "we can combine some of my mom's southern comfort food with Kaycee's Midwest meatloaf, burger, and sausage platters to make a whole new menu. Then we promote his apple pie, and my peach crumble, downplaying the cherry pie since no one knows how Rosie — rest her soul — really made it."

"I dunno," Bill said, sitting behind the desk in his backroom office. "It wouldn't feel like Rosie's if we did all that at once."

"Bill," said Wilma, "We all loved Rosie, but it's time to face the facts. This place hasn't felt like her since we lost her."

"She's right, Bill," Kaycee chimed in. "We need to shorten up the menu and find new ways to energize the locals again."

Bill shook his head and cupped his face with his hands. So this is the beginning of the end, he thought. Or maybe, it was an end to the beginning.

"Bill..." Wilma brought him back from drowning in his thoughts again. "We can't put this off anymore. You pert'near have three, maybe four months left if we're lucky."

He knew she was right. If he stayed the course, drifting along in a daze as he had been for the past four years, there wouldn't be anything left to save. He sighed in surrender and lifted his heavy head to give them his blessing. But instead of his eyes landing on Wilma as he intended, he looked right past her.

"She's right," Kaycee added. "Let us help you save this place."

"Can I help you?" Bill asked.

As he said it, Kaycee and Wilma turned around. There was a man standing in the office doorway. He was plain and unassuming, starting to bald and wearing a short-sleeved button-down plaid shirt and tan slacks. He was looking in at the three of them — sizing them up, if Bill didn't know better. He scratched his head.

"It's upstairs," Bill said, standing. "The bathroom. You're looking for a bathroom, right?"

"No," the man shrugged.

They were all standing now, with Kaycee folding his arms over his chest.

"Are you a customer?" Bill asked.

"No," said the man. "I'm not a customer."

"They were closing the upstairs when we came down," Kaycee said. "Want me to show him out?"

"Yeah, that might be a good idea," Bill said before redirecting to the man. "Is that all right with you, mister?"

"No, I don't think so," he said while coming to some conclusion. "I'm not leaving. Nobody's leaving."

"Come again?" Kaycee asked, unfolding his arms.

"Nobody's leaving," he said. "We'll all go upstairs together and get the other two."

"Why would we do that?" Bill smirked.

"Because it happened right here," he said, pulling a pistol from a belt holster.

Bill guessed it was a .380 based on its size, a small six-shot weapon. He had seen one when he bought his own gun years ago. He purchased a Colt for the diner instead but then locked it up at home after Rosie urged him not to keep it around.

"Yeah, I get you," Bill said. "You want the money? Money we got. It's down here."

"Do you have chains for the doors?" asked the man. "If you do, I want the doors chained. And then I want everybody together."

"You betcha," Bill said, holding up his hands. "We'll play it that way. But maybe you don't need everybody. Let Wilma here go, and the waitress upstairs, maybe?"

"You don't understand," he said, shaking his head with a pained expression. "It happened right here. Nobody can leave."

They did as he said, heading upstairs and then collecting the remaining busboy, John, and waitress, Mandy. They did as he asked and chained the doors, first the front and then the back. There were several times that Bill considered rushing the man — and he imagined Kaycee was doing the same. But it always ended the same way, with Wilma or Mandy lying dead on the floor along with anybody who rushed him.

"All right," Bill said. "The doors are chained. Now what?"

"Everybody into the kitchen," he said. "It will be safer in the kitchen."

"Okay," said Bill. "Maybe John could turn off the outside sign too. You know, nobody wants to attract attention."

The man considered the request. He nodded.

"Go ahead, John," Bill said.

John knew what Bill meant. The panic button was right next to the signage switch. When he returned, he gave Bill an affirming nod. The police would be on their way.

"It's done," John said.

"Now what?'" Bill asked the stranger.

"We wait," he said. "And pray."

Bill looked at his watch. Five minutes, he estimated. They would get there in five minutes unless all the officers were already dispatched elsewhere. It seemed very unlikely in a city like Sioux Falls. So Bill assumed all they would have to do is hold it together for about five minutes until a squad car rolled by.

"Why is he doing this?" Mandy whispered to Wilma.

"Hush," said the man.

"This doesn't make any sense," Mandy said to him. "What do you want?"

"It happened here," the man said. "It's happening now."

"We'll be all right, Mandy," Bill cast a reassuring smile with the hope it might stave off any pending hysteria. "We'll just wait and pray."

There was a rattle at the front door as if someone was testing it. Three minutes, Bill thought. Three minutes and no siren. It couldn't be the police.

There was another rattle at the back door, which made him frown. Did they send two cars? What was going on?

They all heard the whoop of a siren, faint in the distance but clearly coming in their direction. The hostages looked at each other, comforted by the idea the police were on the way. But Bill was less sure. If the police were minutes away, who was outside?

"You called the police?" asked the man, looking at John.

"What?"

"You called them," he said, wildly waving his arm. "No, no, no, no!"

The rattling at the front and back of the building was growing louder, more urgent. Someone was trying to get into the diner. Someone at the front. Someone at the back. The rattling grew into pounding. The glass in front was cracking. The lock in the back was breaking, and the door was putting a strain on the chains.

"You don't know what you've done," he said, shaking his head at John. "Everybody into the cooler. Everybody get in now!"

Where there was hesitation before, there wasn't any now. All of them were confused and frightened by the sudden attack on the diner.

The five of them filed into the cooler, with Wilma making the sign of the cross as she dragged Mandy inside. The young waitress started to lose it, openly crying. John was right behind them, followed by Bill. Kaycee took the longest to climb inside, trying to crane his neck to see if he could see something in either direction. He couldn't.

"There's no time," said the stranger, giving him a push and prodding him inside.

As Kaycee pulled the cooler door shut, they all heard the police siren wind down in front of the store and several shots fired. But the noise and chaos were all gone with another tug on the door. Kaycee, not taking any chances, dropped a wooden plank between two metal slats built into the door. The stranger looked at it and then at Bill.

"It was Rosie's idea," Bill shrugged. "She wanted a safe room for tornadoes and terrorists, she used to say. This is what I came up with to appease her."

They were happy to have it. Whatever had been on the outside of the diner had found its way inside. Despite being muffled, the destruction drew closer until the crashing and banging found the cooler door. Kaycee put his broad back to it, knowing it probably wouldn't help but pushing against it all the same. John joined him, and even Bill felt obliged to put a hand on it in support. They could feel it, whatever it was, whatever they were, trying to get in.

"What's out there?" Bill raised his voice, panic welling up inside as he felt the force of it.

The stranger looked at him blankly as the lights flickered. The cooler was failing, and the air and lights weren't likely to last. Mandy was crying hysterically now, with Wilma whispering the Lord's Prayer in a failed attempt to calm her, drowned out by the roar and the pounding on the door.

With Bill's free hand, he grabbed the Saint Christopher's medal he always wore around his neck. Rosie had given it to him a little more than a year before her death. He was saying a prayer now, too.

But then as suddenly as it had all started, it stopped. The lights flickered on. The cooler kicked in and cast a gentle breeze of cool air over them.

Nobody said anything. They stood frozen in position, uncertain and unwilling to believe it was over. It took several minutes before they began to relax, muscles powering down as Mandy's cries eased from screams into sobs.

With a nod from Bill, and the stranger ready with his weapon, Kaycee and John opened the door. There was nothing outside to greet them except the still evening air. When they stepped out, they saw the damage. The diner looked like a small tornado had struck it. The structure wasn't damaged, but everything was tossed about.

"How did you know?" Bill asked the stranger.

"I just knew," he said. "I just knew, like I know about your wife."

"What about my wife?" Bill frowned.

"She says the diner is done, hun. Sell it in nine years," said the stranger.

Bill took a step back and leaned against the wall to hold himself up. His Rosie said that? It didn't make sense. None of it made sense. Suddenly, he had a few dozen questions rolling around in his head but didn't know which one to ask first.

He never got a chance. John was calling them all to the front of the diner. Outside the broken windows, the strobing red and blue of police lights lit up the street, but there wasn't any officer to be found.

"You said it had happened here, but what exactly happened?" Bill said, turning back toward the stranger.

There was no one there to answer his question. The stranger was gone.

FORGET ME NOTS

West Virginia 1971

Rosa was watching the light slowly move across the ceiling as the day took command of the dawn. It was a quiet morning, with fewer birds than usual despite the fall migration.

The untamed wood and meandering tributaries of the Indian Fork River attracted diversity to the area. Yellow goldfinches, blue buntings, and white-breasted nuthatches were among her favorites. The variety of colors, much like the changing season, kept her attention for hours as one day spilled effortlessly into the next.

A soft knock at the door interrupted Rosa's thoughts, which were always centered on the present as they felt so much easier to hold onto than the past. She didn't say a word as the door was gently opened. A younger woman entered, head leaning in before floating in with a smile.

"Hi, Rosa. How are you today?" beamed the young woman.

"I'm fine," said Rosa, returning the smile.

"Great. Did you sleep well?"

"I did, thank you," said Rosa.

"My name is Sophia," she said. "I'm here to keep you company today."

"That's nice," Rosa said. "I'd introduce myself too, but it seems you know my name."

"I do," said Sophia, pulling a chair up to the bed. "How about we start with breakfast."

Sophia presented a small menu, talking Rosa through the options because she was uncertain of what to order. Occasionally, Sophia would add an observation and make suggestions, such as adding strawberries to the oatmeal or maple syrup to the flour pancakes. Rosa was impressed by the recommendations, not only because of this woman's attention to detail but because she was right. There was no question that strawberries were her favorite berry, and even a spot of the maple syrup made the thin, crepe-like pancakes remarkable.

After breakfast, the two of them chatted about the changing season. It wouldn't be long before the winter would rob the world of its colors, transforming autumn's fiery reds and browns into winter's whites and grays.

"I have an idea," Sophia said. "Why don't we capture those colors today so we have them for tomorrow. What do you think?"

"How are we going to do that?" Rosa asked.

"Maybe we can paint," said Sophia, uncovering an easel and canvas that Rosa hadn't noticed before.

"Oh, dear," Rosa said with surprise. "I don't know how to do that."

"Sure," Sophia encouraged her. "I think you'll be pleasantly surprised by what you can do."

"You really think so?" Rosa hesitated.

Sophia just smiled and helped Rosa into a chair by the window and positioned the easel so the view would inspire her. With Sophia's gentle instruction and reassurance, Rosa began mixing colors and spreading the pigments across the canvas. She was surprised how quickly she took to it.

In the beginning, Rosa worked very hard to match the fall colors outside. But toward the end, she started embellishing the landscape by painting a foreground that was more representative of spring. There were yellows and golds, violets and blues, reds and burgundies. In front of these colorful arrangements, she painted a row of trilliums, white petals open to reveal crowns of gold, and a small row of mouse's ears, tiny blue flowers with yellow irises.

"Trilliums were always among my favorites," Rosa said, sitting back with a look of satisfaction. "One time, I painted a sea of them drifting lazily to the horizon as far as the eye could see."

"You weren't the only one who loved them," Sophia said. "Your husband Jermall loved them too. You remember?"

"He was such a handsome devil," laughed Rosa. "Always gruff and manly on the outside, but as soft as a kitten on the inside. Yes, he loved the trilliums. Anytime I snuck them in a painting, he'd smile and say I sprinkled my canvas with simple beauties. Simple beauties."

"He sounds like a wonderful man," Sophia said.

"Oh, he was. He swept me off my feet, and I never came down," she said. "He was quite a dancer. We even met at a dance, did I ever tell you that?"

"You mentioned it once or twice," Sophia winked. "I think you told me you went dancing after a protest of all things."

"What else are you going to do after a protest?" Rosa laughed. "People always think that time stood still during the fifties and sixties, but we had to live too. Sometimes we would go out dancing right after we reminded people that those who are equal before God ought to be equal in the classrooms too."

"And there you were, right there beside them, making history," Sophia said in admiration.

"I was a teacher raising a daughter, so I didn't have much choice," Rosa said. "People don't talk about it much around here because West Virginia was unique. We were the northernmost Southern state or southernmost Northern state, depending on how you looked at it. So our protests were never violent like in Arkansas or Mississippi. I think most folks, white or black, were kind of relieved to get over with it if you ask me. I mean, in our neighborhood, it didn't matter where you came from. Greeks, Russians, Germans, Jews, whites, blacks. We all played together. We just couldn't go to school together until we fixed things up. Well, you know. You remember."

"Yes, I remember," said Sophia said. "Of course, I was very young at the time."

"Oh heavens, listen to me," Rosa said, catching her breath. "I'll get myself all riled up if I'm not careful. And you are such a dear for letting me go on about these things before your time."

"It's no problem, Rosa," said Sophia. "I love hearing you talk."

"Remind me to tell your boss just how lovely you are," said Rosa.

"You'll have to drive all the way to Parkersburg if you want to do that," said Sophia. "I don't work here."

"Oh, you're a volunteer?" Rosa asked, then considered her words. "Isn't that funny. I just remembered one of my daughters has the same name. Sophia."

"Isn't that funny," said Sophia.

"Sophia?" Rosa said, seeing her daughter for the first time.

"Yes, Momma?"

"Oh my heavens," said Rosa. "What a day. What a day. Tell me what you've been doing. Anything will do."

For the rest of the morning and well into the afternoon, the two of them knitted memories together like a quilt. Wherever Rosa's mind found a purl, Sophia would cast-on another stitch so it wouldn't slip away. The edge of each new row was cast off and away, and they scrambled to catch another piece of Rosa's past.

"I'm so happy you came today," Rosa said. "But all this excitement has worn me down, I'm afraid."

"It's okay," Sophia said. "I love all the time that I can get. It's been a good day."

"The best day," said Rosa. "I can't remember one better. Will you come again tomorrow? Another good day?"

"The best day," Sophia said, leaning in and kissing her mother on the cheek. "Goodbye, Momma."

"Goodbye, my precious girl," said Rosa. "I'm so proud of you."

Sophia almost said something else, but then thought better of it. She let Rosa's words stand as the last thing said when they parted this time. What else could she say, anyway? Sophia knew Rosa's mind would leave everything behind again as soon as she closed her eyes. And Sophia knew she would have to be the one to step back in tomorrow, setting aside all emotion for the hope of another good day.

She turned, putting a hand to her face so Rosa couldn't see the tear in her eye. Today was the best day, just like yesterday, just like tomorrow. And then she closed the door as gently as she opened it, walking out with the memory of her mother painting simple beauties as far as the eye could see.

BAD THINGS

New Hampshire 2018

Crabby's central location and the Nashua River overlook drew an eclectic crowd most weeknights. They would come in gentle overlapping waves: a few old geezers sipping ports or lagers, families ordering fish and chips wrapped in newspaper, college students filling pitchers and tasting IPAs, and finally the bikers and seedier souls that typically crashed the place before last call.

Rauly had already called an Uber and sent the establishment's regular barfly, Jimmy Calvert, home for the night. That left two unusual suspects sitting at a corner table at the back of the bar, occasionally looking up at the silent flickering images of all-night news but mostly looking down and nursing their bourbons. He didn't like them and strained not to stare them down while polishing the last few rocks glasses.

One was a squat, middle-aged man with a receding hairline and flush, pug-nosed face. The other was taller, lanky and lean with sharp, angular features and squinty eyes. He was the one who had regularly made eye contact with Rauly earlier in the night — a smug, slanted grin as if they shared an inside joke and Rauly was the brunt of it.

He folded the bar rag and dropped it on the work station behind the bar. He planned to politely ask them to drink up so he could go home, but John came out of the backroom before he did.

"If you want to cut out tonight, go ahead," John said. "I can get the rest of it."

"Are you sure?" Rauly said, throwing a nod to the men in the corner.

"Yeah, I got them," he said. "You want a drink for the road?"

"No, I'm good," Rauly said, flatlining his hands. "Five years good."

"Sorry, I forget," John said, shaking his head. "I sure as heck don't know why you do it yourself. I mean, whoever heard of a bartender who doesn't drink?"

"Yeah, yeah," Rauly said, lifting and kissing the small cross he wore around his neck. "See you tomorrow?"

"You can count on closing," John said. "Too many breaks, and you'll get soft."

"I'll take the odds on that," Rauly said, already heading into the kitchen while giving a glance back to the corner. "Just don't let them stick around too long."

The skinny guy gave him another grin, and Rauly winced. The freak.

Rauly washed his hands in the sink and poked around in the refrigerator. The cook had left him some pasta and sauce in a takeout container. He grabbed it along with his coat and headed out the back door.

He immediately noticed a dark gray SUV idling near the back door. The driver looked at him, taking a long drag off a cigarette pinched between thin lips framed by a short cut goatee. Rauly kept a wide berth as he walked by until he felt the cigarette butt flipped in his direction.

Rauly turned around and looked down at the ember. He took a step and crushed it with the heel of his boot and headed toward the bar.

"Where do you think you're going, pal?"

"Me? I'm going back to get my coat," Rauly said.

The driver opened his door, blocking the path. Rauly stopped rather than go around.

"You're wearing your coat," he said.

"Oh yeah," Rauly said, looking at his jacket and rolling his eyes. "Not the brightest bulb, I guess. It's okay. I got good eats."

Rauly lifted the takeout tin as if to smell it. The driver watched, smiling at him, amused by the idiocy of it. Rauly leaned in, shifting the weight off his back foot, and fired the dish into the driver's face with his left hand. As the cold pasta, sauce, and tin blinded him, Rauly brought his right hand around and hammered the driver several times in the temple, fist following him down as he went. The driver was out.

Rauly reached into the man's jacket and fished out a Colt 1911. He was happy to hold one again, appreciating its single action, straight back pull, and crisp trigger. The driver had taken care of it, adding a thicker rosewood grip, three-point sights, and a shorter barrel.

He slipped it into his pocket and headed to the back door, pausing to listen but not hearing anything. He unlocked the door and slid inside, making sure the door shut quietly with barely a click. Then he attempted to recall clearing angles that were once second nature.

The last time he entered a building and expected resistance was more than eight years ago, serving as a U.S. military advisor in Uganda. The target was Joseph Kony, a prophet and a guerrilla leader who supposedly carried spirits within him. Kony couldn't be killed, and they never did kill him, but being stationed there did kill something inside Rauly.

He made it home with a drinking problem, haunted by the mutilations he saw. Returning home too late to be by his dying mother didn't help. He drifted away from friends after losing her, eventually pushing past his sister to hide from his shame, taking refuge in backstreet bars and the dark side of depressed towns that dotted America.

He hadn't given any of it much thought in a while, but he found his sister's face crashing through his mind now. He carried her look of disappointment with him everywhere. Her rejection of him was made complete when he called to talk about Step 8. Maybe, he thought, this would be it for him — no more pain and heartache.

Once inside, he found a vantage point to peer into the back office. He could see John was sitting in a chair in front of the desk, expression blank and absent of color. The two men were standing, flanking the aging manager. They were talking quietly, but Rauly surmised it was a death sentence.

He crept up to the office door, drawing the Colt. At the last second, Rauly stood tall and pushed the door aside. He was smiling when he did it as if his re-entry was a happy accident.

"Hey," he said.

Both men turned. The taller one looked at him, slacked jawed, and started reaching behind his back. Rauly fired a single shot into his skull and spun the gun around on the shorter man. He was putting his hands up, a knife glinting in the light of the lamp. Rauly shot him in the chest.

He pocketed the gun, crouched to retrieve the knife, and freed John by cutting through the duct tape that bound the manager's wrists to the arms of the chair. John didn't look at him. His gaze fixed on a space beyond the door.

"Let me get you out of there," Rauly said. "You okay?"

Coming to life, John suddenly wrestled his hands away as Rauly freed them. He shook off the help. He didn't stand, but his body stiffened. He surveyed the room.

"What did you do?" he asked in accusation, looking at the bodies.

"I dunno. Saved you?"

"No, no," John groaned. "You think these guys are the only ones? Everybody will be coming down on this place now."

"What?" Rauly said. "These guys were going to hurt you."

"I didn't hire you to be some hero," he said. "I hired you because you're a washout. A nobody. A guy who doesn't notice things."

Rauly stepped back. The adrenaline was still surging in his veins as his emotions tumbled from concern and confusion to realization and anger.

"They would have would hurt me, sure," he said, getting up. "But now? I don't know what I'm going to do. This is bad, bad, bad."

"We still have to call the police," Rauly said.

"No, we're not calling any cops," he said. "I got to get out of here. I have to get my family out of here. And you, you'll get out of here too if you know what's good."

John circled the desk and opened the drawer to retrieve the .38 Special the owner kept there. Then he bent down to the safe and opened it.

"What about the third guy?" John asked. "What happened to him?"

"You know?"

"There's always a third guy," he said. "Look. All this? My fault. I shorted them on the cleaning last week so they had to come in and give me a show. I was ready to take it, and then everything would have been fine. But now? We're all dead."

"I didn't know," Rauly said.

"What? You think managing this place makes me enough money to afford nice things?" He frowned. "My boat? The golf membership? My kids' braces? No. That's life. You do what you gotta do."

"Does Joe know?"

"No, but he will," he said. "Somebody will have to pay for this mess, or he'll find a Molotov walking in the front door. Might even be better if he does. Get it over."

Rauly watched as John scooped out the contents of the safe.

"Severance," he said, holding up the gym bag and heading out the door. "You're on your own. Cut loose if you know what's good."

Rauly was left standing alone in the office, looking down at the two men. Boston mob? He didn't know. It didn't matter. He had to call old Joe and tell him to call the police.

After hanging up, Rauly walked out. He wasn't surprised to see the SUV gone, reinforcing his decision not to wait. More than anything, he needed a night to regroup and decide his next move. He wasn't ready for it, but a crisis had come for him anyway.

His instinct told him to disappear, but was that a choice? Wasn't that what he had done all his life? Maybe it was time to learn the lesson and do something different. Stand up tall and hold his ground, even when the devil knocked in the door.

Rauly pinched the bridge of his nose. He turned away from the river and toward the parking lot. Tomorrow couldn't come soon enough.

THE ENGAGEMENT

New Jersey 1981

It was all supposed to be easy. Well, maybe easy isn't the right word. Everybody expects to be nervous when they propose marriage. And I already knew I was going to be a bundle of nerves. There were times I even wondered if I'd go through with it.

So I did what I always do when I'm faced with these situations. I make a plan, and then I rip up the plan, and then I redo the plan all over again. The general idea is that if I can get mired down in the details, then I don't have to think about it. It keeps things simple, which is why I expected it to be easy. The more plans I made, the easier it would be.

Even a few days out, I felt amazingly confident. I was going to ask Katie to marry me and she was going to say "yes," and we were going to start this amazing life together. It's fate, right? Something inside of you just clicks when you find that one special person who completes you. That's how I felt about Katie from the start.

We met at a professional coaching center. I was there because I was in a career transition and exploring this crazy idea to become a personal coach. I mean, it made sense at the time. I fit all the criteria. People usually come to me for advice. I always see great potential in everyone. I'm a big fan of healthy relationships and a balanced life. Me and a thousand people just like me, sure. It was worth a shot.

Katie was there for a different reason. She was working as a human resources specialist and wanted to advance her career. This place also had a program specifically for human resources personnel, teaching them how to improve their presentation, deliver more value, and boost employee effectiveness. It's almost like coaching, except it's human resources.

When she walked in for the first time, I was sitting in the corner of the lobby, just reading a book. It was called *Feeling Good: The New Mood Therapy* by some psychiatrist guy. It was supposed to help lift my spirits in the face of being laid off. There was no one else in the room and I was reading the same paragraph over and over again, so I looked up, not wanting to come across as rude. I mean, it was a coaching center after all, and they were always encouraging us to be present and have a presence.

I must have done a decent job of it because she gave me a little smile after she signed in at the front desk. Then, even though there was no one else in the room, she picked a chair next to mine. Well, not next to mine, but one over from mine, so there was some space between us. Still, it was pretty obvious she was interested.

At least, I thought she was interested. Then it only seemed like she wanted to be friends. In fact, that's all we were for a long time. She even started dating another guy a few weeks after we met because I was too shy to tell her how I really felt. Or maybe it was because I was too busy coaching her, even though I wasn't her coach, and she was too busy being coached.

The reason doesn't really matter, I suppose, because the guy cheated on her. It really made her a mess. It was an ugly breakup. She said she had never felt so betrayed. I remember she even told me how she had lost complete faith in love.

So I backed off from dropping any hints for a while. It didn't seem right, and my hints weren't working, anyway. But then we started running in slightly different circles, given that I lived closer to where I grew up, The Shore, and she always lived in Newark. It wasn't that I wasn't interested. It was just the opposite. She had stopped talking to people we both knew. She got a new phone but didn't transfer her contacts. The only time I really saw her was when she was speaking at some luncheon or event or conference.

She would share her ideas about human resources and motivating people, and I would wait patiently until she was finished so she would see me there. But she never put two and two together, which was probably my fault. I was always pretending to meet up with friends wherever she happened to be a guest speaker.

It was at one of these conferences, however, when I finally had the nerve to get her number. It wasn't easy, but I got it from one of the conference planners and then called her that night. She told me that I was lucky she picked up. Most of the time she ignored unknown callers. I was also fortunate because we talked for hours.

She shared everything with me. How she was struggling to recover from the broken trust. How she tried to go out with other men, but it never seemed to work out. How her dad had cheated on her mom when she was growing up. And how I was the first person she had shared her true feelings with.

I shared some things with her too. How a girl in college hurt me. How hard being laid off from my first job really was. How even though I always told her the coaching gig was going great, it really wasn't my thing. I felt much more confident working in tech, which is where I ended up. She seemed surprised I was sharing so much but really appreciated it.

So that's when I told her how I had felt from the moment we met at the coaching center. She didn't say anything for a long time, like she was trying to piece it all together or sort through all those hints I used to drop. That's when I decided to make my first big move with her.

"If you give me a chance, I will never hurt you," I said. "I mean, maybe it will work out or maybe it won't, but I want to prove to you that just because someone hurt you doesn't mean you can't trust anyone else. I'll show you how to trust again and make you happy. And if I fail you, and you want to leave me any day, then I won't stop you."

Everything changed from that moment on. It was like she had been waiting her whole life for someone to say those things. And I had been waiting for her to make a connection between our hearts since day one. The wait was still worth it.

It's hard to find the words to describe what's it like to spend several months with someone you love. You feel a fluttery excitement every time they walk in the door. You feel electricity running through your skin when you touch. You feel relaxed after making love and wake up when they do. You know when they've had a bad day and how to make it better. You talk about the future and what your kids might look like.

We had all of it, which is why I thought proposing would be so easy. I saved up for a one-carat round engagement ring, bordered by ten tiny stones on each side of the band. I booked a dinner for two at Café Matisse, which is a beautifully appointed restaurant with these colorful Impressionist-style paintings and chandeliers. I had placed an order with a nearby bakery, an assortment of pastries, so we could steal away after dinner in a limousine that she didn't even know about. It would take us home to her apartment in Newark and drop her off, or us, depending on how things went.

Aside from those mile markers, there were a hundred smaller details: what I should wear, which watch was most reliable, what should I say, and when I should say it. I even practiced in front of the mirror, pretending to reach out for a dinner roll before turning my hand over to reveal the small black velvet box. It was all coming together.

It was supposed to be easy. Sometimes I tell myself it would have been easy had I not seen the "Spiritual Reading" sign after picking up her ring from the jewelers. But I did see it. I saw it out of the corner of my eye, passed it, and made a left-hand turn from the right-hand lane even though I always hate it when other people do that.

The woman there didn't really look like a fortune teller. She was just an attractive, middle-aged woman with dark hair and these startlingly green eyes. She didn't wear a costume like some psychics do, just jeans and a blouse. I even asked her about it, and she told me she could borrow a scarf from one of the other women if it made me feel better. We both laughed about it.

I told her I was going to propose to my girlfriend in a couple of days. She smiled and said Katie was lucky to have such a thoughtful guy like me. She could tell by my face and then my hands, once she held them and turned them over. She asked me to sit down and shuffle some oversized cards while I thought about my life with Katie.

Then she took the cards and laid down the Knight of Pentacles, which was supposed to be me. Then she laid ten more cards, one at a time. The first six created a cross over the card representing me, and then she placed four more alongside those before talking me through each one. I remember each one like it was yesterday, but only the last card really mattered.

She let out a little gasp when it came up, an image of a depressed man in a black cloak standing by five cups. The three he was facing were toppled over. What did it mean? I must have asked her ten times before she told me. She said that this card, in relation to all the other cards, told her that while Katie was going to accept my proposal, our relationship would end tragically in about three years.

What the heck, right? It's not exactly the thing you want to hear two days before you ask someone to marry you. I was pretty upset. I told her there was some mistake, then I asked her to start over, and then I told her nevermind. I left.

I still had all my plans to lean on, but I was a wreck for the next two days. I avoided Katie, making up excuses while always pushing it off to the big night when we would meet up at

Café Matisse. Even when she told me she wanted to talk to me about something, I asked her to wait.

Maybe it was the reading, or maybe it was just the mounting pressure, but dinner didn't start off right. Instead of all that pent-up excitement that had run through me like a lightning bolt for months, I was filled with a sense of dread. What do you do when you know the end of a story and it doesn't end the way you want it to? Do you keep reading or rip up the pages?

I wanted to rip them up. I wanted to rip everything up. I wanted to rip open the little black velvet box that I was turning over and over in my pocket and hurl the stupid ring across the room. So what if it hit the lady wearing that ugly blue peacock dress at the corner table?

It was so overwhelming that I wasn't really paying attention to Katie anymore. We were sitting there like two statues facing each other. I couldn't take it, so even though they hadn't even served our salads, I reached out for the rolls like I rehearsed and she, unexpectedly, covered the top of my hand with her hand before I could turn it over for the big reveal.

"John, I don't know how to say it, so I'm just going to say it," she said. "I've been trying to talk to you for the last couple of days because the doctors have found an abnormality in my uterus. I have uterine cancer. They don't know how they missed it."

"What?" I said. "But they can treat that, right?"

"Yes, yes, they can," she said. "Usually. But mine is very advanced, which changes everything. Even if I were to survive, we could never have the life we imagined. No children, for one thing."

"We could adopt," I said, reflexively.

"Our love life wouldn't be the same," she said. "And I don't think I'm going to be a very happy person in the months ahead. When I think of what I'm losing, what we're losing, it's almost too much to bear. Maybe, maybe we should take a break for a while."

I didn't expect it. I didn't expect any of it, so I just sat there for a moment. She might have even still been talking to me, but I didn't hear her. All I could see was the damn man in the black cloak, looking at those three spilled cups.

"John?" she said, asking if I was even there anymore.

"I went to a fortune teller the other day," I said. "And the last card she showed me was this card with a man in a black cloak looking at three spilled cups. For the last couple of days, all I could think about were those cups. But there weren't just three cups in the picture, Katie. There were two more that hadn't been spilled. I think I'll take those."

So I turned over my hand and asked her to marry me.

You know, in my dreams, I always imagined we would knock things off the table and kiss in all the excitement of a cheering restaurant. We didn't. We just sat there across from each other, our two hands interlocked with the ring, and quietly cried for the years we had left as much as the ones we had lost.

PAPA GHEDE

Louisiana 2014

She was sitting in his bedroom when he came up. Her back was to the door, face to the bureau mirror, his brush in her hand.

"You look just like your mama sitting here," he said.

He startled her, but she tried not to wince. She hadn't expected him home so soon. Maybe she should have. Twenty dollars doesn't go very far on Bourbon Street.

"You're drunk," she said.

"I'm not so drunk to miss you coming around," he said. "Why else would you be in here?"

"I broke my brush, and I came in to use yours."

He smirked. "No, you wanted to surprise me."

"If wishes were fishes ..."

"... you'd give me some kisses." He finished with a laugh.

"That's not how it goes," she said, watching him in the mirror but not turning around.

"That's how I say it goes," he said with a hint of anger in his voice.

He took another pull from his bottle, leaning up against the door and admiring her. She could feel his eyes crawling up one exposed arm to her neck, and prayed he didn't detect a tremble. Fear excited him, and she was already flush with it.

"Did you go to the Quarter and get what I said?"

"I got something," she said.

He was talking about a pink teddy he had seen in the window of Victoria's Secret. She was talking about something else. She held it in her lap and covered it with her right hand. Then she slowly raised the brush with her left and set it back on the bureau.

"Maybe I could brush your hair," he said, shifting his weight off the door frame. "Or maybe you could show me what you got."

"Sure," she said, lowering her eyes so she didn't have to see the hungry expression on his face anymore.

A floorboard creaked behind her.

"Which one?" he said. "Brush your hair? Show me something?"

"I'll show," she said.

"And you won't fight me this time?"

"I won't fight you no more," she said with a break in her voice.

He reached out to put his hand on her shoulder. She could feel him closing in along with his stink. He smelled of sweat and smoke and stale beer.

"Good."

With one hand, she tucked a knot of hair she pulled from the brush into the figure in her lap. Then she slowly started to angle her body toward him, as if the idea were her own, but keeping her hands hidden until the last possible minute. He stopped.

"What you got? What you got there?" he asked, eagerly.

Then he saw it too late. His face expressed only a momentary flash of recognition as her arms spread like the expansive wings of a brown pelican. In one hand, she held a voodoo doll. In the other, she fisted a knob pin, more than five inches long, capped on one end with a skull carved out of bone. She brought her hands together, driving the sharp end of the pin deep into the poppet's head.

He howled, throwing the bottle aside and grabbing his temple as if his head was exploding from the force of it. She imagined the white burst of pain that started just above his ear and penetrated his brain.

She twisted and twisted, encouraged with every shake of his head. He was screaming with every stab and twist. She cried out in a mix of anguish and relief. The abuse was finally over, she thought. She was sure of it, until his shrieks turned into snorting laughter.

"Oh, you got me," he said, looking down at her. "Except it don't work that way."

He raised his right hand and backhanded her across the face. The blow knocked her off the chair, spinning her around. The doll scattered across the floor and she chased after it, scrambling, throwing elbows and knees forward.

He grabbed at her flailing legs and caught one shoe. She kicked him away, losing her shoe in the process. It didn't matter, she thought. She had the doll again and was stabbing at it.

"The definition of crazy is trying the same thing over and over and expecting a different result," he said, loosening his belt from his pants. "It ain't working."

He was on her, grabbing her throat with one hand and punching her with a buckle in the other. He was saying something about making her pay, but all she could think to do was stab and stab and stab at the doll.

And then he stopped, his eyes wide in disbelief. She looked down at her own hands and saw a small ribbon of blood from where she had stabbed through the doll and into his chest, the sharp end of the skull-capped pin slipping between two ribs.

"It don't work that way," he said, pushing himself off her.

Or maybe it did, she thought, working her way up. What had the Mambos told her?

"When we lose all sense of reality, only illusion and delusion remain."

"You have no ti bon ange," she spat on him and turned out of the room.

She grabbed her pre-packed satchel and was out the front door. She didn't see a soul outside, except for a dark, odd little man smoking a cigar. He gave her a smile and a tip of his high hat before continuing on his way. Had she turned around, she would have seen him enter her uncle's house behind her.

THE STANDOFF

Arizona 2017

She felt the heat from the morning sun on her face as she squinted at him. It felt too hot for this time of day, the desert air biting at her exposed skin. Whether it was global warming or the coming confrontation, she couldn't tell. Pins and needles.

He was a big man, drinking in her frailty. His hands were glued to his hips, a broad straw hat casting a long shadow that made him look all the more formidable. He could be on her in a step. He could break her with a snap.

"I let you stay here," she said, German accent as heavy as the pitchfork she held in her hands. "But no more."

"I fix fence," he said, offering it up as more of a question than a statement, with a Mexican accent as heavy as her native tongue.

"No, you broke the rules."

"What rules?"

"No illegals."

"No illegals," he countered.

"They broke the fence. They tried to get into my house."

"No, they come to my house. They're all gone."

By his house, he meant the mobile home she had lent to him at the front of the property in exchange for doing yard work. It was run down, with a front porch that sagged under every step. The rooms inside smelled of mildew every time it rained, which is why she had moved all her old clothes into one of the other dilapidated mobile homes on her property.

"I don't want any trouble," she pressed.

"No trouble."

"No *Militsiya*," she said, her thoughts tumbling through the words. "No Gestapo."

He shook his head, frowning.

"Police."

"No police," he said, putting up his hands. "I fix fence."

He didn't understand. She wasn't calling the police. She didn't want them to come around. Gestapo. *Militsiya*. Police. They were all the same to her. They forced her from her home, turning her family's farm into a headquarters during the war. They forced her and her sisters into hiding, rape gangs with badges, before they could escape to West Berlin. They always ask too many questions behind their fake smiles, just like the local sheriff when her grandson requested a well check because she didn't answer the phone.

"I don't want police," she said, remembering how the sheriff suggested a nursing home. "No concentration camp. No commune. No prison."

"No police," he said. "I fix fence."

"You have to go because she has to go." She motioned to his mobile home with the pitchfork.

"Another chance," he said, smiling and taking a small step back. "You see."

"She stole my dresses." She scowled, years of anger boiling up inside her.

"One dress." He held up a worried finger.

He didn't understand. One dress. Ten dresses. One hundred dresses. The number didn't matter when you never threw anything away. Racks of clothes. Boxes of wigs. Bags of papers. Knickknacks and figurines. Three homes and a trailer, some rooms filled floor to ceiling.

She kept everything because she knew what it was like to have nothing in Germany. Even her childhood was given away washing Russian uniforms for a few rubles a week. She had nothing when she escaped to West Berlin, just a promise from her sister that the circus would save her life. It gave her a life instead. She met an American soldier. He had given her a dress and then abandoned her when she was two months pregnant. The soldier was Hispanic too.

She waved the end of the pitchfork at him.

"*Nein*," she said. "You go. *No schutz*."

He took a hesitant step away from her advance. Her pulse quickened, confidence rising with every inch he yielded. He was just like the man who left her, making promises and giving dresses. Only this time, they were her dresses.

"*Ich hasse dich*!" She lunged. "I hate you!"

But this time, he didn't give any ground as she thrust at him. He sidestepped the tines and grabbed the handle, trying to wrest it free. He pulled and pushed; pushed and pulled. On the third yank, she fell away from it and landed on the ground, clutching a burning wrist.

"You crazy," he railed, raising the pitchfork above his head. "We should have killed you last night."

"*Baller!*" she screamed. "*Baller!*"

Her German shepherd rounded the back porch of her home, looking for a ball. He ran forward, teeth bared, stopping just in front of her. His body was low, ears back, and tail down. The man held the pitchfork aloft, poised to stab her dog if not her.

"You crazy," he said again, but this time in surrender. "You don't know our struggle."

He spat and lowered the pitchfork, tossing it down. The dog eased, licking her wounded hand.

"It's good," she said. "You good dog, Spike."

The man left her there, heading off toward his home. The pair of them would be gone by the afternoon, leaving her all alone again. She was used to it. Her son died before his twentieth birthday, leaving her and a different American solider who had stepped up to be her husband. He died five years ago.

"We all struggle," she whispered, getting up.

She slowly started walking back to the house. She had to bandage her hand before it was time to feed the quail. They always visited in the late afternoon. They were her quail inside the fence.

AS IT SEEMS

Kansas 1971

The storm shelter had already felt cramped with five people and a black Cairn terrier, before Rose's father invited the family of three inside. The new arrivals were wet, the storm having added to its fury in the 25 minutes since her family had descended into its depths, more than twenty feet below the surface.

Not counting the steep stairwell, the single room was a ten-foot by twelve-foot rectangle of thick, reinforced concrete that her father had paneled with wood planks to feel more like a basement than a tomb. Her parents had covered one side of the room with tack paper-lined shelves packed with food tins, bottled water, and survival supplies. The other side of the room was dominated by two metal fold-up bed frames with four-inch-thick mattresses and standard-issue Army surplus blankets.

The top bed was folded up against the wall, making room for the brunette who was lying unconscious on the bottom bunk. The young man, her boyfriend, sat on the edge of the bed, pressing a wet compress to her head. She had been injured by flying debris after they had abandoned his MGB Roadster in favor of the Sorell family farmhouse ten minutes before. It was only by chance that he saw the elevated opening of the storm shelter while circling the house and looking for help or an unlocked door.

With the bottom bed occupied, Rose's mother had taken to standing against the back wall, adorned with an American flag, and waiting patiently for the young woman to show any sign of regaining consciousness. Rose's father, Albert, was still perched on the steep corrugated steps he had climbed to let in the newcomers while Rose sat on the floor, attempting to calm her terrier after the shelter had been opened to the cold, damp wind that whipped through the tiny space.

"Well, would you look at this," the man in the suit muttered as he surveyed the space, temporarily blocking his daughter and wife from entering. "There's no place to sit."

Down here, or what most people called the Sorell storm shelter, wasn't built for comfort. It wasn't even built as a tornado shelter, which explained its excessive depth. It was constructed in 1961, about the same time children were first being taught to "duck and cover" under their desks, and paid for with a small mortgage on the farm and a government bomb shelter grant.

The only grant stipulation was that the bomb shelter had to be clearly marked for residents to find in the event of a nuclear attack. The Sorells were among the first in the area to install such a shelter, with Albert considering it more part of his patriotic duty to fight Communism than any fear of fallout. He always assumed that America's sheer tenacity to fortify its citizens would provide more protection from World War III than any actual infrastructure.

Nonetheless, he signed up immediately and put the local contractors to work. They dug deeper and retrofitted what once was a root cellar and tornado shelter, transforming it into a certified bomb shelter, not that anyone understood what was "certifiably" needed to survive a nuclear winter in '61.

"It wasn't built for comfort," Albert said, encouraging the family to move down. "But we paid off the ten-year loan last year, and we'll all be safe until the storm passes."

"Is the dog friendly?" asked the man, reaching out with a cautious hand and holding his daughter back with the other.

"Mostly," Rose said, despite feeling a growl from somewhere deep inside the terrier.

"Well, I'm going to tell my daughter to steer clear, anyway. She's allergic," he said. "What's his name?"

"Toto," Rose said.

"Seriously?" snorted the man. "I suppose your name would be Dorothy, then?"

"Her name is Rose," said Albert.

"All right, I guess that makes sense," he said, smiling at his joke. "No harm done. We're still in Kansas, after all. I'm Walter, Walter Loman, and this my wife, Dolly, and daughter Sally."

Walter ushered them into the corner by the stairs as he introduced them, but took a protective stance. His wife and daughter had dressed comfortably for travel, but he wore an unassuming beige suit and a brown tie. It was clean, slightly oversized, and dated.

"We were driving to Albuquerque from Chicago when the storm hit," he continued. "I wanted my family to see what the wild west looks like."

"That's a long drive, mister," the boy said. "You driving the whole way, or are you trading off with the missus?"

"Oh, it's not so long," he said. "We stayed in Topeka last night. Thought we could make it to Clayton."

"Clayton?" said Albert. "Never heard of it."

"It a small town that was part of the Santa Fe Trail," he said. "I don't imagine we'll make it today, though, even if I do drive the whole way. I have a lot of experience driving. I represent Encyclopedia Britannica. Heard of it?"

"We have a set of those at school, except the other kind," the boy said.

"World Book," Walter guessed. "They're fine if you can find a set under five years old. Ours are considerably more scholarly, and we send updated volumes at no extra cost."

"Hey, Russell?" Albert grinned at the boy. "Did you hear the one about the housewife who answered the door when a stranger knocked?"

"No, sir," the boy said.

"She asked if he was an encyclopedia salesman. He replied, 'No, ma'am, I'm a burglar,'" Albert said. "'Oh, thank goodness,' she says."

"Yeah, a good one," Walter said with a forced laugh to feign solidarity. "What's wrong with the girl?"

"She was hit on the head," Russell said. "Ms. Sorell was kind enough to patch her up, but she hasn't regained consciousness yet."

"Fine folks," said Walter. "But you never know. This is where an encyclopedia might come in handy. H for head injuries."

"Daddy?" Walter's daughter Sally asked, looking for his attention. "My eyes are itchy."

"It's probably the dog," he said. "There's not much air circulation down here."

"You're welcome to try the ventilation system," Rose said. "It's a hand crank."

"Yeah, I bet it is," said Walter, walking over to it. "And a radio? It would be good if we could get some weather updates."

"Radio won't work down here," Albert said. "There's something in the soil and there's too much soil anyhow. Don't worry, though. We can still hear tornado warning sirens down here."

"Comforting thought," said Walter, folding out a hand crank from the unit.

As he turned, it began to whirl like a muted air raid siren that wasn't all that different from the sirens they were listening for from some distant tower outside. The sound made Rose uncomfortable and Toto even more so. He began to bark at Walter Loman, who had worked up a good speed despite breathing heavily for the effort.

"I don't know," he paused. "I don't know if it will do any good."

His daughter was crying now; a soft whine. Dolly told her not to rub her eyes, but it was too late. She reflexively irritated them even more. Toto continued to squirm, finding the eight-year-old girl as good enough reason to bark as the whirl of the ventilation system.

"Can you shut the dog up?" Walter said.

Unsure of what to do, Rose gave Toto some slack. The terrier took it and pranced over to the corner of the room, beginning to squat. The pungent smell of it filled the room.

"Come now, I've just about had enough," Walter said, looking at his wife as she covered her nose and mouth.

"He didn't mean anything by it," Rose said. "I'll clean it up."

"I'll get it, Rose," Albert said. "We have a bucket for anything like that, his or ours, makes no difference."

"It's not good enough," Walter turned to Albert, raising his voice. "The growling. The barking. The allergies. It's just too much."

"What do you propose we do with him?" Albert snarked. "It will be another hour or two before the storm passes."

"He's a dog," Walter said, grimly. "He'll figure it out."

"No!" Rose protested. "Daddy."

"Don't worry, Rose," he said. "Nothing's going to happen."

"Come on, Mr. Loman," Russell chimed in. "You can't be serious."

"You bet I'm serious," he said, pulling something from his pocket. "This hole in the ground is bad enough. I'm not going to let some mutt make it all the worse. Hand him over."

"No!" Rose blurted, pulling Toto back to her and covering him with a protective arm.

The revolver in his hand wasn't large, but its short barrel didn't have to be in close quarters. Rose wasn't sure what kind of gun it was. Her father had only taught her how to clean and shoot rifles and shotguns, weapons that made more sense on a modern farm. What Walter Loman was pointing indiscriminately at them was something else, probably purchased for self-defense.

"Calm down now, Mr. Loman. Let me talk to her," Albert said, looking at the gun and then turning to his daughter. "Rose, it's all right. It doesn't look like we have a choice."

"He'll die out there, Daddy!"

"Let's give him more credit than that," he said, reaching out to take the dog and pass it to Loman.

As he passed Toto to the salesman, he paused long enough to look Walter in the eyes. He wanted the man to see the smoldering fire starting to ignite inside him. Albert might be older, but hard work had maintained some of his failing strength.

"The girl can shut up too," said Walter, muzzling the terrier with a clamped hand as he climbed the stairs.

He was halfway up when they heard the muffled whines of a siren somewhere outside. The sound was a steady drone, rising and falling every few seconds. Loman took one step down again. But as he did, there was a distinct knock on the shelter door. Three solid raps before a more frantic, urgent pounding. With Walter on the stairwell, no one moved toward it.

"Someone's out there," Albert said. "You going to get it?"

Walter didn't move. He seemed frozen, consumed in thought.

"If there's a tornado close by, it's the same as murder," Albert added dryly.

Walter looked at him with a sense of uncertainty, let Toto go, and climbed the stairs again. The gun was still in his hand when he opened the storm shelter doors. The smell of rain blew in with several gusts of wind. They could hear the door close again, and Walter coming back down the stairs.

A large black man followed. His denim jacket and overalls were wet; his boots made a sucking sloshing sound with every step.

"I'm so glad you all..." he said, stopping mid-sentence as he looked at the expressions of everyone in the room and then back to Walter. "What's all this?"

"Move over there," Walter said, pointing with the gun. "Move over there with the rest of them."

"Hey now," he said. "I don't want no trouble."

The lights in the shelter flickered. The sirens faded in the background. Rose wasn't sure if the storm above had drowned it out or if the three-minute mark had lapsed. Some people always assumed they were safe when the siren stopped, but it wasn't right. Most weather warnings only lasted a few minutes.

"Great," Walter muttered. "Now, we have a dog and a drifter stinking up the place."

"My name is Percy, if you don't mind," he said, hands elevated.

"It's all right, son," Albert said to Percy. "Come on over here."

"Just put the gun away, Mr. Loman." Russell stood up. "It's time."

Walter looked down at the gun and then around the room, his face mirroring the agony of his captives. He seemed unsure of how everything had escalated. The shrinking room, the thinning air, the crying girl, the barking dog, the disinterest of the farmer ... he didn't know. It all pressed in on him, now compounded by the addition of another unfriendly.

"I shouldn't have let him in," he concluded. "You never know about people. He could be anyone."

Outside, the storm roared. The rattling of the shelter door was joined by the hammering of some unknown debris. All eyes looked to the ceiling as the lights flickered again, except Rose and Percy. She looked down to comfort Toto in her lap, and Percy's eyes locked on the barrel of Walter's gun. It had dipped with a relaxed wrist as he considered whether the threat above was greater than any imagined threat in the room.

"It's right above us," Walter whispered, looking at Albert for clarification. "You hear it, don't you? It's right above us."

"It's all right, Mr. Loman," Albert managed, hands open.

"Don't you see?" His lips curled back, showing angry teeth. "We'll all be buried alive down here. All because of that storm."

Rose looked up at him, tears in her eyes.

"No," Rose said. "We'll be buried alive down here because you're the storm."

He looked at her and leveled the gun. His panicked face was becoming pale and placid as he made some terrifying resolution. Toto growled as the light flashed again. The bulb popped, plunging them all into darkness.

As it flashed, Rose saw Percy making a move toward Mr. Loman, reaching out with a hand before his body followed. There was a scuffling. Something fell onto the stairs. The clatter of metal on cement. The sound of punching meat. Moans of agony.

Rose pressed her hands to ears, expecting to hear gunfire. But she never did. It became silent, except for the heavy breathing of men.

The next sound she heard was accompanied by the smell of sulfur, cutting through the mixture of sweat, dank excrement, and damp basement. Her father was lighting a kerosene lamp. A soft light illuminated the room as he locked the glass housing over the flame.

Percy had pinned Mr. Loman, and Russell was busy tying the salesman's hands.

The storm was subsiding, but no one spoke until Albert climbed the stairs and opened the shelter door to a pale gray sky. The rain was light and smelled clean. Toto broke free from her arms and scrambled up the stairs in delight.

When the rain stopped, Percy Booker was the first to say his farewells. Albert had offered to hire him on to help fix the damage the tornado had done to the northeast side of the house. Percy declined, saying he would rather not be around when the police officers showed up with questions. Besides, he said he had a train to catch.

They were sorry to see him go. Everyone was sorry, except for Mr. Loman. He had been right all along. You never know about people.

SCREEN DOOR

Wisconsin 1981

Every summer we migrated north with the birds, flocking to a family lake cottage deep in the woods. My grandfather had built most of it: thick logs fashioned into a home and painted green; big bay windows on the west side to catch the reflection of the sun off the water; a screen door on the east with a squeak that said welcome home.

It was a retreat where family members gathered to remember some things and forget others, caught up in all the charm and challenge of living in the moment. Who would win at penny-ante poker? Who would pull in the biggest fish? Who was old enough to claim their right of passage by plunging into the water and swimming a mile to the other side of the lake? Who would lose their marshmallows in the bonfire made from an old boat that had outlived its purpose?

It was a place with backwood rules. Flush for two but not for one. Flip the bail closed on the spinning reel before the lure touches the water. Never buy bait because it's easy enough to dig up nightcrawlers in the morning or net minnows in the early afternoon. Expect to clean what you catch unless it's a muskie. Never let a screen door slam, and expect someone to call after you if you do.

"Don't let the screen door slam."

The last time I shut it quietly behind me, my grandfather was half the man I remembered. Lymphoma had stolen most of him. We didn't take the boat out or pick wild berries or climb the watchtower. There were no accidents reported on my uncle's radio or trails to mark or gardens to tend. We settled on telling each other a few good stories before he lifted a broom above his head for exercise.

It was the last time I ever saw him, and the last time I ever walked through the front door again. The cottage was sold by his second wife a few years later, compounding everyone's sense of loss with reoccurring emptiness that comes about every summer.

Looking back, I should have slammed it.

A HOLE IN THE WALL

Hawaii 2020

"**W**ell, that's better," she said, sitting cross-legged on the damp ground so she could see him.

"You're a doctor," said the teenage boy, peering in through the other side of the hole.

"Don't be silly," laughed the girl, brushing stray hairs back from her face with a gloved hand. "I'm not old enough to be a doctor."

"I wouldn't know," said the boy. "You're all covered up with that mask and gown."

She folded her arms and shrugged, feeling self-conscious for the first time. The boy wasn't wearing anything like it. He was dressed in blue jeans and a green aloha shirt with white flowers and light green stems, just as he would be on any other day.

"I suppose you wouldn't know," she admitted. "But I'm just like you — a student without a school to go to while we stay at home."

"Oh," said the boy, considering what she said. "So what's with the getup?"

"My parents don't want to take any chances," she said. "I put this on any time I go outside. And sometimes I wear it inside when my father comes home from work."

"That's funny," said the boy. "We don't do anything like that."

"Are your parents essential workers?" she asked. "Mine are essential workers. My father works at a bank, and my mother works at Kope Lani. It's a cafe."

"I know Kope Lani," he said. "We've gone there. It's good."

"You think so?" she asked. "I can make you something from there. My mother brings things home all the time. Tea? Coffee? A milkshake?"

"Oh," he said, realizing he was feeling a little bit worn down and could use a pick-me-up. "Do you have any Kona coffee? It's so delicious."

She made him some with their Kona peaberry chocolate-covered coffee beans, one of the cafe's most popular brands. Then she had to work out the next problem. The fence between their two houses was very high, and the hole wasn't big enough to fit the entire cup through. He had to settle with taking small sips through a straw.

"Thank you for the coffee," he said."I've never tasted that flavor before, at least not brewed like that."

"I'm glad you like it," she said. "It's my favorite. Do you want to taste another favorite?"

He wanted to, but said he was good. He just wanted to enjoy her company.

She was too excited to accept his answer and ran into her house anyway. She came back a few minutes later with a croissant and a small jar of Lilikoi butter. For the next twenty minutes, she tore off little bits of the croissant, slid it across the butter, and passed it through the hole.

They even made a game of it. He would lean into the fence so she could pop it right into his mouth. They laughed every time she missed, so sometimes she missed on purpose.

The two of them spent the rest of the afternoon like that, sitting in the sun and taking turns peeking through the hole. She told him about her parents and how they left for work each morning and came home tired every night. She told him how she loved art, making tiny clay jars and painting colorful boats that navigated the dark blue waves and white ocean spray. She said her favorite subjects were history and literature, and how she wanted to write children's books.

He told her about his childhood on Kauai, and how they had moved to the Big Island just before the lockdown. His father had worked on a farm, but now he worked from home, and his mother was a marine biologist. He liked scuba diving and surfing. And he also liked books very much. One day, he'd travel the world.

They shared some of their favorite things about the islands too. He always had a fondness for the aviation museum with its flight simulators, films, and aircraft. She always loved the Bishop Museum with its rotating exhibits for kids. They both loved swimming with dolphins and wondered when they might get back to their normal lives.

When the day got late, they both heard a car driving up her driveway, and she suddenly jumped up in a hurry. She did a little bow and thanked him for the fun afternoon, and then apologized for having to help make dinner before her father got home.

"Come back tomorrow," she said as she scampered toward her house.

He was just as happy to have a new friend as she was, so he returned the very next day. She was already waiting for him, with fresh Kona coffee and croissants with Lilikoi butter. After breakfast, they spent the morning reading chapters from their favorite books and listening to music made by their favorite bands. By the afternoon, he came up with the idea of playing the Kōnane board game together — with each of them setting up a board and mirroring the moves.

The playdates quickly became a ritual of sorts in the days that followed. Every night, they planned something to share about themselves from the way things were before, making each and every day a new discovery. They made up games. They laughed over charades. They acted out entire plays. Anything they could think of to pass the time.

"I've never had so much fun with anyone," he told her. "I might even be falling in love with you."

"Don't be silly," she said. "You've never even seen me without a mask."

"I don't care about that," he said. "I just want to be with you. Maybe I can ask my parents to invite you and your parents over for dinner?"

"Do you think they would?" she asked, suddenly delighted by the prospect but not believing it. "Everybody's so afraid right now."

"Of course they will do it, Kalena," he said. "We're neighbors. It will be all right. I'll ask tonight. You'll see. My parents think everyone is overreacting anyway."

"You don't know what that means to me, Kekoa," she said. "I've been so lonely."

"Don't worry," he said again. "You'll see."

"Kekoa?" she called out before she turned toward the house.

"Yes," he answered, leaning in to see her one more time.

She didn't say a word. Instead, she slowly pulled the mask down off her face and smiled. He thought she was the most beautiful girl he had ever seen.

He couldn't wait. He bounded into the house and asked his father to invite the neighbors over for dinner. His father was a little surprised by his son's excitement, but he thought it was a great idea, especially because they never had a chance to meet anyone after the move.

His father even waited outside for Kalena's father to come home and extend the invitation. But the effort was short-lived. Kalena's father stopped him from coming any closer than the mandated six feet. There would be no socializing until the governor lifted the state-wide lockdown, her father had said. The decision was final. Stay home.

The news crushed the boy, and he tossed and turned most of the night, finally falling asleep after reassuring himself that everything would work out. He would comfort Kalena in the morning. It was just a matter of patience. The order couldn't last forever.

It was a beautiful blue day when he woke up, and he quickly brushed his teeth and combed his hair, only slightly apprehensive about telling her the bad news. He was still excited to see her until he discovered he wouldn't see her today. The hole, their hole, had been boarded over on the other side.

"Kalena," he called out. "Are you there?"

"I'm so sorry," she said, sounding incredibly distant on the other side of the fence. "I've tried, and I've tried, but the boards will not budge."

"What happened?" he asked.

"My father was so angry," she said. "I've never seen him so upset. He said we were selfish. He said people are dying, and we shouldn't be so selfish to go on living. He said I can't have anything to do with you anymore."

"It's all right," he said. "We'll get through this together."

"I don't want to be selfish anymore," she said, not hearing him. "Kekoa? Do you know the legend of Ohia Tree and the Lehua Blossom?"

"Of course, we learn it as children," he said. "The volcano goddess Pele was rejected by the brave warrior Ohia in favor of Lehua, so Pele turned him into a twisted tree."

"And Lehua was so heartbroken that the gods took pity and turned her into a tree flower, joining them forever," she whispered.

"That's why we don't pick those flowers or the heavens will cry over those lovers being separated," he said. "What does that have to do with anything?"

"I love you, Kekoa," she whispered.

Before he could respond, the first drop of water landed on his forehead. He looked up. He hadn't noticed the clouds move in or darken. It was going to rain.

WHERE'S THERE SMOKE

Oregon 2019

Jeremy came down the stairs heaving two overpacked brown suitcases along with him. He paused when he reached the bottom step, setting the luggage down to regain his balance, and adjusted his glasses.

His wife, Stephanie, stood at the bottom of the steps looking at a painting that complemented the front entryway of their home. It had been a long-time family favorite, greeting people at the front door with big, bold red-and-orange flowers splashed across the canvas. It created the illusion that you could peek underneath them and see the soft sand and brilliant blue of an ocean sky beyond. If he didn't know better, he would have thought she was considering whether the light did the painting justice where it hung or if it might look better over the family room couch.

"What are you doing?" he huffed.

"Do you remember when we bought this together?" she asked. "It was before the kids. I think when we were visiting Sausalito. Wasn't it? We took the ferry over from San Francisco."

"We talked about this," said Jeremy. "We can only take what we can't live without."

"Are you sure? I'm not so sure," she said. "So many memories, Jeremy."

"It won't fit," he said, attempting to maneuver his way around her. "None of the paintings will fit."

"I know," she fretted. "Just let me have this moment."

"Steph, we're out of time," Jeremy said. "Where's Samantha?"

"She's in the Forester," she said. "You go ahead. I'll be right there."

When he opened the door, the acrid smell of burning redwood and conifers hit him in the face again. It was stronger than before. And while he wasn't sure if it was because the fire was closer or the wind had shifted, it didn't matter. They should have evacuated hours ago.

A week earlier, they thought weekend rain and a drop in temperatures marked the end of the fire season. But a lightning strike similar to the one that started the Chetco Bar Fire two years ago changed everyone's calm into calamity. What began as a lonely column of smoke on the horizon had turned black as it raced along the eastern side of the river and threatened to spill over the hill and consume a handful of the northernmost houses, which included theirs.

"We don't have time," he urged her. "If the fire cuts off the river road, we won't get out."

"Fine." She pursed her lips.

Jeremy pushed the last of the suitcases into the back of the Forester, his daughter reminding him that her rabbit cage was already wedged as far forward into the passenger seat as possible. Mister Brambles, much like herself, was already feeling pinched in the tight confines of an overpacked vehicle.

"Don't worry, Sam," he reassured her. "It's only a short ride to Smith River."

They had booked a pet-friendly motel for two days before sorting out where they wanted to go during the evacuation. Stephanie had wanted to continue on into Crescent City, but he eventually won out by describing the motel as a sort of base camp to get their bearings. The best outcome would put them out a couple of days. The worst would have them driving all the way to his sister's place in Santa Rosa, which seemed increasingly likely based on the fire report that finally convinced him to start packing and the red glow on the ridge that he watched all night.

"I still think I should drive," Stephanie said, climbing into the passenger seat. "You didn't sleep at all last night."

"No, I'm fine," he said, leaning on his last reserve of adrenaline. "The seat is already adjusted anyway."

That was it, he thought as he turned out of the driveway and onto the access road that would take them to the river road. By sometime tomorrow, there was a good chance they would be homeless, and the reality of it wasn't even sinking in; he was still sorting through twelve years of accumulated treasures, things, and junk in his head.

"Did we remember my grandfather's flute?" he suddenly asked.

"Can we live without it?" she said.

"Come on, Steph. Cut me a break." He sighed. "He carved it by hand during the war. You know that ..."

"Look out!" she screamed.

As they were bounding down the empty access road, likely the last of their neighbors to evacuate, a beat-up red Ford Ranger came roaring up toward them in the opposite direction. The two vehicles would have collided had he not been able to turn onto the Mulligans' driveway.

Their Forester skidded to a stop on the gravel patch leading down to the neighbor's house. The Ranger kept on, not even slowing down to see if they were all right.

"Is everybody okay?" Jeremy said, looking for confirmation despite his daughter's crying.

"Yeah," Stephanie said, reaching back to reassure Sam, and then looking at Jeremy. "What do you think that was all about?"

"I don't know," he said. "Why would anybody be headed up to our place?"

"Unless they're part of a fire team," she said with no conviction. "You know, volunteers."

"I think we both know they aren't volunteers," he said, mulling it over.

"Then turn around," she said. "We have to go back."

"What difference does it make?" he asked. "Everything back that way will be gone by tomorrow."

"Don't say that. You don't know that," she said, raising her voice. "Turn around and go back, Jeremy. You've had your way on everything else. Don't let those men break into our home. Go through our private things. Go through your daughter's things."

"Daddy, I'm scared," Sam chimed in, causing a momentary silence.

"All right," he surrendered, turning the steering wheel and heading back up. "All right."

Nobody spoke as Jeremy drove back up toward the house. He was driving considerably slower than he had been on the way down, which was probably for the best. Smoke had started rolling down from the ridge, creating a dense haze in the air. He pulled off to the left side of the road about twenty feet from the driveway.

"I thought you were going to drive by," she said, questioning. "Why are we stopping?"

He gave her a look but didn't say anything. Then he leaned over and opened the glove compartment and reached in for his Glock 19, a gun he had only fired once in his life.

"I'll scare them off, but you and Sam wait here," Jeremy said as he stepped out.

Jeremy cut through the trees along the driveway, angling in toward the front of the house. As he approached, the smoke grew thicker, becoming dense, acrid fog that felt heavy to breathe. The nearby cracking and popping of trees, underscored by a roar of flames pushing the air higher, was closer than he could have ever imagined.

As expected, the Ranger was parked outside, and the front door had been broken in and left open. Jeremy took a breath only to choke on smoke as he stepped out from the trees and approached the door. He held the gun up like they taught him at the range, except his shoulders were flung too far forward and his knees bent too low. He was slowly shuffling up to the Ranger, his heart pounding and eyes tearing up from the assault of smoke and fear, when one of the men he had seen in the truck came out of the house with two trash bags, one in each hand.

"Whoa, whoa, whoa," the man said, eyebrows raised, chin forward but smiling. "Whatcha doing here, chief?"

"This is my home," Jeremy said.

"And what are you going to do with that?"

Jeremy pulled the trigger. When nothing happened, they looked at each other momentarily, and the looter rushed him. Jeremy racked the slide while he stepped back, whimpered, and fired the gun. The Glock popped off three shots, the first high and the second two into the man's chest after Jeremy adjusted for the hump-back grip.

The man fell back onto the ground as Jeremy's face lost all color. He staggered, almost dropping the gun until the second looter called out from inside the house. Jeremy returned to his awkward pose.

"Hey now, let's all take it easy," the other said, peeking out from the frame. "Did you kill him?"

"I think ... I couldn't help it," Jeremy stuttered. "He jumped at me."

"I'm not armed," said the man.

"You're in my house," Jeremy said, still shaken. "You broke into my house."

"Yes," he said. "It was going to burn down anyway."

"It's still my house," said Jeremy.

"We're going to burn right along with it if we stay on much longer," he said.

"Come on out then," Jeremy said. "Hands up."

"Let's work this out before I do," he said. "It's a real shame about Earl. He was a good friend of mine. But maybe it's best you and I just go our separate ways."

"What do you mean?"

"I mean, you put the gun down, and I'll come out," he said. "Then, I'll get in my truck real slow and be off."

"Our things are still in your truck," Jeremy said.

"I suppose I can unload it," he said.

"All right, do that," Jeremy said.

The man came out, hands up. He was older than the man Jeremy had shot. His hair and beard were disheveled, but there was a kindness in his drooping eyes and the deep lines carved into his forehead. He slowly ambled to the back of the truck.

"I just have to get my work gloves on," he said, reaching behind his back.

Jeremy fired. He only needed one shot. The man looked at him dumbly, disbelieving. He didn't say anything. He just dropped the work gloves that he had tucked into the back of his belt, held his chest where the blossom of blood started to seep into his shirt, and fell to the ground.

He looked at Jeremy, a questioning expression frozen on his face. It was a question Jeremy couldn't answer. Was it because the man reached behind his back? Was it because he was witness to the other accidental shooting? Was it because Jeremy felt violated? He didn't know. He barely remembered squeezing the trigger.

Jeremy sat down on the driveway, put his hands to his face, and sobbed. When he regained his composure, he looked at the two men, and then up at the hill where he could clearly see flames creeping over the ridge. He had to get his family out.

A few minutes later, Jeremy opened the door of the Forester and climbed into the driver's seat.

"Did you stop them?" Stephanie asked.

"They weren't there," he said, reaching over and putting the Glock in the glove compartment.

"But we heard shots," she said.

"Something spooked me, but it wasn't anything," he said, turning the key in the ignition without looking at her. "The house, though, it won't be there tomorrow. Nothing will be left tomorrow."

Stephanie sank back in the seat to digest what he told her as he started down the mountain again. She tried to ask him a few more questions, but he didn't say anything. He was too focused on the road and what he left behind.

PUNCHING AND HUGGING

Maryland 1990

Eldon Moss sat in the antechamber of the church, eyes down and looking at the tile between his knees. His hands massaged his temples, trying to knead away the hangover before it took hold as a migraine.

He had been that way for twenty minutes, praying to a God who felt conspicuously absent, but maybe He wasn't. The ceremony had been delayed as the manor's staff attempted to clean up the grounds. An early morning shower had made the lawn muddy and runny.

Eldon pressed his head harder. It was a terrible day and he was getting married.

Outside, guests were navigating the wet grass and choosing sides. Ushers gently asked if they were there for the bride or groom and led them on to the right or left block of white folding chairs. The guests would then hesitantly slide into one of the aisles along hastily thrown plastic runners, check the chairs for moisture, and cautiously sit down. Each of them would then slowly sink into the dampness.

Eldon couldn't see it, but he imagined their growing impatience, with guests looking over their shoulders and hoping to catch a glimpse of the wedding party. The flowering lattice arch that would frame the couple's ceremony had lost their attention long ago.

He could conjure the image of his aunt perfectly, having flown down from Connecticut, sitting with the knees of her white pantsuit pressed together, pensively tapping her watch in disbelief. His mother, wearing something flowery and flowing to capture her free spirit, was likely wringing her hands in fretful worry. And the minister — if you could call the new age non-denominational female prophet that his future wife had chosen — was pacing back and forth on the sidewalk where the wedding party stood just out of sight. She whispered to them that as long as they kept to the stone path, there shouldn't be any muddy missteps.

Six hours earlier, he had given in to a high school fantasy with someone other than his fiancée, slipping under the patchwork quilt that covered a double bed in a room considerably smaller and quainter than the one reserved for him and his future bride. They had been the last two standing after three days and nights of pre-wedding obligations — the welcome party at the inn, the early morning couples shower, the bridesmaid luncheon at the Milton Inn, the Susquehanna State Park picnic, the wedding rehearsal at the manor, the rehearsal dinner at the bistro — and the constant tug-of-war between upscale and comfortable that defined the chasm between their two families. It was adding up to a small fortune covered by a joint loan taken out by the newlyweds, just as binding as the marriage license.

Her family had initially offered to pay on the condition that the wedding was held in Baltimore. Never mind that he and his fiancée, his immediate family, and most of their friends lived in Pittsburgh, with the balance of guests all arriving from north of New York. They had complained that her older's brother's wedding had cost a small fortune because it was held in the bride's hometown of Savannah. Now it was their turn to capitalize on tradition and claim their daughter's hometown advantage.

Eventually, he and his fiancée had compromised to avoid an outright boycott that would have left the guest list impossibly lopsided. They agreed to be married in Maryland, but not Baltimore, and her family was asked not to contribute a dime as a signal. They refused to be bought, influenced, or otherwise coerced for the balance of their lives.

It became a matter of principle that clouded the wedding plans from that point on, right down to the rain-sodden ceremony that was about to take place — if it ever took place. Joan's family might not have been writing checks, but they still insisted on criticizing every place, plan, or accompaniment. He almost managed a smile while wondering how they might critique his latest indiscretion but then quickly slipped back into his red-eyed, head-throbbing depression.

With each passing minute, he sat there with the taste of the pre-wedding affair still on his lips; he was losing his nerve to go through with it. And, he guessed, if he were losing his nerve inside the private confines of the church's antechamber, then he would only feel worse standing at the outdoor altar, looking past his bride-to-be and her maid of honor, to the bridesmaid he had tangled up with just a few hours ago.

After everyone else had rightly tapped out last night, the two of them had taken a midnight walk down to the marina, something reminiscent of another after-party walk taken years earlier to an all-night convenience store in search of smokes and snacks. They tripped along, talking of old times that seemed further and further away with each passing day toward the wedding date. The pair of them — friends through high school — were closing doors on the past with idle conversation until they came to the last door he had never closed.

"Tell me, El," Summer smiled, the moonlight reflecting off the river. "Any regrets, requests, or last wishes before your untimely demise?"

"That's a pleasant way to look at it," he said. "It's not a funeral."

"Sure it is," she said, punching his arm. "It's the last rights for everything that came before."

"What do you want me to say, exactly?" he said. "That I should have climbed Kilimanjaro before getting married?"

"Something like that," she said, leaning into him.

"Yeah, right," he huffed, reading between the lines. "You made it perfectly clear we were only friends."

"Remember when you left your shoes under my parents' bed?" She laughed. "They were all concerned about them until I said they were your shoes."

"That's me," he said. "The consummate gentleman."

"With me, maybe," she teased. "Sorry about that."

"Sorry for what?" he asked.

"Sorry I made you my friend," she said. "I lost so many that I didn't want to lose you."

"You're not helping," he said.

"Kiss me," she said, pulling him closer. "Kiss me before it's all too late."

He did. They did. For ten minutes on the waterfront, they shared a moment that both of them had always held somewhere deep inside, a forbidden door neither opened. When they stopped and stepped back, they said nothing before hurrying back, hand in hand. He wouldn't even be missed because he was supposed to be sleeping in a different room before the wedding, anyway. They had planned for him to bunk with the best man. He bunked with her instead.

"You don't look so good, El," said his father, breaking the spell as he leaned in to say they were minutes away.

"I don't feel so good," Eldon said.

"So who threw the first punch?"

"It wasn't a fight," Eldon said. "Unless you're talking about Jack, Daniel, and Coca-Cola."

"Funny, I didn't think those three would leave you as white as a sheet," he said. "Maybe I should ask it differently. Who threw the first punch, you or Joan?"

"I don't follow you," Eldon said.

"Somebody did something, or you wouldn't be stumbling through the last few days drunk or hungover," he said. "Somebody threw a punch, and there's been trouble ever since."

Eldon considered. Take away last night, and his dad was right. There were several punches thrown during the four-year courtship, starting with him breaking off the relationship early in favor of a college freshman who had turned his head. He wasn't trying to throw a punch. He was trying to do the right thing, breaking it off with Joan before turning his attention elsewhere. They broke up, but Joan hung on.

"I suppose I did," Eldon said. "I dated that dark-haired girl when we split the first time."

"Doesn't count," his father said. "But it did to her, I suppose."

"There was the time she stayed with you and Mom after we got back together," Eldon said. "You remember. She went out with my friends, but caught a ride home on the back of a motorcycle with some other guy."

One of his friends had called him before Joan had left for the airport the next day. She had gone out with a bunch of them, drank too much, and dared two party drop-ins that no one knew to take her for a ride. They did more than donuts in the parking lot of the local supermarket before dropping her off at his parents' home.

"Yeah, I remember," he said. "And then you forgave her. You made up."

"I thought it was payback for the breakup," he said. "Maybe I deserved it."

"Maybe," his father said.

Eldon inventoried his memory for more missteps between them. There was the time he invited a bar band to their apartment for breakfast, mostly because he was trying to impress some girl he met. Nothing much had happened because the girl fell for the frontman, but Joan had made a big deal about the mess and smashed tangerines.

There had been Rachel, one of the girls he was friends with in college. She had a crush on him, but he wasn't interested. Still, Joan eventually barred her from their apartment anyway, one of a handful never to be invited over if she wasn't home.

There was that fling she might've had with a coworker. His one-night rendezvous with an old girlfriend. Joan leaving him stranded at a nightclub and locking him out of the apartment. His bad decision to ask the strippers to come back to his bachelor party. Her spendthrift existence that left them without a phone for the week.

"Punching and hugging," his father said, watching his son tally round after round.

"What?" Eldon said, looking up for the first time.

"There isn't going to be a clean slate with this ceremony," he said. "Once the first punch is thrown, people have a nasty habit of making it the rest of their lives — punching and hugging, breaking up and making up, as long as they stay together."

"There's something else?" Eldon asked, holding his arms out to convey the totality of it.

"Not everybody has to be like your mother and me," he said. "Or her mother and father, for that matter."

"It's too late," Eldon shrugged. "Everybody's here."

"It would take more courage to walk out there and call it off than it ever would to say 'I do,'" he said. "It's your call. But either way, time's up."

"All right," Eldon said.

The sun outside was bright, and he held up a hand to shield his eyes. There was a smattering of claps as he approached the arch with his best friend, a college friend, and his soon-to-be brother-in-law. The bridesmaids followed: Joan's best friend, Summer, and his cousin.

Summer was as radiant as ever, as if nothing had happened between them the night before. She was the same girl who kissed Eldon full on the mouth the moment he had introduced Joan as his girlfriend. *You can't have him if you can't get used to this,* she had said. *Some friendships can't be broken.*

Eldon stood on one of the stone pavers and swayed offbeat from the music. His father gave him a hesitant glance, warning him one last time that it was now or never.

As the bridal chorus sounded and all heads turned from him to Joan, basking in all the attention as she and her white dress glided to the altar, Eldon made his decision. It was her turn to throw a punch. He prayed for it to be a knockout.

ALL YOUR JOYS

Massachusetts 2019

Kameron Lee Parker peered out his bedroom window and across to his neighbor's house. There was something different over there, set between the upstairs window pane and the always-closed blinds.

He squinted at it — a symbol of sorts, inked or painted on a small canvas and positioned to be seen from the yard of his home, not by the occupants. He had never seen anything like it.

At its center, there was an all-seeing eye in a triangle with rays of light emanating from it. That image was, in turn, framed by a larger circle with an overlapping five-pointed star. Each point was adorned with a horseshoe. The ends radiated outward.

He didn't like it. Everything about it felt wrong.

The blinds wobbled and he jerked back, sinking deeper into his room. He half-expected to see one of the slats flip up like they sometimes did. They didn't.

Maybe the movement came from one of the cameras he sometimes forgot about. The neighbors had added them a few weeks before, one camera for each window.

"Why do they have to be like that?" Kam had complained to his mom when he saw them installed. "I don't want anybody watching me all the time."

"Can you blame them?" she retorted. "You robbed them."

"It wasn't like that," he said.

"No? They welcomed us into this neighborhood with open arms, and you broke into their home." She was angry at him again. "That's called robbery."

He didn't mean for it to happen. One thing had led to another. When he told his friends that his new neighbors were headed out of town, Kavon told him to case the place.

"You're the one who moved on up," Kavon said. "Or maybe you ain't one of us anymore."

"They're my neighbors," he said.

"They're my neighbors," Jerome mimicked and added a singsong. "Moving on up."

Kam cased the place the next day, crossing into their backyard, where the bushes and trees provided the most cover. He knew what to do. His friends had shown him before.

He looked through each window at an angle, surveying the frames, locks, and tracks. The very last window looked the most promising. It had a well-worn latch. The window was also set into a recessed wall on the far side of the house for added concealment. He leaned right up to the glass and looked inside. Then he looked up for anything out of the ordinary but couldn't find anything. It would be easy.

He pushed off the frame and backed up to consider the other windows, looking up to the second floor. No, he thought as he returned to the most promising prospect, the window on the recessed wall would do. They may as well have left a key under the front mat.

"It looks easy enough," Kam had said, after calling Kavon back. "They're gone the weekend. Their kid has an out-of-state lacrosse tournament."

Kam took another look outside as if seeing all over again. Except this time, all he saw was the big leering eye. One eye placed in a window, camera eyes set in every other window. They were sending him a message. Those crazy people were watching him.

He fumed. They had been watching him from the start. Every time they pulled up when he was standing outside the back door of his house, they watched him.

"Everything all right?" the man would ask him. "Are you locked out or something?"

"Do you need any water or anything?" the woman might say.

"Let us know if you need any help," the man offered once.

"Why does he sit out there all the time?" the kid whispered to his mom.

"Hush," she said. "It's not our business."

She had been right about that. It wasn't their business. It was embarrassing enough that his mom made him sit out on the stoop to punish him. Sometimes she made him stand out there with nothing to do. Sometimes she made him take a textbook, which he didn't read anyway. Sometimes he would curl up on the stoop and sleep.

After a while, the neighbors stopped asking and started casting suspicious looks instead. Sometimes he would duck behind a tree when they came home. Sometimes they saw him and turned away. Sometimes they didn't see him. There were no more waves, smiles, or paper plates with chocolate brownies.

His mom had done that. Every day, she would find another excuse to send him to the stoop: his grades, his chores, his curfew, his sister, his attitude. He landed a week outside just for telling her off. She asked where he went the night before. He said it was none of her business where he went or how long he was gone. That's how it escalated.

"If you aren't going to live in this house, then you aren't going to live in this house," she said. "Give me your key. You can leave when you want, but you can't come home when you want."

"What? You're nuts." He laughed at her, not believing it.

"Don't wake me, your sister, or Evan to let you in, either," she said. "If you're not home by curfew, wait outside until we open the door."

And that was that. He had to wait for her to come home from work after school. He had to sleep outside if he came back too late. He had to sit out on the steps anytime he said or did anything she didn't like. It wasn't long before he was out more than in.

He was out when the neighbors packed up their Subaru Crosstrek for the lacrosse tournament that weekend too. Kam knew what they were doing because he had seen it before. They would take a dozen short trips from their garage to their third car, loading up luggage, sports gear, lawn chairs, and a fold-up wagon. The man had a system to it, fitting everything together like a jigsaw puzzle.

They looked like a family, not a care in the world. It was easy to dislike them for it.

His own family had fractured after his dad decided to walk out on his mom for a younger woman. Shortly after, his mom picked up a new boyfriend. His sister was shuffled between two houses. He was mostly left alone.

Unlike his sister, he didn't have to be shuffled. He hadn't spoken to his father since the separation, except when his dad asked if he wanted to visit.

"You walked out," he said. "Keep walking."

Contempt is what convinced him to commit the robbery as much as fitting in with the friends he left behind. What did these people care? Their insurance would cover whatever happened.

Besides, his friends weren't after everything when they shook a place down. They were in and out, looking for easy scores — cash, credit cards, jewelry, and any other opportunities.

Kam went downstairs to look out the kitchen window. From there, he could peer into a few of the neighbor's lower windows undetected. He had watched their house from this same window before the break-in, looking for any signs that someone might be watching or stopping by to check on the house.

Someone was downstairs in the kitchen now. He couldn't see who it was because the blinds were pulled three-quarters shut. But he could see something being done, gloved hands working a slip of paper out of a honey jar that the woman had placed on the window sill the day before.

What did she say when he was pulling weeds in the yard?

"This is your sweet life today," she had said, holding a jar of honey out in front of him from her porch. "But come tomorrow, all your joys will wither."

"Yeah, whatever," he had said. "I'm not supposed to talk to you anymore, so please don't talk to me."

She didn't say a word after that, only smiled and touched one finger to her eye. He thought she was referring to the video camera that had caught him in their home. Now he was wondering if it meant something else. Did it have something to do with the eye in the window? Did she give him the evil eye?

Someone once told him that there weren't any witches living in Salem during 1693, but there were plenty who lived among them now. Not that it mattered. He didn't believe in witchcraft. Growing up in Roxbury, the only magic he had ever seen was the day the MBTA bus system ran on time.

Then again, maybe it didn't matter what he believed. People who lived in Salem believed it. Somehow all those Massachusetts Bay Colony killings had transformed the entire town into a paradoxical tourist destination. One side sold T-shirts that proclaimed "I got stoned in Salem." The other side claimed this was a spiritual epicenter where real witches made pilgrimages.

Was that what he saw now? A spell? Gloved hands working a sticky slip of paper into a pile of ash, dust, and dirt so that all his joys would wither. Hadn't they already?

"Kameron!" his mother screamed over the high-pitched shrieks of his sister. "Kameron! Help!"

He bolted up the stairs, taking two at a time. Then, at the top, he took in the impossible scene. His pit bull had sunk its teeth into one of his sister's ankles. Jambar was pulling her out of Kam's room as she grabbed the door frame to stop him. Kam's mother was standing only a few feet away in her bathrobe, unsure of what to do. Her mouth was still moving, but her body was frozen.

"Jambar, no!" Kam yelled and rushed at the dog. "Let go, let go!"

"Help me, Kam!" His sister cried in a heaving sob. "It hurts! He's hurting me!"

Kam grabbed the dog's collar, but Jambar wouldn't let go. He worked his hands into the dog's mouth to pull its jaws apart, but he couldn't get a grip, its teeth slick with saliva and his sister's blood. With every attempt to free her, Jambar only tightened his grip with a low growl, occasionally giving Syrai another yank when Kam relaxed.

"Do something!" his mother was shouting at him. "Do something for once in your life!"

As he got up from the deadlock, his hands followed his eyes to the baseball bat next to his dresser. It had been sitting there since he fished a baseball out of his sports bag to smash his neighbor's window. Now he was picking it up to do the unthinkable.

It took three heavy blows before Jambar finally let go. His growl turned into a whimper on the third swing. He released her ankle and slumped against the wall, giving Kam's mother just enough room to sweep in and scoop up Syrai.

"Oh, baby girl," she said. "Are you all right?"

She answered with more sobs, pointing at the dog that had mauled her. Then she made eye contact with her brother. Her eyes met unexpected anger.

"Why did you go in my room?" he said accusingly and drawing his mother's attention.

"What? Your dog just attacked your sister, and this is your thought?"

"He wouldn't have done anything if she had stayed out," he said.

If she weren't holding Syrai, she would have struck him. He could see it in her eyes.

"I have to take her to the hospital," she said.

"I'll go with you," he said.

"You can't," she said, giving a nod to his ankle monitor.

"What about Jambar?"

"It's your dog," she said, pushing past him. "Get out of my way."

He was going to ask her if she was going to the hospital in a bathrobe, but he thought better of it. Maybe she would grab something from the laundry room. Maybe she wouldn't. He couldn't think straight.

He felt lightheaded and sat down next to his dog. Jambar's head was warm and sticky where Kam had struck him. He could feel the tears welling up in his own eyes.

He stood up to shake the sorrow off and, as he did, his eyes looked out the window and across the back lawn to the neighbor's house. Even in the twilight, he could see the big eye staring across at him. It could see everything.

"You did this," he whispered, before reaching down to pick up the bat.

Everything had seemed to go so smoothly the night he and his friends had broken into the neighbor's house. He had used a baseball to break the window, reaching in with his long arms to undo the latch. He tore off the screen and slid open the window.

It wasn't until he climbed inside that he saw the one thing he missed when he cased the house earlier. There was a camera positioned in the far corner of the family room, a tiny green light in the distance.

He walked toward it slowly, hoping to blend into the shadows, then reached over the lounge chair and pulled it from the shelf. He walked it back to the broken window and passed it back to Kavon before making his way to the front door, where Jerome was waiting.

Since it was his score, he went upstairs to the master bedroom. The choicest items are always in dressers — jewelry, cash, credit cards. The first forty dollars was even sitting out in the open. Then he worked his way down the drawers, coming up empty until the last one. He found a cheap poly-frame service pistol and about a hundred rounds.

He was about to work his way over to the closet when they called him. They had dug around the laundry room and come up with keys for two cars left behind.

Kam flew down the stairs after them. Jerome was already starting the silver Nissan, leaving the black Audi A4 for him and Kavon. Kavon backed it out of the garage, but Kam took the wheel once it was on the street. He didn't have a driver's license, but to the spotters go the spoils. The A4 was his, right up until he wrecked it a few miles away. They had the Altima a little longer. The cops picked it up a day later.

Kam tightened his hand around the bat. Those people. It was their fault, all of it.

It was if they had cursed him the minute he and his family moved into the neighborhood. He started getting into trouble more often. He hadn't seen the camera when he cased the house. The Audi was too much car to handle. He was picked up just a few minutes after coming home the next day — spotted sitting on the stoop as if nothing had happened. He gave up his friends and the location of the cars when he was questioned. The judge sentenced him to house arrest. His dog inexplicably attacked his sister. Maybe they had cursed him.

Kam stormed out of his house and across the back lawn to the neighbor's house. He no longer cared if the cameras saw him coming or not. Looking back, he should have.

When Kam shattered the same window he broke on the night of the robbery, he saw the woman waiting for him this time. She was smiling at him, touching a finger to her eye. The warding spell worked, knocking him out onto the lawn.

All he could remember after that was lying there in pain until the familiar pulse of red and blue lights cut through darkening twilight. All his joys withered in the sinking sun.

FOUR FATHERS

Georgia 1968

As much as Rosalee tried to pretend she was on a grand adventure, she knew the trip to Macon, Georgia, wasn't a vacation. They were going to see him, and he was the reason she was clinging tightly to the broken neck of her stuffed rabbit — one of the last remnants from her childhood — as trees with broad leaves swallowed up the open roadside. The familiar helped her feel safer.

She and her mother had reached the motel in the early afternoon, about an hour-and-a-half after the last time-killing distractions had run their course. From the wide open back bench seat of the 1965 Buick, she had played the Alphabet Game, I Spy, and Name That Tune for what seemed to be a hundred times. Then she lost interest as even the hit songs like "Hey Jude" and "The Dock of the Bay" on the radio became drawn out and melancholy.

Her mother turned it off and left them listening to the gentle whoosh of traffic through the cracked window that had become their reality. It lulled Rosalee into a trance as she lay back on the seat and put her stocking feet up against the window.

She had wanted to sit in the front, but her mother wouldn't allow it. The back was the safest place in the car for twelve-year-old girls with stuffed rabbits. Besides, her mom reasoned, you don't have to wear a safety belt in the back. Get comfortable and close your eyes or read your book, she would say.

"Well, well. Look at the time," her mother had said as she unpacked the suitcase. "We'll see him at the hospital, get it over, and go for an early dinner."

"Okay," Rosalee said, shaking off some of the cobwebs that had formed in her mind while lying down across the back seat.

She wanted to say no, but couldn't find her voice. She had heard about him. Some good things. Some bad things. Most of them from her grandmother when her mother was at work or out of earshot. But her mother avoided talking about him during the drive from the motel and down the long corridors of the hospital.

"Don't be nervous," her mother said, pushing her through a door and quickly walking away.

She took a few hesitant steps toward the man in the bed. He was lying there, staring up at the ceiling and pinching the bridge of his nose like her grandfather did when he had a headache.

"Hello?" Rosalee called out.

"Well, hello there," he said, pulling himself up with his elbows, reaching for some glasses on the small table, and fighting the IV line attached to his arm. "Come on in and let me get a look at you."

She did as she was told, walking closer to the bed. She assessed him as he assessed her. His skin was dark, baked by the sun, and with a yellow cast. His eyes were tired, sunken. His hair was short and wavy, matted by lying in bed. His chin was firm, supporting a broad smile. He was smiling at her.

"Good, good," he said, spinning a finger in the air. "Twirl around a bit."

She did as she was told again, holding the flower-print sundress to her sides as she did. The spin relaxed her, and she giggled on the third turn.

"My, my, my," he whistled. "You're as pretty as your mother."

Rosalee blushed when he said it. She wasn't sure why but felt the heat of it.

"Don't tell anybody," he added, leaning in toward her. "She was always my favorite, your mother — the one who got away."

"Why'd you let her?" Rosalee asked, all smiles.

"Now, there's a good question," he said. "I didn't want to; I didn't. I was dispatched to Spain and you and your mother were supposed to come and live with me. She changed her mind."

"Was it because of the photo?" she asked, remembering the picture of him her mother had shown her. He was younger, standing by a beautifully exotic woman behind the statue of an elephant. They looked happy. They looked together.

"You know about that?" He choked a laugh. "I caught hell for it from your mother, I did. But it wasn't what she thought. It was part of my cover. I was over there, helping the Spanish restructure their infantry and Airborne divisions, but I was doing something else too. It was complicated."

"Grandma said you were a spy," she said. "She said they made you a spy because you spoke so many languages. Do you really speak seven languages?"

"*Das ist mir Wurst.*" He laughed.

"What does that mean?"

"It's German. It means this is sausage to me," he said. "It means I don't care about that, and you shouldn't either."

She wrinkled her nose. "Then what? What should I care about?"

"You should care that you're my only daughter," he said. "That's why I called for you. I wanted to see you. I wanted to talk to you, to know you, to give you something none of my children, your brothers, will ever have. You want to know? Come over. Pull the chair over and sit by me."

She hesitated. The chair was on the other end of the room, next to another bed. Nobody was in the bed, but it belonged to someone. It was unmade and stank.

"Don't worry," he said. "He won't be back for a while."

She walked over cautiously, surveying her surroundings as if it might be a trap. When she was satisfied, she snatched the back of the chair and pulled it quickly over to her father's bed. He laughed as she did it; the chair legs squeaked as the rubber resisted the floor.

"You would make a terrible spy, Rosalee." He laughed.

She frowned, but then she laughed too. He wasn't as scary as she thought he might be. She settled in next to him.

"I'm going to be honest," he said. "It was a good thing I wasn't in your life so much. I'm not a very good father. I was a better soldier. Your youngest brother, Gilbert, he'll never even know that, but I want you to know it."

She didn't know what he meant, but then he explained it to her. Gilbert was only six years old, and the only father he knew had already put the military behind him. In Gil's eyes, his father wasn't much more than an auto mechanic with a bad disposition.

Gil's father left for work with a hangover every day and knocked off early so he could make happy hour at the neighborhood bar that was within crawling distance of their house. Sometimes Gil's mother would join him. Sometimes she wouldn't. It depended on how well they were getting by. But that's all they did. They got by.

"I'm not proud of it," he said. "But that's who I am to him, and maybe it's all he'll remember. I don't know. Maybe his mother will tell him something better, but that's all we have. There are a couple days of real happiness every year buried in the mundane."

Her older brother, Lorenzo, he told her, had a different father altogether. Lorenzo's mother had met him shortly after returning from West Berlin. He had been stationed there for three years, fully expecting World War III when the Soviet Union blocked all road and rail travel in or out of the city.

"I figured I was something back then," he remembered. "I had been drafted as a boy from a small town in '46 and was coming home a man with big city experiences in '49. After all that time with German women, I fell for the first American girl I met when I got back."

Except, the relationship was cut short when the U.S. Army needed to send men in green to an out-of-the-way county called Korea. When he had left, he was itching for the fight he never had with the Soviets. When he came back, he wasn't the same man.

"Korea got to me. I think it was all the refugees more than anything. They were always hungry, cold, and miserable; and they would always evac an area when we did and follow along. This one time, there were these five little girls, none of them over the age of nine, who came into our camp. They didn't have any shoes or socks, so we let them sit by the fire. A couple of us fed them rations that night, but I couldn't help but wonder if we were just making them suffer a little longer before they wandered off again, maybe freezing or starving to death anyway. We didn't know." He looked at her, taking in her expression. "Jeez, what am I thinking? I shouldn't be telling you this."

"It's all right," she said and put her hand on his arm.

"I was over there a long time," he continued. "I knew I couldn't be a father when I came back, so I told her so when I got home. I tried a few times. But each time I came home, it was worse. I was distant. I was distrusting. I was a hurricane of fear and hate, scaring her and my son. So I did the best thing I could do. I stepped aside."

Lorenzo's mother eventually married a doctor, and Lorenzo was following in his footsteps.

"When I met your mother, I was a different man," he said. "I guess you could say I was the best me."

They had met at a military dance, modeled after the ones previously hosted by the USO through the Korean War until the program fell to feminism. It was unofficial, but the women were still coached to help the men have a safe and memorable time to ease them off what they called the "rigors of combat." That meant they should keep the conversation simple, and a little flirting wouldn't hurt either.

"Your mom told me right off that she was much too young and had too much to see before settling down," he mused. "She changed her mind after a few weeks, and we eloped. Her parents were so mad, but it was the right thing to do. I was on leave between Vietnam and my next assignment, awarded the Bronze and Silver Stars."

"You're a hero?" she asked.

A company had ambushed his platoon in Vietnam, but they had only lost one man because of what he did. After a rocket ricocheted off their truck and the VC stormed it, he managed to drop out the passenger side of the truck and circle to flank them. He caught them off balance and chased the remaining VC into the brush, pushing them back and then engaging a larger force until reinforcements could arrive.

"I was a hero until they kicked me out," he said. "But that happened here, stateside."

"Why would they do that?"

"I got in trouble," he said. "I was drunk, short a few dollars, and wanted some beer to finish off the night. So I did what they taught me to do. I wrote a fake check. They might have let it go, I suppose, but it was not my first time. Three times a charm."

"Oh," she said, not understanding the appeal.

"Drinking always got me into trouble," he said. "I drank to kill time in Germany. I drank to kill the hopelessness of Korea. I drank to kill the enemy in Vietnam. I drank to kill bad dreams in Spain. And I drank to kill my regrets in Georgia. I guess it was just a matter of time before drinking killed me."

"Does it hurt?"

"Yes," he said, looking at her and then squinting. "No. Sometimes I forget about it."

"Maybe you'll get better."

"No, sweetie," he said. "I'm not going to get better."

"Is that why you wanted to see me?"

"Something like that," he said. "I guess I just wanted you to understand. Gilbert's father is just a washed-out auto mechanic. Lorenzo's father was a shell-shocked kid. And another boy in Germany, his father is an unknown GI. But you, Rosalee, your father was a charming war hero who swept your mother off her feet. If you remember that, no one can take that away from you."

She didn't say anything. There was nothing to say. She simply took his hand in hers and held it, tracing its lines and callouses. She would have liked to know them better, those hands and the man attached to them.

"Rosalee," said the gentle voice of a silhouette from the doorway. "Your mother is waiting for you in the visiting room. It's time to go."

She cast a glance over her shoulder at his wife. She looked impatient and pleasant at the same time, one hand on her hip and her weight on one foot. She was tapping it lightly.

"He needs his rest," she said to nudge her along. "Maybe you can see him tomorrow."

"I'll remember," she whispered, patting his hand and then gently resting it on the bed.

She wanted to hug him and say goodbye, but her war hero had fallen asleep. She stood up and quietly walked to the door where his wife was waiting. She would never see either of them again.

THE SAMARITAN

Indiana 2016

The boy came up behind her as soon as the school bus pulled away. He was lanky, wearing sweats but walking with the club swagger of a 19-year-old with a fake ID.

"Hey, baby," he said, trying to get her attention. "What'chu got planned this afternoon?"

She heard him but pretended not to hear him. It was always the smarter play to ignore leers, jeers, and catcalls. She pressed her earbuds in deeper, head down, feet forward.

"You pretty," he said, circling around alongside and walking backward. "You know that? You're real pretty."

She angled herself away from the boy, twisting her shoulders while walking past him at a slightly faster pace. Anyone driving by would have wondered if she was in trouble or if they knew each other. She was distressed, but the boy's age and posture suggested a remote familiarity.

"Hey, I'm talking to you," he said, grabbing her arm. "You too good to talk to me?"

She wrenched her arm away, the expression on her face changing from pretending to be absorbed to startled. He wasn't interested in misogynistic flirtations. He invaded her space, triggering her fight-or-flee response. She wanted to escape, pressing the notebooks she carried closer to her chest. He followed, unrelenting, drifting back and forth between schoolyard harassment to aggressive taunting.

He grabbed her again, this time insisting she turn and face him. Fearing she would lose her notebooks, she stopped and turned around. He let go but made it a point to move closer than she was comfortable.

"Leave me alone," she insisted, never looking up at him.

"See that, we talking now," he said. "That's all I want."

"Leave me alone," she said again with more conviction before turning away and picking up her pace. The boy skipped along with her — laughing, scowling, demanding.

The scene was beginning to attract attention. A car slowed, surveying the situation and trying to determine if they knew each other. It sped up only when a second vehicle, an old Ford Bronco, pulled alongside the pair and rolled down the window.

"Is everything all right?" asked the driver.

"Yeah, man," the boy said, blocking her advance. "Lovers' quarrel. Isn't that right?"

"Miss?"

"It's nothing," she said. "He's going to leave me alone now."

"Don't be like that," the boy insisted. "Tell him I'm your boyfriend so there ain't trouble."

"I can give you a ride if you need it," the man said.

He was older, with a receding hairline and whisks of gray, taking over what was once a full head of chestnut hair. His beard was well trimmed, but his denim clothes better matched the condition of the compact SUV, dirty and unkempt. It was hard to read if his appearance meant hard worker or drifter.

"I think I'll be okay," she said.

"Yeah, see that," the boy said and put his arm around her. "We're making up."

The sudden invasion of space was to much. She pushed past the boy and fled toward the passenger side of the Bronco. The boy looked surprised as she opened it.

"Hey, it's cool," he said. "I'll leave you alone, just don't go with creepy guy."

The man grinned at him and flipped him off, stepping on the accelerator and making a U-turn toward the direction she had been walking. He looked in the rearview mirror and then pressed ahead.

The Bronco's cab smelled, a toxic mixture of oil, rust, dirt, and stale cigarette smoke. She wanted to keep the window rolled down, but he insisted it was too cold. She fished for her aunt's number instead and started to text her.

"What was that all about?" he said, looking her over.

"I don't know," she said. "Some guys are just like that, you know."

"Yeah, I suppose," he said. "Good thing I came along."

"You won't have to take me far," she said, looking down at her aunt's response. "My aunt is going to pick me up on the corner, about a mile-and-a-half down."

"My name's Eric," he said, offering her his right hand.

It looked dry, fingernails dirty despite being ripped to the quick. She hesitated before reaching over to give it a shake. It was cold and firm.

"I'm sorry," she said. "My name's Janice. That boy shook me up."

"Did you know him?" he asked.

"No. I mean, I've seen him before, but he's never bothered me," she said. "You try to shrug these things off or wonder how to avoid attention."

He frowned. "So you're not flattered or anything when someone notices you?"

"No, not always," she said, shifting her weight slightly against the door.

"I won't call you pretty then," he said with a wink. "It's a secret."

"It's not that much farther," she said, feeling the air in the cab grow thick.

Neither of them spoke for a minute, creating a sudden uneasiness as small bits of dust shook free with every bump and swirled in front of the windshield. She wanted to roll the window down. She wanted to turn on the radio. She wanted to walk the rest of the way. Her eyes darted around, from the glove compartment to a grumpy bobblehead bulldog stuck to the dash.

She'd made a mistake, she thought. The dog nodded, reading her mind.

"I understand these things." He nodded. "We have rules nowadays. You can't call pretty girls pretty. You can't look at them or talk to them or touch them. You can't even expect any gratitude when you save them. Nope. We have rules."

"You can pull over anytime." She was talking faster. "I think I see my aunt right up ahead. The white car, right there. I can't thank you enough."

"You can," he said, stepping on the accelerator and driving by the white Hyundai.

"What are you doing?" she asked, eyes growing wide. "That's her. She's right there."

"Old rules were easier," he said. "You do something for someone, and they owe you. You see something you want, and you take it."

"What are you talking about?" she asked, her words coming out as a squeal, hands reaching for the steering wheel in an attempt to feel in control. She hadn't a chance.

His right hand came up in a punch that rocketed through her head, sending it backward into the passenger side window. Her head spun, eyes blurred. He punched again.

As she slumped in the seat, Eric looked back in the rearview mirror. He was being followed, but daylight savings was on his side. It would be dark soon, not that he expected much from the driver who was already falling behind.

In the Hyundai, Rosalind was reliving the last few minutes all over again. She had received a frantic text message from her niece, asking her to pick her up on the corner. She had mentioned some Samaritan coming to her rescue and described the SUV.

When Rosalind first saw the Bronco, she immediately felt relief. Whatever frightened Janice enough to catch a ride would be over by the time they got home. Maybe it could be explained away as a misunderstanding. Girls have a much more acute sense of danger these days than when she was growing up. They saw wolves everywhere when most men were lucky to be a step above strays.

Except the Bronco did not stop. It slowed as it approached the designated corner and then inexplicably sped up. At first, she thought her eyes were playing tricks on her, seeing two silhouettes scuffling in the front seat behind the grime-smeared windows.

As she followed at some distance, her first call was to her husband. He wasn't available, so she told him to track her phone as soon as he got this message and that Janice was in some kind of trouble. The second call was to the police.

She had told them she was reporting a kidnapping and then started answering a barrage of questions. Her niece was abducted. The vehicle was a blue Ford Bronco, but dirty enough to look tan. It was headed east on State Road 26.

What scared her the most was what she couldn't answer. She didn't know what was said. She didn't know if the man was armed. She didn't know what he looked like. She couldn't remember what her niece was wearing that morning. She had left for school before Rosalind had woken up. She didn't have a license plate, and with the sun sinking in the west, it was unlikely she would be able to decipher it.

That's when the nightmare happened. The gas light was already illuminated before Rosalind had left the house. And while she wasn't one to risk driving around on fumes, she had only expected to drive a few blocks. A chime now accompanied the warning light, and she started to cry as she watched the Bronco take a right turn while she had to continue straight into Rossville for gas.

The police wanted her to stay on the line, but she didn't want her fading battery to die. She told them where she was and hung up to get gas. They suggested she stay until officers arrived, and they would canvass the area. She told them they'd better canvass the area, but there was no way she would wait a minute more than she had to.

She spent the rest of the night looking for any signs of the Bronco, up and down dark farm roads until the first rays of sunlight appeared over the horizon. It wasn't until the sun was up that she saw the truck abandoned in an open field.

She tried to drive off the road toward it, but her car quickly became stuck. She started walking, first to the SUV, then toward the farmhouse beyond the truck, and then veering off toward a tree line by a creek on instinct. As she drew closer, she could see the remnants of a shack in the back, tucked along the tree line near the descending embankment of the creek.

Her walk became a jog and then a run. The cold morning air protested against her hot breath. She could make out a shape in the structure, an outline of a body with wisps of dirty blond hair catching in the breeze.

"Janice," she yelled before she could think better of it. "Oh, my lord. Oh, my niece."

Janice laid there unmoving, clothes torn and body battered. Rosalind quickly took off her coat as she grew nearer and immediately covered the girl, collapsing into her, and desperately searching for signs of life.

"Oh, my poor child," Rosalind cried before she yelled to no one. "Help. Help me! Help us!"

"Nobody's coming out here," a voice came at her from the far wall, a man emerging through an opening in the back, broken boards that were once a doorway.

He held a coffee cup in one hand, with a girl's necklace spun around his fingers like a talisman, a charm dangling between his middle and index fingers. In his other hand, he wielded a tire iron, the lug wrench extending from his hand as if part of his appendage.

"You did this?" she choked. "Why did you do this?"

"She still alive?" he asked, sounding disinterested but bending down slightly for a better look. "She might be."

"Stay back," she said, hands shaking under the coat.

"Or what?" he smiled and took a drink of coffee.

Rosalind pulled the Sig Sauer P238 from the conceal-carry pocket of her jacket. It was small with a matte silver slide. She pointed it at him with uncertainty.

He raised both hands, still clutching the coffee cup and the tire iron. He was too far away to charge her and too close to run. Even a poor shot would likely hit the target at this range.

"Animal," she snarled, pulling the trigger. The gun made two hollow thunderclaps, the first shot grazing his shoulder and the second fired wide, splintering wood.

The man didn't press his luck. He dropped the coffee but kept the tire iron as he scrambled out the way he entered, leaving Rosalind alone, sobbing, and desperately checking for a pulse. As she searched, somewhere in the distance, the Ford Bronco roared to life and sped away.

INDIAN WRESTLING

Minnesota 1968

Two tribes of boys had drawn up on the creek bank. They were uneven groups, with six comprising the larger of the two and three in the other.

Freddy and his older brother Paul stood behind their friend, who was facing the larger pack with his hands clenched in defiance. Mark was the skinniest of both groups, with a temper disproportionate to his size.

"We won," Mark said, pointing to the crawfish that Freddy held in a jar. "Shut up and pay up."

"There wasn't any winner," said Robert. "Look at its claw. It's broken and won't last the afternoon."

"You don't know that," Mark insisted. "Nobody knows that."

"Come on, Mark," Paul said. "It's not worth it."

"I won't be cheated," said Mark, shrugging off the hand Paul had placed on his shoulder.

"You won't be cheated?" Robert said. "You're the biggest Indian giver around."

"Don't call me that!" Mark yelled. "Take it back."

Rather than take it back, Robert doubled downed on the offense and encouraged the rest of his group to join him. Soon the words became a chorus of insults, with six boys parroting Robert.

While nobody knew for sure, there was always an unspoken assumption in the neighborhood that Mark's father had been Native American. But nobody, not even Mark, knew for certain. All he knew was that his father was killed in a car accident and his mother had left him to be raised by grandparents because she couldn't cope with raising a handicapped boy.

"Stop it. Just stop it," Mark said, meaning it but looking diminished all the same. "Or else."

"Yeah, what are you going to do about it?" Robert said. "Wanna fight me?"

"Nobody wants to fight anybody," Paul spoke up again, trying to use age to his advantage.

He was two years older than any of the other boys, but often joined his brother when Mark snuck off to the creek. Neither Freddy nor Mark was supposed to play in the ravine, so following along seemed to take the edge off the infraction. Since he wasn't a snitch, the least he could do was look after them. Not that it did much good, obviously.

"Let Chief Limps-Along fight his own battles, you dirty kraut," said Robert.

"He's not fighting my battles," said Mark. "I'm in this alone."

"Yeah?" Robert said. "We all know better. You're not only red, you're yellow."

Mark took a step forward and Paul tried to hold him back again.

"No fighting," Paul said. "If you get in a fight, we're all busted."

"Fine, no fighting," Mark said. "But I'm no such thing."

"Yeah?" said Robert, smiling and looking up at the footbridge spanning the creek behind them. "Prove it. Cross the bridge on the outside."

The footbridge was a concrete structure that rose three stories on either side of the depressed creek bed and its overgrown wilderness. A chain-link fence arched over the top of it, making it impossible for anyone crossing to climb the fence and jump or fall off, unless someone attempted to cross the bridge on the outside by using a small one-inch concrete lip on either side of the arch.

Crossing the bridge on the outside had become a common dare in the neighborhood — a test of courage that many had claimed, but no one had actually accomplished with more than one witness. With the exception of Peter, an older boy who lived across the street from Mark, most claims were only backed up in pairs. And once a pair of boys claimed to have done it, there was never a need to do it again in larger company.

"All right," Mark said, surprising the bunch of them into silence.

"All right, what?" Robert sneered.

"All right, I'll do it."

The expression on Robert's face was a mix of disbelief and satisfaction. Disbelief because he never expected Mark to accept the dare. Satisfaction because the kid would probably break his neck if he went through with it.

Mark didn't wait for anything else to be said. He pushed past the pack and headed up the narrow, muddy trail that led up to one side of the bridge. Freddy and Paul folded into the pack, looking up at the bridge where Mark would eventually emerge over the tangle of trees and underbrush that obscured both sides of the bridge from view, assuming he was going through with it.

"Well?" Robert called up the embankment. "Don't keep us waiting."

Mark didn't keep them. After a minute, he shimmied his way out onto the bridge, the toes of his shoes finding an extra perch between the small spaces of chain link and his hands hooking on tightly near his shoulders. His progress started strong but slowed as the distance between the bridge and the fast-turning shallow water below grew. Mark could feel a growing uneasiness as he looked down at the pack straining to see him emerge from the branches and leaves.

"You have to go all the way across," Robert called. "All the way."

As he kept climbing out, the problems became increasingly apparent. The toes of his hightop sneakers were slick after climbing up the embankment, making it difficult to plant his feet securely on the concrete. This problem was compounded by the fact that Mark's left leg was shorter than his right, making it more challenging to reach out and anchor his feet to the bridge. It became clear he wasn't just looking for footholds, but looking for the largest spaces between the links so he could jam his feet into them.

The other challenge was the fence itself. The links were loose in some areas, bowed out where kids had pushed against it to look out over the creek, making them prone to pinching fingers. Many links also had small pieces of metal flashing, making it just as important to watch your hands as much as your feet.

"Come on," Freddy whispered.

"Yeah, come on!" Robert shouted up, turning the quiet encouragement into a taunt.

The other boys followed his lead, yelling up at Mark to hurry up. One of them, and then another, picked up a rock and hurled it up at him in an attempt to prod him forward. He stopped when one of the stones finally hit him in the back. Everybody stopped.

"Don't be a crybaby," Robert said.

"I'm not," Mark said, choking back the tears. "I'm stuck."

It was true. Freddy could see that the point of one chain link had broken through Mark's shoe where the canvas met the rubber toe cap. Mark was starting to panic, attempting to yank his right foot free.

"Give me a break," Robert squawked. "It shouldn't be taking so long. You're chickening out."

"You think so?" Paul said. "Maybe you should show him up."

"Yeah, maybe I will when he does it … if he does it," he said. "I've done it a million times."

The looks on the faces of his friends, however, said otherwise. There seemed to be some uncertainty, with the boy who had previously claimed he and Robert had taken the challenge months ago putting his head down. The truth, it seemed, was that Mark was the only one of either group to have gone so far.

"Fine, I'll show you." Robert frowned and jumped across the rocks to the other side of the creek and then ran up the embankment on the far side. In no time, he was up on the bridge, quickly hurrying along toward the center where Mark was still trying to free his shoe.

The boys below erupted with new shouts of excitement and encouragement as Robert proved that he wasn't going to let a loser get the better of him. Now, both boys were side by side in the middle of the span. Mark had finally freed his foot from his shoe, expecting he would have to retrieve it from the other side of the fence later.

"Back up," Robert said. "You had your chance, chicken."

"No," Mark managed. "I'm going to finish what I started."

Before anyone understood what was happening, Mark and Robert had engaged in a sort of reverse Indian leg wrestling, with each boy kicking the leg nearest his opponent out in an effort to get around him. Sometimes, one would kick his leg out, and the other would block it with his leg. Other times, the two boys locked a leg with a knee or ankle to make the other yield.

It was Mark who eventually faltered, his sock slipping off the bridge while he was kicking out, temporarily forcing him to hold on with only his hands. Robert made his move, sidestepping around Mark as the smaller boy panicked to find someplace to plant his feet. Then Robert crushed Mark against the fence to get by, leaving imprints on the boy's face in the process.

Mark yelled out something unintelligible — a noise the other boys would later describe as a war cry — found some footing, and pushed out against Robert just as his foot came up short and landed on Mark's abandoned shoe. This time it was Robert who slipped, one hand breaking away at the same moment his feet. At first, it looked like he would swing one-handed around Mark until the twisting momentum became more than he could bear.

No one made a sound as Robert fell. Not even Robert as he reached out for Mark's outstretched hand as full awareness overtook him. He was falling until he wasn't falling any longer. There was a snap, crush, and the wet sound of punched meat. There was nothing left to hear except the rippling creek and chirps of red-breasted robins.

The boys below, Freddy and Paul included, all stood with their mouths gaping and then began to scramble. Whether they were scrambling to get help or attempting to flee the scene of the crime, Mark couldn't tell. He was too busy working his way down the bridge.

When he finally made it back down the embankment, he thought Robert was dead. The boy was lying on his back, motionless in the cold water. It wasn't until Mark was standing over Robert that he saw the boy was very much alive.

"You suck," Robert coughed.

"Whatever," Mark said, taking care to help Robert sit up and assess the damage.

Robert was lucky, breaking his leg in three places instead of his back or his skull. The damage was so severe, it was expected that the injured leg would be permanently shorter. Even if they were right, he decided it wouldn't hold him back. What did hold him back sometimes was knowing that the boys he trusted most had scattered after he fell. It was the least likely hero to help him up the muddy bank and get home.

There was never any doubt in his mind what real courage looks like after that. It's not always the one who leads a charge, but the one who weathers it.

INTO THE BARDO

Rhode Island 2017

Officer Hector Almada took another sip of coffee before kicking snow off his boots, pulling down his hood, and slowly entering the small coastal cottage that served as the caretaker's home for the seasonal inn next door. He forced an early morning smile as he went inside, hoping it would preempt any scolding for buying a cup elsewhere since Maggie made notoriously lousy coffee.

"Hey, Maggie, is your guest up yet?"

"Yes, and I've made him some breakfast," Maggie said. "Go on up if you like."

"We appreciate you taking him in for a few nights," he said.

"Just tell me where to send the bill."

Almada nodded and crossed to the stairs. He placed one hand on the railing and paused.

"Has he said anything to you?" he asked.

"No, not really," she said. "He seems like a nice enough boy, but still disoriented by what happened to him. Was he really in the water three hours?"

"More like twenty minutes with an immersion suit," he said. "They found him because he had managed to climb his way into the life raft."

"Darn shame," she said absently before repeating herself with more force and a shake of her head. "Darn shame."

Almada didn't know what to say to her pronouncement, so he climbed the stairs and knocked lightly on the first door to the right. It was where Maggie had made room for the boy since the inn was closed for the winter. The captain of the fishing boat that rescued the boy had asked her to put him up. Their families shared too much history for her to say no.

He felt fortunate for that. Keeping the boy close to Payne's Dock made it easier to boat over from Newport to see him. It also saved Almada from dealing with the ever-growing number of family members who had descended on Block Island, most of them upset that the Coast Guard had suspended the search for the three other men. Those staying on the island took up residence around Old Harbor, a few miles away.

"May I come in?" Almada asked out of politeness as he entered.

The boy nodded, motioning to the round-back chair against the wall with a piece of toast. He was a big kid for his age, maybe seventeen years old, with blond hair like his uncle. He was sitting up, pillows stacked between him and the headboard of the old Cape Cod twin. A breakfast tray cautiously straddled his legs, slightly uneven because of the way he had bunched up portions of the floral-print comforter around his waist. He chewed slowly and then reached for the orange juice instead of the coffee.

"They haven't found them, have they?"

"No, I'm sorry, Logan," said Almada. "They called off the search. I had hoped Maggie already told you yesterday. Three days is just too long."

He shook his head, his tired red eyes taking on a new gloss. He set the toast down and then the glass.

"I'm not surprised," he said. "Bear was dead before he hit the water."

"That's why I'm here," Almada said, attempting to look unfazed by the revelation.

"You a cop?"

"I'm with the Department of Environmental Management, the DEM," Almada said. "We're responsible for investigating boating accidents."

"Okay, but Sandy wasn't crazy, if that's what you think," Logan said. "I mean, I can't explain why what happened happened, but he wasn't crazy. My uncle always had a smile on his face. Always saw the good in people. You know, a real positive guy."

"It's all right," Almada said, reaching out with a comforting hand. "We'll figure things out together. Can we do that?"

"Yeah, okay," he said.

"You know, you've been through a lot," Almada said. "Your head is probably swimming with everything that happened. I know mine would be. So why don't we start somewhere else, like the beginning."

"All right," Logan exhaled. "I can do that. So you mean from when we left?"

"Yes, a fine idea," said Almada.

"We left Galilee late, around 10 p.m.," he said, seeing Almada wasn't following him. "By we, I mean my Uncle Sandy, cousin Pauly, and Bear — Barry Fuller. The water was a bit cold and choppy, but Sandy thought we could get a good haul of flounder, fluke, or other ground fish. The plan was to follow the tide. You know, we pay a lot of attention to the tide because it has to do with the way we fish."

"Of course," Almada said, taking basic notes. "You weren't worried about the weather?"

"We've fished in weather before," Logan said. "It wasn't bad when we turned out around Point Judith at the start. It was a fifty-eight-foot trawler. *Queequeg*'s an older boat but she has always been a beast. My uncle only had a problem with her once, an engine casualty about ten years ago."

"The *Queequeg*, right?" Almada asked, pretending to write. "Like, from *Moby Dick*?"

"Yeah, my uncle said he picked it because we're Irish royalty on my great-grandmother's side," Logan said. "She gave it all up to search for adventure in America. You get it?"

Almada nodded, settling back into the chair and making the connection. Queequeg, the son of a South Sea chieftain, had given up his station to explore the world in the Melville classic. More important than the connection, the boy seemed more relaxed in telling his story, which is what Almada wanted.

The late-night outing started well enough. Earl Sullivan, who everyone called Sandy, wanted to get a good jump on his January catch. There was no reason he couldn't. He had four extra hands with Logan out of school and his nephew Pauly home from college for the holidays. It was the same team that once hauled up twenty baskets in a two-hour tow. A few catches like that in early January would give Sandy a solid jump.

The first couple of baskets looked like good hauls, but nothing that suggested they could expect twenty baskets in two hours. So Sandy decided to head out northwest where he knew winter flounder was more abundant. Logan remembered Bear disagreeing with the decision, not wanting to be caught out in a storm. Sandy told him to flip a coin.

Heads or tails, Bear turned out to be right. While none of them were spooked by the twenty-foot swells that greeted them, his uncle didn't like the way the waves were breaking. So it made more sense to stay ahead of the storm and fish a patch closer to Block Island.

"What did he mean ... the way the waves were breaking?" Almada squinted.

"I don't know," Logan said, remembering. "He told me about the rule of seven or less once. That if a wave's length is seven times or less than its height, it's more likely to break. It was pretty choppy, making the boat roll in a bobbing motion. Maybe that."

"He was spooked?" asked Almada.

'No, I wouldn't say he was spooked then," Logan said, his face losing a little color. "He was spooked as we were coming up on the island."

By the time *Queequeg* reached the fishing spot, Sandy was thinking about calling it a day. The storm was moving in faster, and the swells kept growing, giving the boat a good toss. Logan said he spent most of the ride holding onto the work deck doorway, right up until the time his uncle called him up to the pilothouse.

"Do you see it, Logan?" Sandy had asked.

"See what?" Logan replied, peering out through the water streaked windows.

All he saw were large dark waves illuminated by the glow of the trawler's lights. That's all there was. There were waves and more waves, making hills and valleys that the trawler would climb and fall into, a familiar heave and surge.

"There's something else too," his uncle said. "Look, look. You must see it."

Logan wasn't sure how his uncle could see anything. Light rain and ocean spray sheeted the windows. Outside, black waters bled into the dark sky as the trawler bobbed awkwardly like a toy boat in a bathtub. Then Logan saw a green flash in the distance, a beacon that appeared and disappeared every time the boat reached the crest of the next wave.

"The light?" Logan asked. "Yes, I see it. We must be close now."

"No, not the light. There is something else out there too," Sandy said, throttling the boat up a notch. "There. A smaller white glow, maybe someone in trouble. You see it, don't you?"

Logan didn't see it. What he did see was Sandy growing more frantic, almost demanding as the trawler pitched, heaved, and rolled with the ocean. The boat was racing ahead, Sandy driving the engines. Logan continued straining to see something aside from the occasional flicker of a green beacon.

They were growing closer when Bear came in from outside, wind howling in behind him. The door slammed, but the latch didn't catch. He stood facing Sandy, hands on his hips with an aggressive gait that Logan had never seen before.

"Sandy, what are you doing?" he asked, setting his net gaff down. "Don't you see the lighthouse. There! Look! We're too close."

"What?"

"You can't approach this way," he said. "We're too close."

"Don't you see her? She's right there," Sandy said. "A woman. We have to get to her."

"There's nothing ahead except rocks and shoals!" Bear shouted. "You know this, Sandy. Turn to starboard!"

"No!" Sandy insisted. "There's no time. We have to get there."

Bear reached out and put a hand on the wheel. As he did, a wave hit the trawler, causing a sudden heave and yaw, sending Bear crashing into Logan, whose own feet had momentarily lost their footing. Another wave broke over the bow, spraying the pilothouse windows.

"Get out!" Sandy roared, regaining his balance and taking the wheel. "All of you!"

"No," Bear said as Logan backed up to the pilothouse door, which was still slapping open and closed. "Give me the wheel."

Bear charged Sandy, knocking him away from the wheel to the port side. Bear had the wheel now, throwing the shifters into neutral and throttles down. The boat lurched in response, the engines howling in outrage.

"This is my boat!" Sandy shouted, getting up with the gaff. "You'll kill us all!"

Sandy came at him, swinging the hooked gaff in a sweeping arch just as another wave took the three of them off their feet. The hook caught Bear just above the clavicle, tearing into the muscle. He screamed as Sandy pulled the hook forward and pushed Bear away from the controls.

Logan, unsure of who to help, followed a different instinct altogether. He grabbed the VHF-16 handpiece.

"Mayday, mayday! This is the *Queequeg*, southeast of Block Island, near Mohegan Bluffs."

"Get away from there, boy!" his uncle yelled at him. "Get Pauly and check the engine!"

"Mayday," Logan said, sinking to give himself a lower center of gravity. "Crewman injured. Ship in trouble."

"Do what I said!" Sandy screamed, letting go of the wheel and grabbing Logan's jacket, hoisting him upward with the next wave.

As Sandy shoved him toward the door, something struck the boat, causing it to heave and yaw again. Bear was up now, blood spilling from his shoulder, but determined to help Logan. He landed a fist on Sandy's back, a hammer blow that caused him to turn around, giving Logan a chance to spill out of the pilothouse and into the weather.

He clung to the handrail, making his way to the trawl deck. Pauly was waiting for him in the doorway, black smoke billowing from somewhere below. He grabbed Logan, leaning into the boy's blank face.

"What's going on up there?" Pauly asked.

"I don't know," Logan said, face slack with shock. "Something got into Sandy. They're fighting for control of the boat!"

"What?" Pauly asked, disbelieving before making a decision. "All right, I'll go up and figure it out. You get an immersion suit on. Something hit us, and we're taking on water."

"We hit something?"

"No, something hit us," he said before pressing his way against the wind to the pilothouse. "Get a suit. One minute!"

Logan watched Pauly disappear into the pilothouse before turning into the deck cabin where the suits were stored. He had practiced putting on the reddish-orange suit a few dozen times, but this was the first time he had to do it in an emergency. He sat, pushing his legs in first, and then climbed up on his knees, bracing himself against the wall.

He slipped his left arm in first, then the hood, and then his stronger right arm. The hardest part was always the zipper because the suit's hands always felt oversized and awkward. Get it wrong and he would be dead. The suit was the only protection against hypothermia in the frigid water.

He stood, waddling out onto the deck. The bow of the boat already felt higher than the stern. He took one last look toward the pilothouse, but saw nothing — just the occasional flash of the green beacon and something white and luminescent that appeared as the green light left a ghost trail and disappeared.

Was this what his uncle had seen? He didn't know, and knew he couldn't navigate up to the pilothouse in the suit. He did what he was supposed to do. He jumped into the water while holding onto the hood. The suit made a sucking sound as the air escaped, and it tightened to his body. The *Queequeg* was starting to take on water fast.

He could see a silhouette outside the boat, someone attempting to loosen a life raft before the lights went out. Pauly? Sandy? He wasn't sure. It was too hard to make out much of anything as the cold water burned his exposed face as he rose and fell with the waves, a bobber in the icy blackness.

Almada looked at the boy, who had grown silent. He already knew what happened next. Logan would drift with a growing debris field for almost 20 minutes until a board off the boat hit him. He grabbed onto it and, discovering it was stuck to the life raft, managed to climb into it.

He was upset to discover that the raft was empty, but he knew it would save his life. The captain of the rescuing boat was also working the tide and debris fields when he found the life raft, a faint light through the gloom. They immediately brought the disoriented boy on board and covered him with dry, warm towels.

The search for the missing fishermen would continue through much of the day. Three Coast Guard cutters and another small boat, combing 400 nautical miles around where the trawler was believed to have gone down. Joining them were several other fishermen who knew the Sullivans and a private pilot who had flown out from Cape Cod.

"Do you know what happened to your uncle to act this way?" Almada asked.

Logan shook his head.

"All right," Almada stood up. "Why don't you finish eating and get some more rest. I suspect some of your family will be here to visit soon enough."

The boy nodded. Almada made his way to the door before Logan spoke.

"It's just — it's been real hard. I mean really hard," he said. "But he wasn't crazy. I saw it too. I saw the woman too."

"Yeah, kid," Almada said. "Get some rest."

Almada had everything he needed, except the answer to one question that wasn't for Logan. How could she be back?

TIDY LINES

Montana 1992

There was an idiosyncratic magic in the way the line danced as Nathan finished his upcast and snapped his wrist forward in a downcast. It would loop the air, keeping a tight, graceful arch until he brought it forward, and the fly would sail out across the sparkling ribbons of white water.

As soon as the fly line touched the water, he would tuck it under his index finger and strip it back behind his index finger. Over and over until, snap, he caught his third trout with a whoop and a grin.

He looked back over his shoulder and smiled at us from the water. Heather and I were still attempting to fish from the shore. He was the only one with fishing waders.

"That's three today." He smiled at us as if nobody was counting. Everybody was counting.

Heather looked at her older brother in admiration. I gave an approving nod, attempting to hide my growing frustration.

"You two having a good time?" he asked.

"Yes!" Heather exclaimed.

"Yeah," I said, pulling in my line again.

I wasn't having a good time. We had been standing in a cold river for the better part of three hours, desperately unprepared for what had befallen us.

"Heather said you love fishing," Nathan had floated the night before. "Want to go out tomorrow?"

I had grown up on a lake, so fishing almost felt second nature despite rarely having the opportunity after Heather and I moved to the great state of Arizona. Sure, you could fish small recreational lakes or ponds in and around Phoenix, but it never felt the same as lake fishing in Michigan where I grew up. It took too much effort to find any worthwhile fishing spots, and we didn't have a boat.

At least that is what I told myself. The truth was we had both become urban desert dwellers and getting wet mostly meant visiting friends with a pool in the backyard. It's what we did. We would find out which friends wanted to drink. We were the fishes.

When her brother cast out an invitation to see his new lakefront cabin in Montana, we jumped at the chance. It didn't even matter how ill-prepared he always was for guests.

We had to buy our own bedding for the living room floor when we stayed at his condo in Redondo Beach. We had to fill the empty refrigerator when we stayed at his townhome in Park City. He didn't mean the lake right outside his front door when he asked us to go fishing. He meant fly fishing on the Madison River with only two reels and one set of waders.

"You're not having a good time," he said, keeping the smile but wrinkling his nose.

"No, I'm fine," I said, passing the rod to Heather. "It's different a bit from spin fishing."

"I told you, ten-to-two," he said as if the numbers were an enchantment.

Heather had that look about her. It proclaimed she was a dumb blonde. She wasn't really dumb or naturally blonde, but she used the idea as a self-defense mechanism around her brother. He was the hero. She was the zero.

"Your turn, Jason," said Heather. "I tangled the line."

"Great," I said, looking down at the knots while she headed toward the picnic basket.

It was a good thing Nathan was catching fish. None of us would have eaten without him. He seemed well-suited to the rhythmic and repetitive nature of fly fishing. It matched the rest of his life.

He was a retired Navy pilot, ferrying passengers back and forth between cities for United Airlines. He made six figures, investing most of it into real estate since his divorce a few years earlier. It was methodical, the opposite of the life I was building.

I lived as I fished. You drop a minnow in the water on one line and cast out a specific lure with another. I was an artist, painting abstracts when the mood struck me and working as a graphic designer to pay the bills.

In his eyes, I was floating through a life that was both incidental and accidental. But try explaining that to a pilot. It would be like a spark plug trying to explain its importance to a cog. Cogs seldom question their existence as long as the things around them are in good working order. Airplanes take off from a runway and come down for a landing. Fly fishing has an upcast and a downcast.

"I'm surprised you couldn't pick it up," he said, wading over to check the tangle.

"Hey, first time fly fishing," I shrugged.

"Right." He squinted. "I feel like I picked it up faster."

We called it a day when he caught his fourth fish. There was plenty for dinner, but Nathan didn't head straight home. He wanted to meet up with a friend at a small pub on the way back to the cabin.

His friend Derrick seemed likable enough. He was a petroleum engineer for the Bureau of Land Management, which meant that his team monitored policy, procedures, leasing, and land use with various companies. He was a big guy, and much more down to earth than Heather's Top Gun brother.

Good thing. After the first beer, Nathan broke off with Heather to help him bring back the next round from the bar. Derrick and I became aquatinted, throwing darts.

"Any luck fishing today?"

"No, not really," I said.

"I'm surprised you didn't do better," he said. "People who throw darts usually pick it up pretty quick. You set your opposite foot forward, bring it back, and toss ten-to-one."

I looked at him blankly. Nathan hadn't told me any of it.

"I thought it was ten-to-two," I finally said.

"Not if you want your line to cast out," he said, walking over to retrieve his darts.

Heather and Nathan returned with a pitcher of beer and fresh glasses. They were laughing, acting like siblings who got along.

"Good game?" Heather asked, leaning in to kiss me.

"Yeah, I'm up," I said.

"Nathan," Derrick smiled. "Why didn't you show him how to cast today?"

"Is that what he told you?"

"He said you told him to cast ten-to-two," Derrick mused. "That's a fail."

Nathan took a pull from his beer. He looked at it for a minute before turning toward Derrick to square up a statement.

"He would have failed anyway." He pinched his eyes. "It's what he does."

This was one of the problems people had when they like to keep a tidy line. When life isn't as tidy as they like, they want to cut the knots away, regardless of how much line is left.

I didn't say anything. I imagine I didn't have to. My expression must have said it all.

"Come on, boys," Heather choked as if I had been a participant. "Let's play nice."

Nathan pushed away from the table and headed back to the bar. Derrick excused himself, saying he had an early start the next morning.

"It's nice to meet you both," he said. "I'll say goodbye to Nathan on my way out."

I walked over and pulled the darts out of the board. I didn't need to, but there wasn't anything else to do. Heather walked over as I slowly set them back in the rack.

"Nathan didn't mean anything by it," she said.

"He never does," I said.

"It doesn't matter," she said. "What matters is how we feel about each other."

She had circled to face me, hooking her thumbs into my belt loops. This was where I was supposed to say she was right, how much I loved her, and that it didn't matter. Her brother. Her father. Her mother. They all had tidy lines dropped in the water. The pilot. The accountant. The office manager.

"You know what they say," I finally said. "Marry the girl, marry the family."

We finished the round, and the three of us headed back to the cabin without saying a word. But when we got back, Nathan said the airlines had paged him to pick up a flight. We would have to spend our last day at his cabin on our own.

We did, taking his outboard motorboat onto the lake the next morning. Heather and I had two spin reels poled apiece, one to drop in the water and one to cast out. All the awkwardness of the night before became lost in the morning mist until I caught my first fish.

Heather was jubilant when I caught it, thinking it to be an omen of some sort. I thought so too, which is why I threw it back.

THE CATCH

Texas 1957

The drone of summer cicadas gave way to the steady percussion of hammers on stakes as the boy crested the hill and slid down the loose dirt, leaving a cloud of dust under once-white tennis shoes. There was an entire city being constructed below him, with canvas tents and colorful flags and hastily erected canopies to make a roofline.

Upon reaching the bottom, the boy headed toward an alley between two large tents, passing three partially shaded picnic benches where a half-dozen foreign denizens were having breakfast before the dry midday heat would drive them inside.

"Where do you think you are going in such a hurry, *malysh*?" asked the giant of a man as he reached out and grabbed hold of the passing boy's collar.

The giant tugged him, almost off his feet, and spun him around. The boy's eyes first landed on an oversized leather belt before straining to look up, past the carpeted chest, and at the bearded grin of his captor.

"Oh, leave him be, *grobian*," laughed the young blonde sitting sidesaddle at one of the tables. "He's just a *kleiner junge*. Too small for you. Throw him back until the others arrive."

It was still early, hours before most townspeople would line up for jobs as temporary roustabouts. But the boy knew his chance for a week's work would slip away if he waited.

"I'm not so small," said the boy, as the giant set him down with a laugh.

"Oh yeah," the blonde said, blowing a smoke ring at him. "*Sie grobian*, too, a brute? Okay then, so what is your name little brute?"

"Jimmy," he said, blushing at what reminded him of a lace swimsuit, barely hidden under her open robe. "Jimmy Bishop."

"Well, Jimmy, Jimmy Bishop," she said. "My Russian friend asked you a question. What can we do for you? Or maybe what can you do for us?"

Others were starting to take an interest too as the giant gave him a small shove toward the woman. A tall, lean man with a crown of red hair stared at him over a tin cup of coffee. Another woman, a scantily dressed brunette with exotically painted eyes, gave him a wink. A dwarf in a purple shirt and canvas pants held up by suspenders stood up on a bench, still holding his breakfast plate, to get a better view.

"I'm just looking for work," his voice cracked. "I don't know. Maybe clean up after the animals?"

"Lions and tigers and bears, oh my," said the brunette, placing a hand to her mouth in feigned surprise.

The giant's booming voice led an amused chorus of laughs from the ensemble. Jimmy guessed them to be entertainers. Strongmen and dwarves. Hoop dancers and clowns. Jugglers and snake dancers. Misfits and magicians.

"You like that movie, Jimmy?" asked the blonde, again. "The Wizard of Oz?"

"It's okay." He kicked the dirt by his feet.

"It's okay. He says it's okay," smiled the blonde, standing up and opening her arms. "You ought to be more careful walking around. This is a mysterious playground."

"Marvelous," said the tall man.

"Exotic," said the brunette.

"Magical," concluded the blonde.

"I don't believe in magic," said Jimmy. "I'm almost thirteen."

They laughed again, this time at him. The giant gently pushed him closer to the woman. He could smell the smoke coming off her cigarette. She reached out and gently put one hand on his shoulder. Her blue eyes seemed to become clearer and colder the closer he moved toward her.

"Come closer, and I'll tell you a secret," she teased.

"Come on, Ingrid," said a new voice, coming over. "Leave the kid alone."

Jimmy turned to look at the newcomer. He was fit, and some might say handsome. He wore loose-fitting slacks held up by a thin belt and a sequin-lined vest instead of a shirt. He was smiling, but his furrowed brows suggested irritation.

"He's our friend, Peter, our guest," Ingrid said and licked her lips. "He's a delicious catch."

"Knock it off," he said, opening a path of escape between the giant and Ingrid, and then offering an explanation. "These German circuses, kid. You've got to be more careful."

"German?" rumbled the giant. "Who's German?"

"Ivan's not German, and his name isn't even Ivan." Peter thumbed at the giant. "He's Russian. One rung lower."

The giant offered a non-committal growl.

"You're such *die Bestie*, Peter." Ingrid laughed and flicked her cigarette at him. "Always insulting Ivan. Always spoiling the fun."

"If you're looking for cage work, you can find it in that direction," said Peter, pointing toward the break in the tents that Jimmy had been heading toward before being accosted. "Turn right at the end, then right again, four tents down. Ask for Herr Kruger."

"Thanks," Jimmy said, putting out a hand but finding it was greeted by empty air.

He put his hand down, walked a few steps back, and then turned and ran.

"Welcome to the *Zirkus*, Jimmy Bishop," Ingrid called after him. "Welcome to *Die Wunder der Welt*!"

They were laughing again, their voices chasing him. So Jimmy picked up the pace, feet digging deeply into the well-worn paths cut into the farmer's field that hadn't yielded anything worthwhile since the statewide drought started seven years ago.

It wasn't long before he felt lost, trying to remember exactly what Peter had told him. He wasn't sure, exactly, so he took to asking for "Herr Kruger" as he passed crewmen and roadies. They would reassure him with a general direction, saying "ya" or "goot" as they waved him by.

Eventually, he slowed to a walk. The bustle of building tents had thinned away at the fringe. From here, he wasn't sure where he should go, but he did get a sense of how this makeshift town might look like a magical kingdom, springing up out of the greens and golds of grain fields or desert grasslands overnight.

No wonder people were drawn from all over Texas and neighboring states. They would come by the thousands, the crowd being a spectacle in and of itself. Never mind that most other circuses seemed to be operating on life support as Americans started to tune in for entertainment from their living rooms instead of seeing it live. This one — *Die Wunder der Welt* or the German Circus — was something of an exception.

The promoter billed it as a larger-than-life European extravaganza that would crisscross America's railways only one time before returning to the old world. See it once and never see it again — a real one-of-a-kind novelty in a world mostly interested in mass-produced magic like Slinkys and Hula Hoops.

"Herr Kruger?" Jimmy called out as he poked his head into a tent flap.

He was greeted by a menacing guttural growl and gust of bad breath. Someone had set the case too close to the opening, and a paw sprung out through the bar, snagging his shirt. Jimmy screamed and backpedaled away from the cage, tripping on his heels, and falling into the blackness of the tent directly opposite of this one.

He didn't try to get up at first. He just laid in the dark on the hard-packed dirt, trying to catch his breath and calm a racing heart. There was a coolness in this tent, and it helped him recover from his second shock of the day.

"Get ahold of yourself, kid," Jimmy told himself.

There was a quiet, almost inaudible hum from somewhere in the center of the tent. So Jimmy flipped over onto his stomach and peered into the dark and tried to adjust his eyes to the blackness by ignoring the small sliver of light from the bottom of the tent flap behind him. He could feel a light chill touching his face — not all that different from the air conditioning that his best friend's family had installed two years ago.

"Hello?" he whispered, getting up on his knees and slowly starting to stand.

He took a step forward, hands out in front of him. Somewhere above him, toward the tent's high peak, he caught a splash of golden light breaking up the darkness. He looked up at it, watching it grow out of a few feathered embers and into a graceful golden eagle, circling the tent canopy high above.

Two more splashes of gold accompanied it, taking shape as luminescent partners, with flames trailing feathers and adding more light to the expansive space above.

As the three of them circled, the sides of the tent seemed to fall away, leaving the faint outline of trees marking the edge of the forest hollow. The top of the tent faded into a distant night with constellations blinking beyond the tops of towering fir trees and past the fiery birds that seemed to have brought it all to life.

Even the ground below him began to respond, becoming grass that started at his feet and quickly rose up to touch his knees. Deeper inside, Jimmy could now see a man with a top hat in the center of it all, waving a baton as if conducting an orchestra. Jimmy knew he was the one bringing this extraordinary world into focus.

He gasped at the silhouette of another creature, as large as an elephant but lower to the ground like a lizard. His surprise was loud enough that the man with the top hat took notice. He stopped, turned toward Jimmy, brought both hands together, and pulled them apart with a fizzling snap. Jimmy felt a tugging sensation at the center of his chest as everything went black.

"You shouldn't be in here," said a stranger who had come through the tent flap behind him.

The sunlight that followed after the man was momentarily blinding. Jimmy squinted his eyes, putting up a hand to shield them. He was sitting on the ground again.

"I was looking for Herr Kruger," he said. "I took a wrong turn."

"You took a turn all right," he said, extending a hand to help the boy up. "A bump on the head by the looks of it."

"No," Jimmy said, reflexively bringing a hand to his head to discover a knot just below his hairline. "I mean, I suppose I did."

"Look now," the man said, brushing the boy off. "You're no worse for wear. Let's get you a drink and find Herr Kruger."

"Weren't you in here just a moment ago?" Jimmy asked, pointing to the man's top hat.

"Ah, yes. People see all sorts of things when they hit their heads," he said. "Most people call me Herr Hoffer, but you may call me Anton. Come along now."

"Thank you," Jimmy said. "I haven't been able to find my way."

"That's the beauty of a circus, isn't it?" Anton asked. "You don't find a way as much as a way finds you."

TIME CAPSULE

Maine 2017

Billy resisted the urge to pull his wool jacket closed, walking between his car and the front door of the Bear Paw. It was a chilly fall night with some brisk weather blowing off the Kennebec River, but the bar manager, Charlie, liked to run the local pub hot for out-of-towners even if most of his customers were Mainers. It had something to do with tips, he said. The further away, the better the tips.

So instead of pulling his jacket tighter, Billy picked up the pace and took off his coat as he crashed through the front door. He tossed it on one of the coat racks and headed toward a small opening at the bar.

"Hey, Charlie, give me a Geary's, will you?"

"Yeah, give me a minute on the pour," he said.

Placing an order at the Paw, as they called it, was also an unofficial announcement that you'd arrived. It also allowed people an opportunity to finish part of their conversation before giving you a proper greeting as a newcomer. They welcomed him with a chorus of how-do-you-dos and raised highballs. He obliged them all, hugging a few and nodding to others. By the time they finished, Charlie was back with a beer glass.

"Hey, um, let me be the one to tell you before someone else does," Charlie said. "Look who's set up at the table."

Billy gave him a shrug, indicating he probably wouldn't care. But then Charlie gave an insistent head bob. Billy would have never shrugged it off had he known. His eyes moved quickly past Ed Mailer and onto the woman who was readying a shot.

Her hair was shorter and framed her face, but there was no mistaking who it was. Jessica Michaud — the girl that gave him up for New York City five years ago — was shooting the seven ball in the corner pocket and lining up the nine. He fished two quarters out of his pocket as he walked over to them.

"Winner, if it's open," he said, slipping the quarters under the opposite bumper as she sunk the nine ball.

"Yeah, Billy, of course," Ed said. "I need to eat something anyway."

Jessica didn't stand up right away. She leaned into the table with a sigh before turning around.

"Hey, Billy," she said, brushing some stray hairs off her forehead and out of her eyes.

"Hey, Billy?" He echoed her observation as a question and asked one of his own. "What are you doing here?"

"Honestly, I didn't bank on you being here," she said. "I figured you'd be at Skeeters, if anywhere."

"Preemptive avoidance," he acknowledged. "Good one."

"It's not that," she said. "I just … what did you expect? That I would come back, unchanged, and call up Billy Stevens as if maybe time stood still."

"Why are you back?"

"My mom needs my help," she said. "She was diagnosed with small cell lung cancer."

"I'm sorry, Jess," he said. "I didn't know."

"It's surprising how so few people do," she said. "It's a small town in a small state."

Billy put the quarters in the slot and pushed. The balls tumbled down unseen chutes, lending a period to the end of her statement.

"Anyway, I'm back for the duration, however long that is," Jessica said. "I've been back for about a week and came out tonight to get some air, if you know what I mean. I needed to decompress and not think about it."

"Hey, I get it," Billy said. "I won't push anymore. Let's just play. You can tell me about big city life."

"Okay," she said. "But that might not be my favorite subject, either. And New York City isn't big. It's only about 300 square miles."

As they played, she began to describe a world unlike any he had ever experienced. She talked about the boroughs and neighborhoods, how hard it is to set priorities in a city that wants to dictate them, how many pairs of walking shoes she blew out, and what it's like to get stuck in the subway. She complained a bit about the noise, the smells, the less-than-friendly people. But he could tell she found some beauty in that concrete jungle too.

When she started describing Grand Central Station, he was taken in by her love of it. To her, there was something magical about the dirt and grit. The same could be said about the bridges or the brownstones or the skyscrapers or the ferries or the dizzying amount of choices all stacked upon each other in a city that doesn't think about sleep until the bars close at 4 a.m.

"I had every intention of scaling the big corporate ladder of New York City advertising and earning a corner office like everybody covets there," she said. "But after my boyfriend — yeah, sorry ... I've had several — dumped me in a blaze of glory and left me wondering how to pay for the apartment, all of the anxiety of New York finally got to me, and all I wanted to do was come home. So I called my mom, and instead of offering comfort or words of wisdom, she sent me screenshots of her X-rays."

"Harsh," he said, attempting to look like he was at least trying to focus on a shot.

"That's me," she said. "For better or worse, not the girl who left here five years ago. You?"

"Nothing so exotic," he said. "I graduated like you, felt lost after we broke up and took a job at Cutter's Quarry, mining granite, so all those home chefs have something nice to cut their vegetables on. It's not a bad gig. I've advanced to running the saw mostly."

She smiled at him, and he could feel it cut all the way to his heart. When she smiled for real, her cheeks rose and lit up her eyes. For as long as they held you, he remembered, it felt like you were the only person in the world who mattered in that moment.

"Don't take this the wrong way," she said. "But you look the same. I mean, aside from the scruff under your chin, I feel like I've unearthed the past."

"I get it," he said, shaking his head as the spell was broken.

"What about your stone carvings?" she asked. "Still do anything like that?"

"No, well, not really," he said and then reconsidered and started pulling at a piece of rawhide around his neck. "I have this one piece."

He took it off and handed it to her. Dangling from the leather was a granite dragonfly. While her collection of dragonflies was packed away somewhere, the meaning of this one wasn't lost on her.

"It's beautiful," she said, tracing the wings before trying to hand it back.

"You can keep it," he said. "I kind of made it for you anyway."

She set it on the edge of the pool table.

"This is kind of what I meant," she said, still smiling but pressing her lips together. "Coming back is like opening a time capsule. Augusta is the same. The Paw is the same. Charlie is the same. You're the same. Everything here is preserved like the granite that you dig up every day. But, I'm not the same girl I was five years ago, and … you know, maybe I better go."

"Come on, Jess," said Billy. "Give me a bone here, and let me welcome you home. There's got to be something I can do, even if it's as friends."

"Yeah, you can walk me out," she said, heading to the door. "Thanks for everything, Charlie. Have a good night."

"Hey, he's not running you out of here, is he?" Charlie mused.

"No, I just got to get home," she said. "That is why I came back, mostly."

"Yeah, sorry about your mom," Charlie said. "Let me know if there is anything I can do."

"Thanks, Charlie," she said.

When they reached the coat racks, Billy grabbed his and started to size up which one might be hers. She pointed.

"The blue one from L.L. Bean," she said.

"Really?" Billy raised an eyebrow. "You know they only make the boots and tote bags in Maine."

"So?" she said, crinkling her face.

"So, the coats aren't as good," he said.

She slipped the coat on as they exited together. As soon as they were outside, she gulped in the clean air, and then spun on her heels to face him.

"Maybe we can try again," he said. "I don't know, maybe some Sunday baked beans."

"Billy, look," she paused, putting a hand on his chest, partly to push him back and partly as a gesture of endearment. "I'm going to be too busy taking care of my mom, you know? And what we had was really special. I don't want to change that, okay."

"Ayuh, I hear you," he said. "Like Charlie said. Your mom was a good person. Let me know if I can do anything."

She didn't say anything else. She patted his chest, gave him a downward-cast smile, and turned toward her Jeep

Cherokee. He stood there and watched her drive away for the second time in his life. Only this time, he had an urge to let her go.

TOP RUNG

South Carolina 2013

Kayla pulled the front door of her modest two-bedroom starter home tight and checked it with a push and pull. It was still pitch dark, so she took a few extra minutes to stretch out on the small front porch before her morning run.

Having a later start time was one of several tradeoffs she had made since surrendering her Columbia apartment in favor of a suburban investment a few months ago. City streetlights afforded runners an earlier start time than the mostly unlit, narrow streets of her new suburban neighborhood. Now she had to start in the dark.

She glanced down at her phone before strapping it to her arm, thumbing her exercise playlist to "Backseat Freestyle" by Kendrick Lamar. It was the perfect song to wake up and get pissed off to before a run, transforming what most were calling sexist lyrics into a personal jam. Like Lamar, she had a dream too.

She wanted respect, not because of money or power or possessions — she hadn't earned those things yet — but respect for her mind over the objectification of her body. And in his way, wasn't that what Lamar was going on about? It wasn't just about writing explicit lyrics. He was rebelling against old school cultural symbols.

As far as Kayla was concerned, women who couldn't push past sexist attitudes by meeting men on equal ground were more like her sister, Naomi. Naomi tried to take advantage of male objectification and became a slave to it in the process. At about the same time Kayla was moving into her new home, their mother called up in tears. Naomi was pregnant. The baby's father was just a kid, fresh out of high school with two minimum-wage jobs.

Between the song and the swirling, angry thoughts about her sister, Kayla's heart rate was up enough. She was ready to hit the road and run out three miles. When the feet-moving beat of "Here I Come" by The Roots came on, she jumped down the three porch steps and started her run.

This was one of only two places in the entire world where she felt in control. Here, it was always the same: knees up, feet landing close to center, hands up and down. Her form was near perfect. It had been years since her feet reached out too far in front or elbows flared out to the side like she used to do when she jogged. But she wasn't a jogger anymore; she ran hard.

The second place she felt in control was at the pharmaceutical lab where she worked. Much like running, she would put her head down and write grant proposals, conduct computer analysis, or manage experiments. She wasn't just a lackey anymore; she worked hard.

It was only in her personal life that things went sideways. Her sister's teenage pregnancy. Her dad's deadbeat drinking habit. Her mom's need to control things. Her steady string of failed romances that didn't understand her career. Her old high school friends who drifted away as they had fewer and fewer things in common.

She was picking up the pace now, running past the last few houses on her block and up a small stretch of road bordered by the first park. It was usually about this time she would see another runner, a man in his mid-thirties with a headlight strapped to his head, on the other side of the street. She didn't know his name but found comfort in raising her hand in acknowledgment.

After they passed each other, she turned with the street, keeping the park on her left and the larger one- and two-story brick homes with spacious yards on her right. These homes were all architecturally different, but with similar facades — houses bigger than those on her block with some combination of red bricks, white siding, gray roofs, white picket fences, flower beds, or American flags — the next step up life's ladder.

Then those houses were gone, giving way to a variety of older homes spaced further and further apart. She was getting into her groove now and letting her mind wander back to her sister.

What bothered Kayla most was the selfishness. Her parents would have to cover expenses. They would handle the hassle of prenatal appointments. But they would also give her worrisome looks, eyes always wanting but mouths never asking for emotional and financial support. The "she's your sister" plea was understood.

Kayla knew she was supposed to be there for her sister, but what about her? There were times she wanted to cry or vent or have someone wipe away her fears. College wasn't easy, and paying back the school debt she took on wasn't easy, either. Investing in a home of her own was another major step too. She had sacrificed plenty to do it, including all those pretty boys who came her way with gifts and glib talk.

Naomi hadn't sacrificed anything. She bent over for the first pretty boy who came her way. Would he stick around to be a father? Would the baby have his name? Where would they live? Would they ask about her sparsely furnished extra bedroom? And if they did move in with her, how would a baby affect Kayla's life? Would her sister even make a good mother? Naomi certainly didn't have the sense to avoid pregnancy.

Kayla's thoughts didn't drift back to the road until she approached the first corner with a stop sign. She slowed down, cautiously looking both ways.

A few weeks ago, she made an incorrect assumption that any cross traffic would stop and was almost hit by a Dodge 4x4. The only time she saw its brake lights was after she had paused in the middle of the street to flip the driver off with both hands. The driver stopped in response, clearly deciding whether he should come back for her, and what? Kidnap her like that couple who kidnapped the girl on the television news?

The driver didn't move until she started running again. None of it made sense to her. He was too busy to stop at the sign, but not too busy to feign some intimidation her way. Kayla could see it all play out again as clear as the day it happened — so much so that she didn't see the Nissan Sentra backing out of the driveway until it was too late.

She heard the squeal of tires over the music first. The impact felt light, not even hard enough to knock her off her feet.

It just shook her up for a moment as the driver immediately jumped out of the car, asking if she was all right and muttering something about her coming out of thin air. She didn't care enough to stop.

"Next time be more careful," she said over her shoulder, catching a glimpse of the man kneeling behind the back bumper of his car.

Was he checking for damage? She shook her head, cutting her pace to a slow jog. Maybe she would discover a bruise back home, but she didn't want to stop now. The church's three-story bell tower was less than a block away, putting her just over a mile into her run. After the church was the second park, much larger than the one near her home. She would run through it, then turn back to complete the circuit.

She looked east just before entering the park and saw she was making good time. The sky had just begun its transformation from black to blue-gray. Then, she noticed something else shortly after entering the park — something out of the corner of her eye, shapes moving along the right side of the path.

When she turned her head for a better look, the bushes and trees masked whatever it was from her view. It wasn't until she pulled her earbuds from her ears that she could confirm anything was there. With nothing more than a low buzz bouncing around her neck, she could hear the whoosh, whoosh of something — or a couple of somethings — following alongside her. And any notion that she might dismiss it as rabbits or squirrels disappeared as she focused in on their low, rasping, panting growls.

Kayla immediately picked up her pace, head down, and elongated the length of her stride. While she always ran hard, she was starting to sprint — first fueled by being startled and then by the realization that whatever it was, it was pursuing her, playing with her, hunting her.

She quickly veered left onto a less-traveled park path that would circle around and allow her to double back. Her pursuers, meanwhile, raced up behind her, alongside her, and sometimes racing ahead of her. The low growls and occasional yaps that sounded like chatter threatened to cut her off at the front of the park exit. She pushed harder, gasping for breath as her head pounded, and she broke out of the tree line.

She felt safer, but not safe, as footfalls of padded feet and claws hit the pavement. She pressed even harder, too afraid to look back, eyes locked on the church steeple in the distance, this time from the other direction. As soon as she reached the church, she cut across the lawn and behind the building. She was spent, first attempting to lean on the back wall of the church and then crashing down alongside it, expecting to see a small pack round the corner and attack her.

They never came. Whatever had chased her out of the park had seemed to give up their pursuit. She rolled off the sidewalk and onto the soft grass that framed the church grounds, crying in relief. She laid there several minutes, holding her sides and then looking down at a ruined foot. She had lost one of her shoes during the chase and the asphalt had chewed through her sock and skin.

As the sky ripened from a predawn gray to orange, Kayla picked herself up, inventorying more abrasions from branches she had crashed through in the park. She started limping home.

She was only about a block away from the church when she saw a man in a weather-beaten open crown hat standing behind a pickup truck and kenneling three mangy animals that looked more like famished hyenas than dogs. The man was closing the cage behind the third. Kayla didn't recognize them because she never got a good look, but immediately sensed that these were the animals that chased her.

"You should keep a closer eye on them," she said, her voice strained from the exertion. "This isn't the Appalachians."

"Yeah, they do love to hunt," said the man, shrugging as he turned toward her with a toothy smile set in a wild, unkempt beard. "They couldn't have hurt you."

"So you knew? They scared me half out of my mind."

"Oh, they do that sometimes," he said before pointing to her foot. "You won't make it far on that. Why don't you hop in and I'll take you to where you lost it."

She shook her head, disbelieving. But then she found herself reconsidering with her next step. She would never be able to walk home.

"All right," she said, taking a long look at the animals in the truck bed as she walked around to the passenger's side.

"My name's Sharron," he said, turning over the engine. "Good to meet you. Wish it could be under better circumstances and all that, yadda, yadda."

"Kayla," she said, oddly relieved that she was finally off her feet.

Neither of them said anything as he slowly drove down the block. She was surprised how early in her run she had lost it, long before the dogs had chased her. As they drew closer, she realized where she lost her shoe. The Sentra had hit her, sending her sprawling across the road. The ambulance was on the scene, but it was too late.

"Go on, get your shoe," said the man. "Then I'll take you home."

"Heaven?" she asked.

"You weren't that good." He shrugged a second time.

ALL THE WILD HORSES

North Dakota 2019

Andrea "Andy" Canton rode up on the crest where two other riders had been watching and waiting. Behind her, more than four dozen wild horses, exhausted by the 125-mile trek she had led them on, stood quietly, grazing the hillside. They were content to relax their muscles, taking some time to ward off the weariness.

The two men sat taller in their saddles as she approached. She could tell almost immediately that they weren't ranchers. While their faces were tan, their plaid shirts were too crisp, jeans pressed, dark hair well kept and short under white hats.

"You know you are encroaching on the Fort Berthold Indian Reservation?" said the younger of the two.

"Yes, sir," she said. "At least I hope I am."

"What do you intend to do with these horses?" he asked, casting a hand up to include them all.

"I intend," said Andy, before restarting after thinking about it. "With the permission of the three tribes, I intend to walk them across Four Bears Bridge."

The younger man snorted a laugh but quieted quickly when the elder man reached out and touched his arm. Then the older man pointed to the girl's leg, noticing the injury she had tied off the day before.

"You're hurt?" the younger man asked.

"It's not bad," Andy lied. "It was mostly a graze. A farmer west of Killdeer took a wild shot at me for trespassing, I guess. I think he only meant to scare me off."

"You should have that looked at," he said.

"I will," she said. "As soon as I get the horses across the river."

"You know that the bridge is a mile long?" he said. "And even if you were allowed to walk them over, what then?"

"Then they'll be safe," she said. "The BLM won't round up horses on tribal land. It's outside their jurisdiction."

"You're making some assumptions," he said. "This isn't just open tribal land or the wild, wild west anymore — it's farmland, ranch land, and oil country. Even if you are permitted to cross, I don't see this as the end of your journey, Ms. Canton."

"You know who I am?"

"Everybody in North Dakota knows who you are." He smiled. "And everybody knows that a fifteen-year-old girl took these horses away from one of the few places they have left to roam."

"Is that what they're saying? They weren't going to be left to roam," she countered, her voice taking on a harshness hidden until now. "These bands were about to be rounded up and auctioned off, with some, maybe all of them, sold for slaughter."

"Now they are offering you an opportunity to surrender the horses and all will be forgiven. So while I admire your bravery, I think you should take the deal," he said. "We're all forced to thin a herd at times."

"There's nothing wrong with these horses," she spat. "Every year, the BLM changes the target range depending on some pencil pusher's interpretation. Some years the bison win more acres, and some years a handful of horses do. Nevermind that they're perfectly fine to all share the range together with elk and deer."

"I wish we could help, Ms. Canton..." he started before the elder man raised a hand to stop him. "My father wants me to submit your request to the council. I'll do it out of respect, but I already know what they'll say."

"Thank you," she said as he turned to ride off toward Four Bears.

For what seemed a long time, neither Andy nor the elder man said a word. Both of them sat atop their horses and stared out at the bands as they continued to graze the hillside. The Nokotas were beautiful animals, somewhat larger and rangier than what most people called mustangs. Initially bred by Native Americans and frontier ranch families, they were survivors as long as they had a place to survive.

It was her grandfather that had taught her about these wild horses, or los mestenos as he sometimes called them. He loved them as much as she did, taken by their resilience and grace. He would treat them as equals, much like she would on his own ranch, tasting their water, eating their food.

"You can learn a lot from horses," he used to whisper as they would watch them graze. "They know the secrets of the land better than anyone."

Andy could almost see his face in the sky, looking down on her, as she reflected on the last few days — her first quiet moment since she started their harrowing escape from the badlands. She had felt his presence at the very beginning, a feeling of comfort that left her only when the frightening whirl of a helicopter grew louder on its approach.

The helicopter was coming to corral these bands — the same ones she and her late grandfather had walked beside all her life. They meant too much to her to let it happen, so Andy intercepted them north of the capture corral, leading them into a canyon that forced the helicopter to break off its pursuit.

She knew Cody Williams, the self-proclaimed cowboy who was waiting just south of the canyon, would be upset. He was the BLM's main man, someone who had perfected this maneuver to lead wild horses into a capture corral and used it effectively across the American West. He had done it many times, working all over the western United States — Nevada, Wyoming, Idaho, Montana — boasting more than 200,000 wild horses, burros, and cattle captured.

He argued that anything that sped up their capture was better than the alternatives like capturing them from horseback or water traps. He said helicopters were less stressful on the animals, but Andy didn't buy it. The stress of stockpiling them in holding pens until death negated any argument for fast captures in her mind.

The only existing solution, as much as she didn't like it, was darting them with birth control. It was the only sensible solution so they could continue to roam free — the last stand of an American spirit that was dwindling into history.

So when the BLM announced plans to thin the badlands population, explicitly targeting bands that recognized her as much as she recognized them, Andy decided to do something about it. She set up an intervention before Williams's expected capture point.

That part of her plan worked more quickly than expected because she understood how these bands moved together. Most people thought that taking a lead horse and moving the animals from behind, much as the helicopter did, was the easiest method. But her grandfather taught her that convincing higher-ranked mares to depart an area in a new direction was enough to convince the others to follow.

It worked, but since the initial interception, she felt like her plan was starting to crumble. The land outside of the park, just north of the Little Missouri River, was dotted with fracking wells, most attempting to tap into the Bakken Formation that turned North Dakota into the second-largest oil-producing state in the nation.

Then, once past the wells, she managed to trace the outer edge of less populated pockets. She went mostly unnoticed, using natural washes and tree lines for cover and not resting until just over the hill from where she would thread the needle between Grassy Butte and the Sweet Crude Travel

Center and usher them across the highway. She did it at the break of day, before the long line of oil trucks took over the road. Had anyone been there, they would have seen an unassuming girl who loved nature and art being followed across the highway by a palette of blue roan, black, gray, chestnut, dun, grullo, and palomino.

Her luck seemed to hold even after one family had lent her a helping hand, giving the horses a place to rest and Andy a basket of food that she hoped would last the rest of the journey. Unfortunately, not everyone was so gracious to trespassers.

Outside Killdeer on her second day, she had mistaken an outstretched hand as a welcome, but it was merely meant to ward her away. As she came closer, the man fired a round from his rifle in the air. She held up her hands, slowing her horse to a near standstill. It wasn't enough to appease the man, and he shot again in her general direction.

The bullet had grazed her leg, a passing hornet buzzing loudly before making rocks jump a few yards away. Her brain barely even registered being hit as she turned around immediately and drove her herd back into the rougher terrain. A few minutes later, after she was out of his line of sight, her leg pulsed and her jeans felt damp.

She washed the wound the best she could and then used her bandana as a makeshift bandage. It wasn't sterile, but it was the best she had. Cleaning it with anything more than water or taking antibiotics would have to wait. She knew she had to do it soon, though, and make sure any pieces of fabric were removed from the wound.

"Do you know who Mato-tope was, Ms. Canton?" asked the older man, speaking for the first time.

"He was some sort of chief, wasn't he?" she said.

"Oh, he was much more than a chief. Mato-tope, which means Four Bears in English, was a great warrior chief and a problem solver, much like the Nokotas you have here. I'm speaking of the first Mato-tope, mind you, though the second Four Bears was also a great leader too."

"The bridge is named after them," she said. "And the resort."

"Yes. But Mato-tope has many more stories than a bridge or a resort. You see, he and his tribe always had many enemies. He fought the Cheyenne, Sioux, Assiniboine, and even the Arikara, which are now part of three tribes," said the man. "It was because he had so many enemies, I think, that he came to call the white man his brother. So when they needed food, he would feed them. When they needed rest, he would give them a Buffalo skin to sleep on. When they were insulted, Mato-tope would even defend them from insults.

"But in the end, it was the white man who betrayed him and his tribe. Mato-tope watched almost every one of his family die of smallpox, his wives and all but one child. He watched the destruction of his tribe, braves and warriors, all laid low. He watched them all dwindle from two thousand people to less than a hundred in a matter of months. Watching this, he was so taken by grief that he climbed to the top of a hill to starve, coming down after the ninth day to die. He only wanted to put himself to rest next to his family and ask for the last of his tribe and all neighboring tribes to heed his warning. Do not trust the white man."

"That's a terrible story," she said.

"Ms. Canton, I have nothing against the white man. I grew up on the reservation and then moved away to pursue a career. I came back an educated man to work with the oil companies, monitoring their wells and delivering supplies. I have nothing against them and neither does my son. We understand the world changes and we must change with it," he said. "But, I will caution you against trusting them with a deal or waiting for the council to make a decision. I will lead you across the Four Bears Bridge now and see you off the reservation."

"Where will I go?"

"Once I leave you, head north toward the Des Lacs National Wildlife Refuge," he said. "Bison use the rangeland there, or you can help them across the border. I'm not sure Canada is any more accommodating. Everybody has their own agenda for land."

She understood. She was on her own, alone but not lonely. America was changing and, like many Native Americans had learned, there wouldn't be any room left unless you were willing to change with it. Unfortunately for these beauties, they couldn't learn to be anything more than a horse. They would, however, have their five minutes of fame as Andy and Joshua Whitecloud stopped traffic on the Four Bears Bridge for a herd of about forty-eight horses.

Later, she would learn he was also called Two Bears. He was only half as strong and half as wise as Mato-tope, but twice as modest, he mused before giving her some food and a first aid kit. He wasn't the only one to offer her provisions or keepsakes. Her horses seemed to have rekindled something in the three tribes — a collective memory of a different time that was less forgiving but considerably freer.

SIDELINES

Illinois 1963

He stood just inside the free-throw line with his feet together and his hands comfortably palming the ball. His polyester shorts were snug, burnt orange with a black trim that came together like a sloping triangle at the seams. The style matched his tank. Sweat beaded on his brow, giving away that he had been at it for hours.

It was still early, but the heat already rose in waves off the cement. It would be too muggy to practice in an hour or two. At least, that is what Orson thought as he watched the teen across the street through the chainlink fencing that divided them.

What a punk, thought Orson. It had been this way for weeks. While every other kid in the community had long boarded their bright yellow school buses, this kid was on a neighborhood court shooting hoops. Orson suspected he was a loser like the ones people read about in the newspaper.

They stayed home, trading in education for free time. Sometimes they put in time on the court, but eventually, most of them took it to the couch in the afternoon with that new Colt 45 beer in one hand and a cigarette, or worse, in the other. It disgusted him.

Orson watched as the boy slowly slid his left foot back, keeping his feet about shoulder-width apart. The right side of his body remained aligned to the basket, his knees bent. He popped and released the ball. Orson shook his head as the ball grazed the rim and sailed away.

"Wow," Orson muttered, and then spoke up loud enough to be heard. "I thought you people were supposed to be good at that."

The kid shrugged, never looking, and set out to retrieve the ball. Then he lined up for another shot. The ball hit the rim again; this time it spiked downward in front of the basket.

"Unbelievable," Orson groaned and then called out. "You gotta bend at your knees, not at your hips for heaven's sake."

The boy tilted his head back and shook his head. He walked over to collect the ball, slowly dribbling it back, and then changed his approach for a three-point shot. He missed.

"Don't nail those heels to the floor, Bellamy," Orson said, laughing as his own joke.

"Man, what is your problem?" the boy asked, turning to face his heckler with hands on hips.

"My problem?" Orson said. "Seems you're the one with the problem. Three for ten ain't landing you a spot with the Zephyrs. Oh wait, those boys are bugging out to Baltimore. Good riddance."

"Don't you have something better to do, like a job or something?" said the boy.

"It's my day off," Orson said.

"You've been at that bus stop watching me every day for more than a week," the teen said.

"I have the whole week off," Orson said.

"And you don't have nothing better to do?"

"I'm protecting the neighborhood."

"From what?"

"Hoodlums."

"You're not going to find any here, old man," said the boy.

"Oh, no?" Orson said, standing up and crossing the street. "I'm not finding any basketball players here, either, so how am I supposed to know you ain't a hoodlum? Do you have a name?"

"I don't have to answer to you, soda," said the boy.

"Soda?" Orson laughed. "That's a good one. Maybe you should write for Lucille Ball."

"Look, I just want to be left alone," he said. "If I tell you, will you let it be?"

"Depends if you're telling the truth," Orson squinted. "I have a good fib detector. Are you a fibber?"

"My name is Duval Johnson, all right," Duval said. "I live just south of 40th. That's your next question, isn't it? Ask the colored boy his name and where he lives."

"Just south of 40th? I didn't know any colored families had crept so far north," said Orson. "Pretty soon, you'll be my neighbor."

"Seems we're already neighbors, mister," said the boy.

"Orson. Orson Burke. You can call me Mr. Burke, but mister suits me fine if you're more comfortable with that," said Orson. "Anywho, since we're neighbors, or so you say, you might as well learn to shoot."

"What?" Duval said, disbelieving.

"Yeah, I used to play a little ball back in the day," said Orson as he worked his way over to a small opening in the fence. "I was a starting forward in high school, and played a little college ball too, but never broke away from the B team."

"Mister, I don't know if playing ball with you is a good idea," Duval said.

"Why the heck not?" Orson said, taking off his shirt and tie and laying them across his briefcase. "You chicken?"

"No, I'm not chicken," he said. "I just don't want someone to think I'm mugging you after you slip and fall or something. People are already watching."

Orson turned to see Edith Barker looking across the road at them from her front porch. Orson always chatted her up in the spring when she planted flowers in front of her fence. He waved, and she cautiously raised a hand in return before quickly turning away and going inside.

"Edith won't bother us none," he said.

"She might if she don't like colored people," Duval said.

"What difference does that make? I don't like colored people as a general rule, either, and here I am teaching you how to shoot," Orson said, holding the ball out to Duval.

"Man, you don't make a lick of sense," Duval said, taking it. "So let me be clear. I don't want no trouble. If there's any trouble, I'm out."

"The trouble is you can't shoot," Orson said, walking over to the side of the basket. "So come over here and shoot the ball against the rim of the backstop a few times."

Duval walked over to where Orson was standing. The older man had made a line with his hand directly in front of his position to the backboard.

"I want you to shoot along that line," Orson explained. "If it bounces back to you, you're shooting straight. If it's off left or right, you're doing something wrong."

Duval did as Orson told him, and the ball hit the backboard and broke to the right. Orson snatched it before it got away and bounced it back to him.

"Try it again," Orson said. "But this time, move the elbow of your shooting hand under the ball."

Duval shot again, and this time the ball bounced back to him.

"Yeah, look at that," Orson said.

Duval did it several more times. With each successful bounce back, both of them grew a little more excited at his progress.

"Okay, now let's go back to the free-throw line," Orson said. "Now keep your elbow tucked like you learned and try not to push the ball so much. Your shooting hand needs to follow through with the ball, ending like a swan. Here, let me show you."

Orson took his position on the foul line and made the fifteen-foot shot with what seemed like ease. Duval laughed and retrieved the ball, giving Orson respect for not being as rusty as he looked. Then it was Duval's turn. He missed the first two but began to sink shot after shot with a little more instruction.

"Man, I can't believe this," Duval said. "What do I owe you for these lessons? Want me to mow your lawn or something?"

"How about a game?"

"In those shoes?" Duval pointed at the Oxfords.

"Yeah, you're probably right," he said. "Maybe I'll take a game tomorrow. Why don't we shoot a quick game of horse and call it a day? It's getting too hot."

"Sure," Duval said.

"And let's make it interesting," Orson said. "If I win a shot, you have to answer a question. If you win the shot, you can ask me a question."

Duval squinted his eyes at the older man. He thought they had moved passed distrust in the time they had been training together, but he didn't fight it. He didn't even protest when Orson set up on the left-hand side of the court, making a shot he knew Duval couldn't make.

"Tell me, Duval," Orson said. "What do your folks do to afford a place just south of 40th?"

"Really?" Duval said, slumping his shoulders. "My dad works as a bottling foreman at the brewery, and my mom takes up ironing and sewing jobs around the neighborhood."

Orson nodded as if the answer suited him somehow before he moved to the three-point line and sunk another basket. Duval, still angry by the first question, missed.

"Why do they want to live with white people instead of their own kind?" Orson said.

"That's a heck of a thing to ask," Duval said.

"That's the game." Orson grinned. "Call me ... curious."

"They moved here because it was a better school, alright?" Duval said.

"But you're not in school," Orson retorted.

"No, I'm done with school," Duval said flatly.

"So they moved here, and you dropped out anyhow," Orson summed. "That's disrespectful where I come from, which is right around here, as a matter of fact."

"I didn't drop out," Duval scoffed. "I finished early. Two years early. We're just trying to find a university that will pick me up next semester. That's why I'm out here. They're more likely to take me if I know a sport. All right? Get what you wanted, mister?"

"What?" Orson's smile faded into slack-jawed surprise.

This time it was Orson's turn to miss, an easy one from the foul line. He was playing basketball with a savant of some kind, and not putting a deadbeat kid in his place. It never occurred to him that the kid graduated early, given the kid's color. Duval made the shot. It had been the one they had worked on for more than twenty minutes.

"So now it's my turn to ask a question," Duval said.

"Whatever," Orson said.

"Why have you been dressed for work, sitting at a bus stop with a briefcase, but never getting on that bus, for not just a week, but weeks?" Duval asked with a squint.

"That's none of your business," Orson said, bending over to pick up his shirt and tie.

"None of my business? None of my business?" Duval laughed and addressed an imagined courtroom. "Ladies and gentlemen, the white gent who needs to know where I live, why I live there, what my parents do, where I go to school, and so on and so on, says 'it's none of my business' when the tables are turned."

"Don't make a scene, boy." Orson gave up. "I was laid off three weeks ago, and my wife doesn't know yet. There. Happy?"

Duval's smugness dropped. He felt bad for having asked, even if Mister Burke had it coming. Sometimes you don't need to know about people.

"I don't know how to tell her," said Orson. "She relies on me to, you know, take care of things like that, which is easier said than done when you're a stone's throw away from sixty. Who wants to hire a mid-level manager to finish working the last few years he thought he had left?"

"Man, that's tough," said Duval. "I'm sorry."

"Don't be sorry," he said. "We all get what we deserve. I came out on this court just to razz you because I thought you were wasting something I wish I had. I assumed as much for one reason, and we both know what that reason was. I was wrong to do it. Turns out we started the day where we belong. You're on the court. I'm on the bench."

"Mister, it's no big deal," Duval said. "My dad says times are changing, and change causes friction. If it didn't cause friction, then the result wouldn't be worth it anyhow."

"Your dad seems pretty smart," said Orson. "Keep listening to him."

"He's uptight, like you, so what? One question and you have to tap out?"

"It's too hot to stay out here anymore," said Orson. "And I better go home. It's about time I told Mary Beth the truth."

"Why don't you come back tomorrow, then?" said Duval. "This time, wear the right shoes."

"Come back?" Orson scoffed. "I thought I told you I didn't like colored people."

"Who says I like white people?" said Duval. "I just want to play ball."

"Friction," Orson considered. "Maybe I could use a little friction."

Orson turned on his heel and headed off the court toward home. He didn't turn around when he heard the familiar swish of a ball gliding through the hoop and catching nothing but net, but it did make him smile. Duval Johnson was terrible at basketball, Orson thought, but he was a little less terrible today. Tomorrow held promise.

ON THE FOURTH OF JULY

Delaware 2018

Mr. Braderie always liked to text her little love notes that he called haikus. They were simple little things that didn't always rhyme or even make all that much sense. But Claire enjoyed them anyway — counting them among the flurry of gifts he liked to give her, like the extra $20 from the front pocket of his trousers for babysitting. All she had to do was reach in to earn it.

Of course, the haikus were probably why she ended up in the kitchen of the Braderies' coastal home, sitting on the hardwood floor with her back against the hickory cabinets, tying a tourniquet around her forearm to slow the bleeding. She didn't know what else to do. The knife wound was severe, and the towel she had knotted around it was drinking up blood faster than direct pressure could stop the flow.

The cut was terrible, but she was still alive, which was more than could be said about Mrs. Braderie's brother Stephan, who was sprawled out in the family room. He was dead. Shot twice in the chest. A third shot had gone high and wide.

It was unlikely someone had heard or seen anything. The only neighboring home on this side of the salt marsh was in foreclosure. Even if it had been occupied, the pop-pop-pop that dropped Stephan would have been easily mistaken for the sporadic cracks of fireworks rolling up and down the coast. They were still going on outside, relentless bursts of light followed by the percussion of firecrackers, ground bursts, and skyrockets. The world outside was ignorant of the intruder, including the Braderies.

The Braderies, Russell and Evelyn, were still out watching the diminishing stashes of illegal fireworks being set off over the ocean as they enjoyed a last round of drinks at an outdoor bar. The main events, a Jimi Smooth & the Hit Time Band concert and beach fireworks at dusk, had wrapped up long ago. Claire had expected them to be late because he texted her during the fireworks show.

All these fireworks,
Burning like my desire.
They all burn for you.

She wrinkled her nose at it before responding with an obligatory smiley face framed by hearts. He was a better attorney than he was a poet, but she didn't care. He was partly her attorney, just as the house was partly her house, and the Aston Martin in the garage — the one he would drive her home in — was partly her dream car. She was vested, her high school crush on an older man transformed into a secret romance.

The affair had started innocently enough after they ran into each other at the bookstore. It was the book Claire was buying at the register that caught his interest, Eleanor & Park by Rainbow Rowell.

"Is that what I think it is?" he teased her.

"A young adult romance," she said, slightly embarrassed. "Busted."

"Funny," he said. "I didn't think you would be down for that sort of thing."

"Let's check the list," she said, rolling her eyes for effect. "I'm young. I'm an adult, almost. And I'm a girl. Young. Adult. Romance. Yay."

He laughed, but not in the way most adults did. He wasn't laughing at her. He was laughing with her as if he had seen her for the very first time.

"I see your point." He winked. "I guess I always saw you a little headier than that."

"Well, you know," she added with a blush. "Even heady girls gotta, well, you know."

"Yeah, I suppose they do," he said. "Hey, I have to get back to the courthouse, but it was great running into you. It reminds me how much Evelyn and I need a date night. Are you busy Saturday night?"

"I could check," she said, and then held up the book and smirked. "Probably not."

"Great," he said. "I'll call you later."

"Great," she said, expecting that to be the end of it. But it wasn't.

He took a few steps and turned on a heel. There was something on his mind.

"You want to have lunch Thursday?" he asked.

"What?" she asked, flushing all over again.

"No, I mean it," he said. "I've been working on some poetry, and maybe you can give me your take on it."

"Poetry?" she laughed. "You write poetry?"

"Let's say I dabble," he said. "Okay, I'm a diehard romantic, and diehard romantics gotta, well, you know. "

"Sure, Mr. Braderie," she shrugged, wondering if she should have called him Russell. "It's a date."

He chuckled when she said it, and he clapped his hands together like an excited schoolboy. A date, he reiterated with amusement, lifting his head up, shaking it, and walking out the door. They had made a date.

In the months that followed, they had made many dates. Lunches. Movies. Libraries. Jet skies. Boardwalk fries. Captain Jack Pirate Golf. Parking lots. Motel rooms.

He didn't even care if anyone saw them together. He would introduce Claire as his son's babysitter, which she was, and mention how she was helping him work on a secret project so he could better understand young adults. She was always surprised how many people knew about his haikus and not-so-secret young adult novel in the making. It made for a perfect in-plain-sight alibi, whether he was writing one or not.

It didn't even look suspicious when he saw her across the street at the Bethany Beach Independence Day Parade and crossed right over to her between the 287th National Guard Army Band and 1st Delaware Regiment. Claire had seen him say something to his wife before he did it, and gave her a big wave. It was all in plain sight.

"Hey, you," he said, with a pearly white smile.

"Hey, yourself," Claire said over the chorus of string musicians in black pants and red vests.

"What are you doing tonight?"

"Watching fireworks like everybody else," she said. "Why are you asking?"

"Want to watch Jack tonight?" he said, trying to read her face. "And then I'll take you home afterward so we can light something else."

"You are a bad boy, Mr. Braderie," she said. "I have a life, you know? Seventeen and all that."

"And all that?" He chuckled. "Come by around six."

"If I don't?" she asked, twirling a lock of hair around her finger.

"You'll miss out because I want to talk to you about something," he said.

"Okay," she frowned. "I'll be there. But you should know I don't like surprises."

"Okay," he said, giving her hand a gentle squeeze before turning back to his family and giving them a thumb's up. "Just this once."

Claire canceled her plans for the evening, lying to her girlfriends that she would score an extra $50 for taking the last-minute gig. They made a big deal about it, even if it wasn't a big deal to any of them. Dropping their numbers from four to three would better match them to the boys.

She arrived on time late that evening, accepting what had become a standard awkward moment every time she babysat. Mrs. Braderie would always open the door with a warm smile and curious small-talk questions about school, grades, interests, and admirers. Then Mrs. Braderie would lead Claire into the kitchen, where Jack was already eating dinner — pasta dinosaurs with meatballs in a red sauce — and give her instructions, short dark hair bobbing up and down on her shoulders.

"You have all that, dear?" she would always ask and then correct herself. "Of course you do. You've only helped us out a hundred times."

Claire would stand there, smiling dumbly and looking past Evelyn into some preordained future where she could place one bare foot on the steering wheel of the Aston Martin and the other on the dashboard above the glove box, the leather seats comfortably reclined.

"Now, don't forget. The most dangerous people in the world are cheats and liars," said Evelyn. "I won't have them in my house."

"What?" Claire said, coming back from the daydream.

"Oh, you didn't hear me?" Evelyn said. "Just be honest with me about his behavior."

"Right, Jack," Claire said, breathing a sigh of relief. "He's never any trouble."

"I'd kill him if he were," she said. "This family has plans too big for spoilers."

Claire pressed her lips thin. She knew what Evelyn was talking about. Evelyn was an attorney like Russell, but her passion lay more with politics than the pen. Mrs. Braderie's first stop would be the school board, as she had already won her primary. She didn't care about public education because her son was enrolled in a private school. The position was a stepping stone for higher office.

"All right then," Evelyn said. "Tell Mr. Braderie that I'll meet him in the car."

"You betcha, Mrs. Braderie," she said. "Have a wonderful time tonight. I know you will."

Mrs. Braderie kissed Jack on the forehead and floated out of the kitchen as Russell entered. He didn't even look to see whether his wife was lingering in the hallway. He went right up to Claire and whispered that he would see her later tonight while playing grab-hands just out of his son's sight. Then, without missing a beat, he gave his boy a fist bump.

"See you later, buddy," he said and followed his wife's path out.

Jack was easy as far as babysitting went. After he was done eating, she would pull out a game like Stratego, watch a movie, and read a story. His schedule was by the book, without much variation, but Claire had taught him basic chess moves. If they ever ended up living together, she needed to do something more intellectually challenging than Stratego or Risk. At least he was more advanced than Chutes & Ladders, she always thought.

After tucking him in bed, Claire would clean up and toss herself on the couch and surf DISH Satellite for something mildly inappropriate. It didn't matter what she turned on, as long as she was, which was right about when she received his text message.

All these fireworks,
Burning like my desire.
They all burn for you.

"You've got to be kidding me," she whispered, before turning her phone over and sinking into the folds of the couch, half-watching, and half-fantasizing for the better part of an hour.

Knowing they were going to be late, she could have made it two hours, but that's when she caught a reflection in the corner of the black screen between scenes. As she sat up to turn around and look, her visual cortex filled in the missing pieces. There was a figure moving toward her with a chef's knife stolen from the kitchen.

Without thinking, Claire brought her left forearm up to ward off the knife and came around with a clenched right, hitting the intruder in the temple and sending the knife flying. The move — something instinctive from all the self-defense classes her father insisted she take — saved her life, but only for a moment. He shook off the blow and dove at her, knocking her over the back of the couch and using his weight to his advantage.

They were grappling as she went for his eyes, catching the corner of one with her nails. He cried out, a voice she recognized, and brought one hand to his face while punching her with the other. He hit her again. And again.

Claire's head spun from the blows, white flashes appearing and then dissolving into red apparitions. He took advantage of the fog, pinning her arms with his legs and removing the balaclava.

"Stephan?"

"You brought this on yourself," he said, putting his hands around her neck. "Just go easy. Just give up and go easy."

She had been gasping when he started, but now she could no longer exhale. Both of his hands were pressing harder, and her eyelids were fluttering uncontrollably. Claire finally managed to free one hand from under her assailant's legs, but it only flew reflexively to her neck, grabbing at hands that wouldn't budge. She felt herself fading, sinking deeper into the couch and down into the darkness.

As she was just about to give up, her one free hand fell away and landed on something cold and familiar. She pulled it down from its holster, pointing it up toward his chest. She pulled the trigger.

Stephan seemed to jump up with the sharp retort of the firearm, standing up and falling backward. Claire sat up, coughing, and fired again. He drifted away from her, rolling back and floating off the floor. By the time she fired the third shot, he was already on the ground. The last round went high and wide.

She lay for what seemed like an eternity as she regained her composure and convinced herself she could breathe again. As she did, she noticed that the initial wound was jagged and still bleeding. She pressed it to her chest and crawled into the kitchen, still holding the M9 in her other hand.

Stephan had wanted to kill her and make it look like a break-in, which could mean only one of two things. Evelyn wasn't going to risk her election on an affair, or Russell was done with her. Maybe it was the temporary loss of oxygen, but Claire couldn't pinpoint which was more likely. She still had twelve rounds to find out.

MOCKINGBIRDS

Oklahoma 2006

I was waiting in the living room while the plumber assessed our kitchen sink. It was one of several surprise issues that had popped up since my wife and I purchased a modest single-story home three months earlier. The things you forget to consider when you buy on the quick.

We didn't really have a choice, or maybe I should say I didn't have a choice. Despite my silent protests, we purchased the home to be closer to her ailing mother. My wife's closing argument was unassailable. Since I could work anywhere, living in Vinita was a small sacrifice compared to her hour-long commute between home and a new Tulsa law firm.

I acquiesced. You can't argue with a lawyer and stay married to them. I could, however, argue with everyone else. Arguing was a part of my job, writing political columns and op-eds for an online news and opinion blog. Blogs were a new thing, but I was making a go of it, planning to take full advantage of my wife's twelve-hour workdays.

Except, I wasn't putting in as much time as I wanted. Before the move, I worked at it all the time until "all work and no play makes Jack a dull boy" became a standard joke in our house. During and after the move, I was the de facto adult in charge of going-away parties, packing, moving, unpacking, meeting new neighbors, visiting in-laws, fixing things, and overseeing the fixing of things, just like today.

Since I was too distracted to work with someone else in the house and I didn't want to stand over the plumber's shoulder while he poked around under our sink, I turned toward our "always-on" television, quietly mesmerized by another segment of the twenty-four-hour news cycle that had consumed so much of our lives since the start of the Iraq War. There he was again. President Bush was talking about the war on terror.

"A new Iraqi government represents a strategic opportunity for America — and the whole world, for that matter," he said. "This nation of ours and our coalition partners are going to work with the new leadership to strengthen our mutual efforts to achieve success, a victory in this war on terror."

I was taking mental notes, feeling like there was something right with what he was saying but also so much wrong. The world was a better place, sure, but you had to weigh that against the loss of life and whether our reasons for being there were justified or not. It was a confusing time, especially with the Oklahoma National Guard stationed right in Baghdad. You want to be a patriot, but you also want them all to come home so they can grow up, raise families, and fish with their kids.

"People have all sorts of opinions about him," said the plumber. "But I love that man."

I hadn't even noticed he had come into the living room, so he had startled me. I thought: Oh boy, I better be careful with this one. You never know what people might say when they see the President on television, especially in a town like Vinita, which was mostly conservative like the rest of Oklahoma.

"How's that?"

"He saved my life," he added. "Want me to show you what's wrong with the sink?"

"How did he save your life?" I asked him, not even hearing the question.

"He supported U.S. Vets through AmeriCorps," he said. "They help homeless veterans like me get back on their feet."

"You're homeless?" I asked, feeling a little uncomfortable at the thought of it and then a little guilty for feeling uncomfortable.

Earl Stevens, a.k.a. Staff Sergeant Stevens, was not homeless, but he had been homeless and would have stayed homeless had it not been for an AmeriCorps volunteer who was working for U.S. Vets as an outreach coordinator. The transition didn't come easy for him, either. It took ten months before Earl would accept any help at all.

"I didn't think I needed any help." He shrugged. "The Army had taught me to survive in a desert, so I was pretty content to survive in the desert. It was easy living in such a small world, one where you only have to concern yourself with finding shelter from the heat of day and your next meal to cook over a fire in the dead of night. I would stay out there for months, and I only headed into the city when the loneliness started to play tricks on me. I saw some things, things I wonder if I really saw."

"What about your family?" I said. "Wasn't there anyone you could reach out to?"

"Oh, I have a family," he said. "But the thing most people never understand — and I never realized it until I came home — is that in the Army, during combat especially, they teach you how to make your world very, very small. When you live where the ax meets the stone, there isn't anything to think about except your life, your gear, your rifle, your career, your unit, your orders. And the longer you walk in the valley of the shadow of death, it becomes smaller still: your breath, your heartbeat, your will to keep moving even when you can't move anymore.

"They don't teach you how to be a civilian. Being a civilian makes your world very, very big. It comes with complications: a wife, a son, a job, a boss, a home, a car payment, dental work, grocery shopping, clothing styles, good neighbors, bad neighbors, restaurants, gender sensitivities, social values, skin color, political views, and a procession of ideas, opinions, and observations about anything and everything — even if the person sharing those ideas doesn't know what they are talking about.

"I lived with my family — my wife and son — for the better part of a turbulent year. I said some things and did some things I'm not proud of, but the transition wasn't easy. I had served twelve years in the Army, seen combat in Afghanistan and Iraq, twice. My first tour began in Operation Desert Storm with the Task Force 1-41 infantry — the first to cross the border in 1991— and my last tour ended with the Battle of Samawah in

2003. I was wounded, sent home, and reunited with my family. But it didn't last."

"What happened?" I asked him.

"In the Army, I used to keep a rucksack packed and ready to go under my bed in case we had to bug out," he said, looking at the flickering television screen. "I did the same thing after I got home, too, even though I didn't need it. But one day, I just grabbed it and walked out the front door. I didn't say goodbye or leave a note. I just left and walked out into the desert."

"Wow," I said. "That's some story. How'd the outreach coordinator change your mind?"

"I needed a few dollars and decided to hold up a sign at an intersection," he said. "It was embarrassing. All those people in their cars, pretending not to see me except for this one kid. He rolls down the window and waves something at me. So I go over to see what it is, and it's one of those chocolate bars, the ones that the kids sell to raise money for school and sports. He looked at me and said, 'Here you go, sir, you're one chocolate better than yesterday.'"

"I don't understand," I said, looking for the connection.

"I said the same thing to a kid in Iraq once," he said. "We were all standing around the Humvee and waiting for orders when I saw this kid on the other side of the road. He knew better than to approach us without being invited, so I waved him over to give him a chocolate bar. 'I'm not going to lie and say things aren't bad,' I told him. 'But right now, you're one chocolate better than yesterday. Tomorrow, it's up to you.'

"It's been like that ever since. Temporary housing. Job training. Transitional apartment. Relocation from Nevada to Oklahoma. I'm slowly adjusting to this bigger world, one day at a time, and one day, I pray, it will be with my family again. Only this time, I'll be ready to be the husband and father they need me to be."

I didn't know what to say so I reached out and shook his hand. Then we walked into the kitchen and I helped him fix the sink, handing him whatever he needed for the next twenty minutes. By the time he left, I came to realize that while Earl was working toward a bigger world, maybe it was time I tried working toward a smaller one. So I turned off the television. It was quiet, except for a pair of mockingbirds I had never heard before.

PRECINCT 13

Kentucky 1978

Mike didn't waste any time starting his homework after school. There wasn't much to do. His science teacher had called off tomorrow's quiz because he was taking the day off to have a tooth bonded or something like that. Quizzes were too important to entrust with a substitute teacher, he said.

That left algebra, which Mike thought was pretty easy. They had been learning how to calculate the hypotenuse of a right triangle all week. Twenty minutes later, the Pythagorean theorem was proven ten times over, so he immediately started chores.

He mowed the lawn, emptied the dishwasher, and dusted the front room for good measure. When he finished, he ran into the kitchen where his mom was prepping a roast for supper, asking if there was anything else that needed to be done.

His mom laughed. "Wow, you're a house of fire today."

"If there isn't anything left, can I stay over at Billy's house?" he asked.

"On a school night?"

"I've done all my homework and all my chores. I even mowed the lawn early," he said. "I can eat over there too, his mom said. They're having burgoo."

"I don't know," she said, looking down at her roast. "I thought we were going to watch Welcome Back, Kotter tonight. It should be a hoot. Hotsy Totsy comes back."

"Please, Mom. Pleeease," he begged with a dimpled grin, head cocked to one side.

"Oh, all right." She sighed and smiled. "Next time tell me sooner so I won't cook so much."

"Thanks, Mom!" Mike said, bolting up the stairs to pack a bag and grab a walkie-talkie.

"Bishop One, Bishop One," Mike called. "This is Napoleon, over."

"What's up, Mike?" Billy said.

"Assault on Precinct 13 is a go," he said. "Tell the squad."

The squad consisted of Mike, Billy, Harlan, Andrea, and the new boy, Buddy, who had just moved to Lexington from Louisville, or "Loo-vul" as most people called it. His family had moved down after his father was offered a foreman position at the peanut butter plant. The move was part of what Procter & Gamble called big business integration.

Precinct 13 had nothing to do with law enforcement or anything remotely similar to the taboo movie that only three of the squad had actually seen after Harlan's brother let them sneak into the theater where he worked. But that didn't stop them from appropriating bits and pieces of the John Carpenter film as code words and call signs. Billy was Bishop. Mike was Napoleon. Harlan was Lawson. Buddy was West. And Andrea was Zimmer because she hated the name Leigh.

Precinct 13 became the name they gave to crazy Pat Mitchell's place, the weird mailman who rode around on a bicycle built for two and had, on more than one occasion, been seen peeping into people's windows. The one time he was caught red-faced and red-handed, he said he just wanted to see who was home because he didn't feel comfortable leaving a package by the front door. There were some odd characters about, he said. Someone was home. It turned out to be Marge Abbot in her bathrobe.

Still, neither this incident nor any of the uncommon oddities exhibited by this hulking loner who made everyone feel uneasy inspired their plan. The Assault on Precinct 13 came together when the squad noticed that Mitchell's proclivity to pick up stray cats and dogs had expanded to include neighborhood pets he just didn't like.

Once picked up, Mitchell would tie them to the backyard fence with baling wire, where they would lay, exhausted by the ordeal of capture, until eventually disappearing into the man's home and never being seen again. Billy claimed to have snuck into the backyard to set an animal free once, but all that remained was a paw the cat had chewed off to escape.

Although horrified by the story, the squad knew they had to take action after Billy heard Mitchell had captured two more dogs during the week. One of them — a fox terrier named Sammy — belonged to Elizabeth Puckett. Billy had a crush on Elizabeth, not that the squad needed any convincing, anyway. They had had enough of Pat Mitchell.

About an hour after dark, after the Sweathogs and Kotter stepped in to find their former classmate Hotsy Totsy a more respectable job, the squad sneaked out and met up in a drainage ditch on the opposite side of Precinct 13. Andrea was the last one to arrive. She said she had trouble sneaking into her kid brother's room for his binoculars.

"Sorry," she said, dropping into the ditch.

"It's all right, Zimmer," Billy said. "We were just working out who would do what."

"All I know is that I can't do it," Buddy said. "A black boy trespassing in Kentucky? No, sir. Thank you, no."

"Come on, Buddy," Harlan said. "Lexington ain't like that."

"I can't take that chance," he said. "Before we moved here, my pops told me you can break Kentucky into two parts: Loo-vul takes after the north, but the rest of Kentucky takes after the south."

"Fine," Billy said, taking charge. "Buddy and I will distract him in the front; Harlan and Mike will free the animals. Andrea, you already know, you're our lookout."

"Okay," she said, peering at the house through the binoculars. "He's just sitting there watching Fish right now."

"He has fish?" Harlan asked,.

"No, the TV show, stupid," Mike said. "Look, if you're coming with me, I'm carrying the wire cutters. Hand them over."

"One potato. Two potato," Harlan said. "Kiss my ..."

"Harlan!" Andrea said in a firm whisper. "Give them to Mike."

Harlan passed the wire cutters to Mike. Two pairs of boys set off across the street. Billy and Buddy hustled to the left, taking up residence behind matching metal trash cans. Mike and Harlan ran to the right and crouched next to the hedge that framed the east side of the property.

The plan was that Mike and Harlan would work their way north along the hedgerow and squeeze in through a small opening at the northeast corner of the lot, where the hedges meet at the chain link fence with privacy slats that bounded the north and west sides of the lot. Billy and Buddy didn't have to do anything unless Mitchell headed toward the backyard.

That plan seemed simple enough too, until Harlan learned the hard way he couldn't fit through the back corner opening, leaving Mike to cross the yard on his own. Two dogs were waiting for him: Sammy and a small German shepherd. Both animals were muzzled and tied to the fence with baling wire, just as Billy had said.

The wire was looped around the collar, muzzle, and back paw of each, giving neither dog the ability to move more than a few feet from the back corner of the west fence. As Mike navigated around their prison, the smell burned his eyes, an unmistakable tang of iron mixed with dirt, fear, and neglect.

Mike clipped the wires holding Sammy first, freeing the fox terrier from the fence but also uncovering a new problem. Harlan wasn't there to carry the dog back, and Mike didn't want to cross the yard any more than he had to. Instead, Harlan started calling for the dog in a harsh whisper.

"Sammy. Come here, Sammy." Harlan patted the ground.

The noise wasn't loud, but almost as soon as Harlan began calling the dog, Mitchell's balding head tilted to the right and his eyes moved away from the television, locking in on the far wall as if he was straining his senses to lock in on any uninvited disruptions.

Andrea thumbed the red button of her walkie-talkie as a warning, but it was too late. As soon as she did, the square-jawed beady-eyed creature rose from his recliner and stretched. Andrea's eyes grew wide. Mitchell looked bigger without his uniform, aging muscles still pressed against his white T-shirt and the black suspenders he used to hold up his loose slacks.

He's the man who sniffs the mail, Andrea shuddered. She never believed it, assuming the boys had made it up to creep her out, until the day her mom received a box from Avon. He had given the small box a long sniff before slipping it inside the mailbox, breathing in the scent while savoring, not the smell, but his power to violate privacy.

As he started toward the kitchen in the back of the house, Billy and Buddy rattled the trash cans. Mitchell turned abruptly and looked out the windows. He walked to the front door, shoulders squared up against any threat that might be in front of him. The boys rattled them again.

"Hey!" Mitchell barked as he opened the screen door that led onto his small front porch intending to scare off any small animals. "Hey... hey ... HEY!"

Andrea slid deeper into the drainage ditch and listened. She could hear the boys whispering as they crawled away from the cans.

"Who's out there? Speak up," Mitchell commanded before turning on stocking feet and storming up the porch.

Andrea risked a look after the slow squeak of the screen door was followed by a sharp slap. As it shut, Mitchell was opening a closet door just off the living room.

She had seen enough of them on television news when she was younger to know what it was. Mitchell had an M16 in his hand and was snapping in a magazine. He headed toward the front porch again.

"He's got a gun!" she quietly but firmly hissed into the walkie-talkie, her voice more audible in both the front and back of the house as it crackled through the walkie-talkies that her friends carried. To Mitchell, the crackling whisper in two locations confused him. To the German shepherd, recently freed of its muzzle, it was an invitation to bark.

Mitchell wheeled around toward the house, heading through the front door and to the back again. He was walking quickly, raising his rifle as he entered the kitchen, where he would have a good view of his backyard. Andrea decided to use this as her opportunity to head toward their bikes, about a block away.

She ran most of the way, diving down on reflex when she heard a burst of rattling gunfire. Her heart stopped, disbelieving that Mitchell had fired his weapon. She didn't hear anything after that until Billy and Buddy caught up to her.

"Did you see that?" Billy asked excitedly. "That nut job fired that thing!"

Before Andrea or Buddy could respond, their worst fears were put to rest. Mike and Harlan turned the corner, with Harlan holding Sammy in his arms.

"Where's the other dog?" Andrea asked.

"I don't know," Mike said. "When Mitchell came barreling out the back door and yelled 'last chance,' I threw a rock to scare the dog off."

"I thought he was shooting you," she said.

"He was shooting at us!" Harlan jumped in. "Mike had just dove under the bushes, and that turkey fired into them like he didn't care. 'Last chance' ... pffftttt.'"

"All right, everybody be cool a minute," Billy said. "We can't stick around here. It's too dangerous, so let's just head home. Harlan? Can you ride back with Andrea?"

"Yeah, sure," Harlan said. "You ready?"

"Yes," she said. "But I have a question. Okay?"

"Okay," Harlan said.

"Do you think he'll know it was us?" she said. "We made a mess of tracks."

The four boys all stared at her. Nobody wanted to answer.

"So what?" Mike finally said. "He'll know it was a bunch of kids, but he won't know which kids."

"Yeah," Buddy said. "It could have been anybody."

The five of them considered it, weighing his statement like someone might weigh a pre-packed bag of apples. The weight feels right, but you don't know if any are rotten.

"We'll worry about it tomorrow," Billy said. "Let's bug out."

They put their hands in a tight circle and touched fists before heading out in separate directions: Billy and Mike together, Harlan and Andrea, Buddy on his own. The Assault on

Precinct 13 was a success. The squad had won. But in doing so, Mike wasn't sure that they hadn't lost something too.

Yesterday, he thought monsters were things conjured up from nightmares and easily seen. Today, he knew monsters could be conjured up from anything and disguised as anyone.

THE EXTRA MILE

Alabama 2008

By the time he pulled into the parking lot, Jake's head pounded. He had left home in such a hurry that he forgot his cigarettes on the bookshelf near the sliding glass door. He always kept them there because he never smoked inside, always in the backyard.

He didn't mind smoking outside. The only downside was some accidental forgetfulness, rushing out of the house, and driving off without them.

He intended to leave town in a moment of clarity. His head was spinning from all the trouble being hurled at him through the locked door of their bedroom. She was on the inside, laughing with someone on Jabber instant messaging. He was on the outside, trying to douse his burning head with Jim Beam because that was the only the whiskey they had left in the house. And then he left.

"Two packs of Marlboro Red," he said.

The man behind the counter squinted at him. He was a tall man, thin but fit, with a knowing smile framed by a manicured belt-buckle goatee. His Jheri curls were grown out and pulled back, tucked under a hat emblazoned with a Chevron logo.

"You all right?" he asked.

"Yeah," he gasped, holding the counter, eyes red and sore from crying.

"You don't look so good."

"I'll be all right," Jake said. "Bad time at home."

"Funny," he said.

"What's that?"

"People always pray to God for what they want." He smiled wide, light glinting off the silver cap on a back tooth. "But then when God goes the extra mile to give it to them, they don't want it."

Jake looked at him, head cocked, unwrapping the cellophane off the top pack while pocketing the other. He pressed one of the cigarettes to his lips, tasting the bite of a stray piece of tobacco on his tongue. He had nothing to say, so he slid the change off the counter and put it in the rainy day dish.

"Suit yourself," the clerk said as Jake crashed through the front doors and into the cool night air. "Just ask yourself how'd you end up here?"

With a spin of a Zippo against his jeans and a deep drag, his headache lifted away with the rush of dopamine. By the fourth huff, he felt like he could finally think past the wavering haze from the whiskey he drank a half-hour ago.

"How did I end up here?" he asked himself, putting his hand on the hood of his car to steady himself. Southbound on Highway 20 was how he had ended up here. But he could also see a deeper answer in the red ember of his cigarette.

It was months ago. They were watching television. She was lying on the couch, and he was sitting in the adjacent chair. They used to share the couch a long time ago, but he surrendered it when she insisted on stretching out a few years earlier. He tried to lie out with her, but she said it was too cramped or too hot or too something. It became part of a new normal, one with six inches of space between them because she didn't feel attractive anymore. He tried to tell her otherwise, but she pushed away his compliments as niceties you tell a friend.

"If I put on a dress," she said, "you'd tell me I look pretty."

"You do look pretty," he said.

"Liar," she said.

There wasn't anything more about it. His laudations were dismissed and he retreated into silence. His words didn't seem to mean anything unless they were the wrong words. And more and more, they were always the wrong words.

Nights out were discouraged. Friends were abandoned. Plans remained unmade. Every night between one workday and the next, they would congregate on the living room furniture, eat, watch television, tuck in their daughter, and go to sleep on opposite sides of the king bed that started puckering up in the middle from disuse.

It wasn't a life anymore as much as an existence — a rusty cage of emptiness. He knew he had to get out, break away, and run. He thought about it. He fantasized about it. He prayed for it.

Eventually, she seemed to sense it too, taking up a fitness trainer to finally get back in shape and rekindling hobbies that had little room to include him. Someone had to stay home with their daughter because babysitters couldn't be trusted. She couldn't be trusted, either.

He was downstairs watching television before he decided to go upstairs to see if she was ever going to join him. He originally asked through the door, but then she whispered to someone behind it and then firmly said she would be down later. He gently tried the doorknob, intending to peek in, only to find out that she had locked it. Why would she do that?

It was a question he would ask himself a dozen times while taking a lonesome shot in the kitchen and having a smoke in the backyard. He tried settling into a show once or twice, but found his mind always wandering to what was happening upstairs, right in front of him.

In the end, he pounded on the door and demanded the keys to the car. Irritated by his interruption, she obliged him by opening the bedroom door a small crack and holding the keys out to him. The door was open enough for him to notice that she was wearing a red camisole, but not open enough that he could see the computer screen flashing in the background.

"I'm going out," he said.

"Okay," she said, flipping her hair and looking longingly back at the screen.

"I don't know if I'm coming back," he said.

She didn't say anything, but he could see she wanted to say something. Jake waited for it, but it felt like nothing was ever going to come out of her mouth. Then he noticed she was wearing lipstick he hadn't seen in years. He bolted down the stairs and out the front door.

He could hear her coming after him, calling his name. But he kept thinking it was too late. He was in the car and gone, headed south and out of town. It wasn't until a half-hour out that he patted his breast pocket and discovered he didn't bring his cigarettes.

Now he was sitting in his car, driver side door open, cigarette in hand, with a blue light from the passenger seat interrupting him. She was calling him again. She had called at least five times, but he had let them all go to voicemail.

He didn't move to get this call. He just sat, legs out of the car, and jumped a fresh cigarette with the first. The smoke warded off the smell of the dumpster outside of the Extra Mile.

He noticed they were having a sale on Budweiser, but he couldn't drink anymore. And if he was going to drink, what he really needed was a fifth from the liquor store behind him. It was closed, which was fine with him. Jake couldn't drink until he knew where he was going.

But where was he going? He wasn't sure. All he really knew was that there was a fork in the road before him. One road went home. The other crossed the Tennessee River and into hell.

Jake stepped on his second cigarette when it hit him. He stood up and shut the door, not bothering to lock it. In five long steps, he was through the convenience store door again and up at the counter.

"Which way should I go?"

"Pardon me?" said a stocky Asian leaning back on the countertop, arms crossed. "Can I help you?"

"Yeah, I was just in here ... I was wondering if I could ask your partner something."

"Partner?" he blinked. "I'm working alone tonight."

"No, the tall guy," Jake said, raising his hand above his head, palm down.

"Just me," he said flatly, pushing himself off the counter to stand closer to the register, no doubt wondering if he needed to push the silent alarm.

"Yeah," Jake said. "Sorry."

He headed back to the front door, this time shuffling. The second pack of Marlboro Reds, still in his pocket, raising the question he couldn't answer. Who sold him the smokes?

Jake sat down on the curb across from his car, back up against the Extra Mile. The white lights of the canopy carved out a slice of night. He put his head in his hands to shield his eyes. Who was to say there was a difference between taking one road or the other? Who was to say which was home and which was hell?

He opened the door on the passenger side of the car and flipped open the phone. It was casting a blue light and humming again. It was her.

"Yeah," he said.

"Come home, Jake," she said.

Nothing.

"Come home."

"Yeah," he said. "Not tonight, but I'll be home in the morning."

He closed the phone, circled around, and climbed inside. He started the car and headed south on Highway 20 until dawn. Then he turned around, tears in his eyes, and made up a story about getting up early to get pancakes for his daughter — the glint of a silver tooth haunting him all the way.

SIREN'S CALL

Vermont 2019

Carol was lying on her back, admiring the silver siren charm necklace that her boyfriend Ryan had given her for Christmas the day before. He was lying next to her on his stomach, arms hanging off her bed and hands almost touching the floor as he scrolled an endless stream of memes, messages, shares, and snaps.

"I really love this," she said, holding it up so the winter light from her bedroom window glinted off the smooth surface of the moon that cradled the siren. Then she angled the charm to frame the pair of them in a distorted reflection.

"It's the cut," he said, not bothering to look. "They use a laser to make the shape and accent the angles."

"It was really thoughtful, Ryan," she said.

"Hey, look at Jake," he said, suddenly laughing.

"Is he on a sled?" she asked, rolling onto her stomach to watch.

"Oh man, watch out for that tree!"

Their friend collided with the tree and was sent sprawling. The two of them erupted into laughter. Jake was more adept at phone management than sled management, but he had lost the phone in the collision, creating a dizzying spiral of sky and earth before being enveloped in a gauze of freshly fallen Vermont snow.

As they laughed, the two of them turned their faces toward each other. The laughter subsided, relaxing into knowing smiles.

"He's a sock head," Ryan said.

"Is he?" Carol asked. "I already forgot about him."

"I'm glad you love the necklace," he said, leaning closer. "I'm glad you love it as much as I ..."

The knock at the door interrupted him. It wasn't loud as much as it was insistent, pushing the door open with every rap.

"Twelve inches," her father clucked, poking his head in and looking at them on the bed. "We need twelve inches of open door ... and twelve inchcs between bodies."

"Dad!" Carol balked.

"All right, we didn't talk about bodies, but we did talk about doors," he said. "Hey, I just want you to know that lunch will be ready in a minute ... before Ryan's hunting accident."

"Twelve inches, Mr. Johnson," said Ryan with a laugh. "Got you, Sorry. I mean ... thanks."

Ben Johnson gave Ryan a thumbs up in a failing effort to relate and quickly left, embarrassed by his apparent un-coolness, but the pursed downturn of Carol's lips didn't budge. She shook her head, looking at the floor, apparently disgusted by her father's behavior.

"Hey, you frowning?" he asked. "It's no big deal."

"He has no business setting ground rules," she said.

"Come on," he said, tracing the line of her mouth in an attempt to promote a smile. "It's only a few inches."

"You're right. Of course, you're right," she said. "Poof. He's out of my head."

"Poof," Ryan said, his hand making an explosion gesture by her head. "Nothing's up there anymore."

"Shut up!" she said, and they were laughing again.

Downstairs, Ben walked into the kitchen to help his wife. She was mostly done, already placing sandwiches and sides on a carry tray.

"You don't think Ryan's spending too much time here, do you?" he asked.

"We already talked about this," she said. "She deserves a normal, healthy life. And boys, like it or not, are part of it."

"So, I shouldn't get my shotgun?"

She smiled at him, lifting the tray off the table and turning toward him. Behind him, the dining room table was already set, pitchers full, glasses poured.

"Take this in for me," she said, extending the tray for a handoff.

His fingertips slid under the tray to take it when they heard three distinct thuds outside, shattering glass, and the accompanying whacks against her back. Her face fell slack, eyes looking out into the distance but seeing nothing as she fell forward.

Ben didn't try to save the tray or break her fall. He already knew it was too late. As the tray and then her body crashed to the floor, Ben dropped behind the kitchen island and narrowly escaped a second barrage that cut down pictures by the doorway that framed the dining room.

"Rachel!" he called up to his daughter. "Escape plan B! Escape B!"

Hearing her father's shouts, Carol rolled off the bed and onto the floor. She pulled on Ryan's arm, indicating he should follow her.

"What was that crash?" he asked, perplexed. "What's going on?"

"Bad things. Very bad things," she said. "Just get down here now."

Ryan did as she said, rolling onto the floor while she crawled to her nightstand and opened a drawer. She fished out a 9mm Witness Polymer.

"What the ...?" he said, eyes wide.

"I don't have time to explain, but my family is in the secret witness protection program," she said, working her way toward the window. "We have to get out."

"I didn't even know you could shoot," he said.

"What I really need to know is if you can shoot."

"I hunt with my dad sometimes," he said. "But we've never shot at people."

"Hopefully, we won't have to," she said, looking out. "Look, this is just supposed to be a deterrent, but things could go bad," she said. "I see one person out front, but whatever happened downstairs must have come from the back."

Downstairs, there was the roar from a shotgun and someone screamed out. Carol duckwalked over to the bedroom door and called down.

"Dad?" she asked.

"It's all right," he called. "One tried to enter, but he's out now. There are at least two more in the back, so stick with B."

"We can't assume it will work. There's one out front," she said, choked by a sudden realization. "How's Mom?"

"I'm sorry, Rachel, but we can't think of that right now," he called back. "Stick to B while I hold down the back. What's most important to me is knowing you're safe."

"Okay, Dad," she said, face flushed with distress. "Ryan knows how to shoot. Is your rifle still under your bed?"

"Yes," he said. "Just hurry, they're working something out back here."

Carol led Ryan to the master bedroom, keeping as low as possible and avoiding windows. He followed her blindly, trying to wrap his head around all this new information. His girlfriend's name was Rachel, not Carol. Her dad was probably a criminal, not a grocery store manager. Her family was in a secret witness protection program, not newly relocated from Oregon. And while he didn't know for sure, her mom was downstairs, likely dead.

When they reached the master bedroom, Rachel told him to wait in the hall. The scoped Ruger Ranch Rifle was under the bed, unsecured, preloaded with 21 Remington 223 rounds, and ready to fire. She handed it to him, knowing this survival rifle was probably lighter than any gun he or his father used for hunting.

Then they were down the stairs in a flash, stopping at the base because the angle provided a clear line of sight through the dining room and into the kitchen. Rachel took it in, seeing her father crouched behind the island with a WP870 shotgun that the U.S. Marshals had given their family a few years before.

Her mother was lying between the island and kitchen cabinets. The lunch she had prepared for the four of them was ruined, spread across the floor. Toward the back door, she saw what was probably the arm of the man who her dad said had entered the house, not expecting Ben could arm himself.

Rachel fought the urge to run to her mom and motioned for Ryan to move in the other direction, toward the front living room. As soon as he did, there was another barrage of fire, but this time the shots were wild, ricocheting off furniture and wall decorations.

"How we doing, Dad?"

"Pretty much a standoff until the police get here," he said. "But I want you out before I run out of surprises. See if you can find a way out undercover. Remember, the gun is only a last resort, honey."

"I know," she said, already moving toward the living room.

This time, as she followed the route Ryan had taken, there were no shots fired. It meant one of two things: The assailants were other going to give up, or they had a new plan for another assault. The way Ryan sat poised, rifle to his shoulder, and eye looking out the sight between the branches of their Christmas tree, she suspected the latter.

"I have a shot," he said.

"Take it," she said.

"Your dad said it was only a last resort," he said.

"Ryan, they killed my mom," she said. "And they are going to kill us."

He exhaled and squeezed the trigger. Then he lowered the rifle and turned toward her. The expression on his face told her everything. They were simultaneously saved and damned.

Before he could say anything, she opened the front door, exited and turned left around the corner of the house. She had no intention of abandoning her father.

The two remaining men set on either side of the back door and considering their next move. They didn't notice her.

Rachel crouched on one knee and held her breath. The man turned, seeing her only after it was too late. She fired with several successive pops, and the man went down. The unexpected shots must have distracted the remaining assailant because she heard the roar of her father's shotgun again.

It was over, she thought, and returned to the backyard. Her father was already coming out to meet her.

"Are you all right?" Ben asked.

"No, Dad, I'm not," she said, adrenaline dissipating into tears as she clung to him.

Then her embrace turned to fists, and she hammered him before dropping to the ground, unable to reconcile the need for his presence and the realization that he was the cause of it all. His crimes didn't end with their entrance into the secret witness protection program. He had stolen her life.

They could hear sirens growing louder in the distance. It was the siren's call, foreshadowing a darker, uncertain future.

THE RIGHT CHOICE

Nebraska 2010

Harry Brickett sat back in one of the bookstore's lounge chairs and thumbed the newspaper as his son-in-law browsed the new releases. He was more interested in how Peter chose his fancy books than any of the Omaha World-Herald headlines, but he pretended to read it all the same.

A tall blonde with white highlights cut between Peter and the bookshelf. She was attractive, wearing a light jacket and tight denim jeans tucked into Chloe boots with vintage French floral stitching that would never see the inside of a corral. They were the kind of boots some girls might pair with a sundress, not practical for Nebraska but not uncommon in Omaha.

"Excuse me." She smiled.

"Of course," Peter said, stepping back and reflexively dropping his eyes to make sure his feet avoided her boots.

She looked back at him over her shoulder as she passed. Peter nodded an acknowledgment and opened the book he was holding.

"Too pretty," Harry barked loudly, straining to make it come out as a cough.

Peter shot him a glance, something between a smirk and a scowl.

"Too young, too," Harry muttered.

"It was nothing," Peter said, putting the book back to face his father-in-law.

"Oh, it was something," Harry said. "I saw the way you looked her up and down and up again, Donny Juanny."

"What? I didn't want her to step on my feet," he said, trying to remember if there was any infraction.

"She had feet, he says," Harry muttered. "Amazed you noticed."

"You two getting along?" Rebecca asked, coming up behind Peter and hugging him with her one free arm.

"Just talking about feet," Harry said, thick with sarcasm.

"Oh, Dad, don't sound so cranky."

"I told you I liked the bookstore at the mall better," he said. "This plaza is dying, and I can't escape these books — ideas and stories about people and places and doing things. At the mall, I can walk around and leave you two to all this uselessness."

"Uselessness?" Peter laughed.

"Come on," she said to her father, changing the subject. "I'll buy you a cinnamon roll."

"A cinnamon roll," he said, considering. "Are you trying to kill me?"

"Half a cinnamon roll," she countered, emphasizing the half.

"Great, I suppose," he said. "You're only going to half kill me."

She helped him up out of the chair, and the three of them moved into the cafe. After they settled, Peter assured her that he didn't need anything so she went to the counter to place their order.

"So, Harry, tell me," Peter said with a smile. "What do you have against books?"

"I don't have anything against them," Harry shrugged. "I just don't see the point. I mean, if it's not a farmer's almanac or going to teach you something, it's just an escape from reality. I happen to like reality."

"So you don't read for enjoyment?" Peter asked.

"Enjoyment?" Harry laughed. "What's there to enjoy? All these books are the same — a stranger comes to town and does heroic things or a stranger leaves town to do heroic things. Now that you know that, you don't need a book. I saved you twenty bucks. Say, maybe you can afford to buy the cinnamon roll instead of my daughter."

"Oh-oh," Rebecca said, sitting down with two drinks, napkins, and a cinnamon roll cut neatly in half. "This table looks tense all of a sudden."

"Harry was just telling me how he doesn't like books," said Peter.

"Of course, he loves books," Rebecca said. "You used to read to me every night."

"I read them for you, not me. It was so you could go off and get that pre-wed degree," he said. "I drove a Hostess cupcake truck route for 40 years. Other than looking up thiamine mononitrate, I didn't need to read."

"You're just being difficult."

"My point is, Peter, books are fine for you and my daughter, but not most people," Harry continued. "They fill heads with heroic notions, and that's not life. There's nothing heroic about sitting in a tractor traffic jam or picking up a Runza for lunch. There's nothing heroic about delivering Twinkies and Ding Dongs to convenience stores."

"You forgot Fruit Pies," Peter said in jest, with a hint of mockery.

"Yeah, those too," Harry said, growing more agitated. "Most people go through their entire lives, day in and day out, without ever needing to be heroic. I never did."

"Dad, you know that's not true," she said.

"What?" Peter asked, leaning forward, suddenly interested. "You never told me this."

"Yes, Harry Brickett is an honest-to-goodness hero," she said.

"I was not a hero," he said, clearly troubled.

"Yes, you were. You saved that boy's life." she said. "Billy Myers."

Harry slammed his hand on the table. Everyone in the cafe turned to look.

"Don't say that name again," he said, starting to stand up until Peter put a hand on his shoulder to ease him down. "Don't say it again."

"Billy Myers was a five-year-old boy who tried to save some ducks he thought were frozen on the pond," Rebecca explained. "He fell through the ice and almost drowned. Except my dad ran out onto that ice and rescued that boy from the water, and then resuscitated him before anybody could call 911. It's what inspired me to study medicine."

"I had no idea," Peter said in admiration. "Why don't you want anyone to know that?"

"Because that's only part of the story," Harry sulked.

"No," Rebecca said. "That is the story."

"I don't understand," Peter said.

"Robert Deacon Myers, his full name and the only name I think of when someone mentions him, didn't need to be saved," Harry said. "In 1992, at the age of 20, he robbed and killed a gas station clerk before driving over to his girlfriend's house to kill her parents so they could elope. After that, they set out across the state and were tied to all sort of heinous crimes."

"I never heard of that," Peter said.

"Of course you haven't. You didn't grow up in Nebraska," Harry said. "The state only tried Robert Deacon Myers for the first three murders and then swept the other stuff away. But we know better. The first woman governor of our great state wasn't going to sit idly by and allow Kansas to be saddled with another Starkweather scandal — not when the first three convictions were enough to earn Myers the death penalty anyway."

Peter grimaced. He had never heard of Myers, but he knew of Starkweather. Charlie Starkweather was a spree killer who murdered at least eleven people across Nebraska and Wyoming in the 1950s, starting with a service station attendant who wouldn't sell him a stuffed animal and then the family of his fourteen-year-old girlfriend, Caril Fugate.

The similarities between the Myers story and Starkweather story immediately struck Peter. He wondered if

Myers had modeled himself after the original homicidal couple, taking bits and pieces from the litany of films they had possibly inspired — The Sadist, Badlands, Kalifornia, and Natural Born Killers among them.

"That's who I saved. He was another Charlie Starkweather, maybe even Starkweather reincarnate," he muttered before looking up at his daughter. "I can't believe you even brought it up."

"We've been over this before," she said. "You aren't responsible for what he did fifteen years after you saved him."

"Oh no," Harry said, looking at Peter. "Let's say you're a British soldier serving in France when you come across a wounded German. You could shoot him, but you decide to spare his life and let him escape. Maybe you feel pretty good about yourself. Maybe you pat yourself on the back. Maybe you change your mind twenty-one years later when the man you let go ends the world as we knew it by starting World War II."

"Robert Myers didn't end the world as we know it," Rebecca said.

"No," Harry said. "He just ended my world."

For the first time since he met Rebecca's father, Peter could empathize. Harry wasn't bitter about living an ordinary life so his daughter could have an extraordinary one. He was haunted by knowing his one heroic moment was also his most tragic.

"I have to agree with Rebecca," Peter said quietly. "Life is riddled with ambiguous outcomes. You may as well lay the blame on his great-grandfather for having children. Who knows what other consequences may have occurred if you had let him drown.”

“Dad, see?” She was squeezing his hand.

“I’m 78 years old.” He frowned. “What do I know?”

“You know how to raise a daughter,” Peter offered.

“I wasn’t asking you, I was asking myself,” Harry said. “I know I like the bookstore at the mall better. That’s what I know.”

Rebecca’s shoulders slumped in defeat as Peter tried to give her a reassuring raised eyebrow. It’s all right, he thought. Give him time to process what I said. Heck, we could all use some time to process everything that was said.

“Okay, let’s get you home,” she said.

Peter grabbed the books Rebecca had picked out and walked them over to the register. Rebecca helped her father to the car. The air outside still held the crispness of early spring. When they got to the car, she turned around and hugged him tightly.

“What was that for?” he asked.

“That was for the fifteen years you saw yourself as a hero,” she said. “It was the light that guided me through high school and my first four years of college. I couldn’t have done it without you after mom died. And if I do half as good raising my daughter as you raised me, I consider myself blessed."

“So, you’re finally pregnant?”

“Yes,” she beamed.

“I was wondering when you were going to tell me.”

“You knew?”

"One of the books you asked Peter to buy is about raising babies, isn't it?" he asked and then winked. "I'm old and stubborn, but not slow and stupid."

"Are you happy for us?"

"Ambiguous outcomes." He chuckled. "I'm happy that you're happy."

They hugged again, longer this time, and with more reciprocity. By the time Peter joined them, they were waiting for him in the car. And while he was surprised to see Harry sitting in the front seat when he came out, Peter knew where he sat didn't matter.

THE SWEEPER

Mississippi 1972

In the early fall of 1972, Medford Evans made the rashest decision of his life. He loaded up his family and all their belongings into a light blue Volkswagen minibus and headed south before the first midwestern snowfall. His wife protested at first, but her young filmmaker husband had the upper hand, claiming this was the only chance she would ever have to meet his extended family.

They would stay for winter, like snowbirds, and then migrate north again in the spring. That seemed like just about the right amount of time to Medford. With McGovern out for busing, civil rights, and thousand-dollar giveaways, he anticipated plenty of sit-ins, boycotts, and protests. He could cobble a film about rural racism during a heated election year and then accept the teaching contract he was offered in New Haven.

After all, Mississippi was among the last to resist school integration, holding out until the 1970 U.S. Supreme Court decision that dismantled all "separate but equal" school systems. Despite how swiftly desegregation happened after the ruling, Mississippi somehow escaped all the violence that plagued the 1960s. But Medford guessed that might change before the election. There must still be pent-up anger over the court ruling that forced compliance, he surmised.

"Times are changing," Medford told his wife. "They're just not changing fast enough."

He desperately wanted to be part of the movement, enough to hastily paint a peace symbol in white on the back passenger's side of the minibus a week before their departure. His wife protested about this decision too, fearing for their son's safety, but Medford shook it off as too hard to undo. Let them stop me, he said. Let them.

His wish came true while passing through Tennessee. A county deputy sheriff pulled him over, curious why another Yankee agitator was looking for trouble in his state. The officer didn't believe the peace symbol came with the bus, but politely told Medford to keep on keeping on.

"Watch your speed now, son," said he told Medford. "People who rush about can find themselves in all kinds of trouble down here."

"I'll take it under advisement, officer," he said before slowly pulling away.

"You do that," said the officer with a hat tip.

After that, the trip was uneventful, a slow and methodically winding tree-lined drive through small towns nobody ever heard of like Doskie, Burnsville, or Leedy. His cousins lived outside Parlor, another tiny township without the benefit of a main street or downtown. Like many of them, most were defined by a small cluster of buildings. A general store, gas station, and Baptist church had sprung up around one of the many crossroads that crisscrossed the state.

"This is it," Medford said to his wife, a grin sweeping across his face as he pulled into the gas station. "My cousins live closer to Mackeys Creek. But this is, for better or worse, Parlor, Mississippi."

"Looks nice," June hesitated. "Quiet, maybe."

"Let's hope not too quiet," Medford said, thinking of his film again. "Why don't you take Robert inside for a treat."

Medford took his time, talking to the gas station attendant and getting his bearings. He had only visited Parlor once before in his life. He was only ten years old when his uncle died of the flu, and his memory of the family trip for the funeral of his mother's brother was fuzzy.

Neither the gas station nor the church had been built back then, making the general store seem out of place. What he did remember were the two flags flanking the front doors. An American flag on one side and the Mississippi state flag, with its Confederate battle standard, standing alongside in unity and silent defiance. These flags, the statue of the store's namesake Confederate Colonel Evander Grier just inside the front doors, and the long candy counter where he and his cousins would pick out ten candies for a penny stood out to him like beacons in the fog of time.

While the microbus was being tended to by the attendant, Medford crossed the street and headed toward the front doors to see how much he remembered. He felt like a rudderless boy returning as a purposeful man. He would be the one to smother Mississippi's smoldering hatred by sharing it with the world.

It was only the squeak of a loose floorboard as he crossed the threshold that changed his thinking and slowed him down. June had turned to look at him, casting a warm smile as she helped Robert pick out candy from a long counter fronted by out-of-place casserole pans.

An older man was helping them. He wore his glasses upon a deeply receding hairline. He wore a grayish-blue store smock, not unlike the ones Medford remembered from his boyhood. The man was explaining the finer points of each flavor to his son, who was rapt with attention.

"Good afternoon," the clerk said, looking up with a smile. "And let me be the first thank you for bringing your fine family into Grier's General Store."

"Thank you," Medford said, smiling back at the man before giving the statue to his left an uncomfortable glance.

"They have cinnamon sticks," his son beamed at him before pressing his hands to the glass again.

"I remember," Medford said, surveying the store as he crossed over.

Behind the counter, Grier's General was stocked floor-to-ceiling with cans, jars, and boxes of grocery items — a haphazard blend of name brands and homemade recipes. They had stacked paper products on top, with some dangling off after the clerk or someone else had hastily retrieved a case for a customer without benefiting from a step stool.

From the counter, he could look out over the rest of the store, an eclectic assortment of shelves with produce in the front that morphed into what Medford might describe as country convenience. The hammers, saws, and other hardware were pegged to the back wall. A black man was meandering between the aisles with a push broom, humming something softly that Medford couldn't quite make out.

"It looks the same," Medford said. "The store, I mean. I came here a few times as a kid."

"Well, you know what they say," he said. "If it ain't broke."

"Don't fix it," he finished.

"So what brings you back to Parlor, Mr. Evans?"

"Oh," Medford managed before an apparent explanation occurred to him. "My wife told you. That makes sense."

"Pardon?"

"Nothing," he stumbled. "I mean, we're visiting family. The Crages?"

"Oh, Jack or Earnest?"

"Both, really," he said.

"So, are you staying at the new house or the old house?"

"I'm not sure," he said. "I imagine the old house. It's the only one I remember."

"Earnest's place then," he said. "I have a pickup for his wife Bessie if you want to take it out for me. It would save them a trip."

"Of course," Medford said. "And you are?"

"Mr. Homily," he said, extending a hand. "Lark, if you want."

"Nice to meet you," Medford said.

"You might also take along a bottle of punch," Lark said, motioning behind the counter. "And I know Earnest and Bessie do love a strawberry rhubarb pie if you can manage. That is why you stopped in, isn't it? Didn't want to pull in empty-handed."

"Yes," Medford said unconvincingly. "Good idea."

"You're welcome to start a tab if you're planning to stay awhile," he offered. "The Crages are pillars of this community, fine boys with fine families."

"No, I'll pay cash today," he said and then reconsidered. "But we are planning to stay awhile, through the holidays and maybe winter."

"Good," Lark said. "Good for you."

"I was also wondering if you know anybody who's hiring?" Medford asked. "I mean, I have a project, but having some walking-around money, well, you know."

"Oh, what project?" Lark asked.

"I'm a filmmaker," he said.

"Filmmaker," Lark considered. "You mean like Hollywood?"

"Yes and no," Medford said. "I'm making a documentary. Who knows? Maybe I could include the store and get it some exposure."

"I don't know," Lark smiled. "We're not all that fancy. But I might be able to help you with walking around money. Why don't you talk to Bill over there and see if he could use a delivery driver."

"That would be swell," Medford said. "It might even be perfect if the hours are irregular."

"Talk to Bill. If he says okay, I'm in too," Lark said with a wink. "Don't worry, though. He won't bite. He's too old."

"I'll do that," Medford said, before turning to his wife. "I won't be but a few minutes."

There was a different kind of skip in his step as he approached the old black man who looked lost in thought as much as the work. Medford was already angling the delivery job as an opportunity. It would put him in contact with scores of people from across the area, folks who might be willing to go on the record. Who knew? Maybe old Bill would be the first one.

"Hello," Medford said. "Hello, I say."

"Hello yourself," Bill said, looking up with a grin, missing one tooth behind the canine. "How can I help you, mister?"

"Bill, my name is Mr. Evans, and your boss wants me to pick up with you as a delivery driver. He said to talk to you first," Medford explained. "What do you think?"

"Is that so?" asked Bill. "That's what he said?"

"Yes, sir," he said. "What do you think? Should I take the job?"

"Well, let me think about that." Bill paused, scratching his chin. "You look fit. Are you up for hard work?"

"Sure," Medford said, mocking a muscle. "Take a look."

"I don't know. You look a little averse to it," Bill bit his lip. "You have a good attitude?"

"The best," Medford said with a laugh like it was a joke between good friends.

"You averse to early mornings or late evenings?" asked Bill as Medford nodded along. "And you ought to know it doesn't pay much."

"Well, I don't know," said Medford. "How much do you get paid?"

"Me?" Bill laughed. "I don't get paid nothin' until Mr. Homily gets paid."

"What?" Medford shook his head. "That's not right."

"I know," said Bill. "And I'm the first one in and the last one to leave, puttering around with the broom, stocking shelves, dusting that statue, taking care of maintenance, you name it."

"You can't find another job?" asked Medford.

"Get another job? Would you look at me?" Bill asked with a frown. "No, sir, I'm like a slave to this old store, and I have been all my life."

"Would you go on camera and say that?" Medford asked, seizing the opportunity. "I mean, we could talk about it all. Maybe I could even film you dusting that old statue. I'm a filmmaker, and this is exactly the kind of thing people want to see."

"Yeah?" Bill looked at him, wheels turning behind those glassy eyes. "I can see that now. I bet you would. You would bring the whole Department of Justice down here, just like they did when Kennedy was in office."

"Yes, that's exactly what I'm thinking," Medford said, dropping his voice to a whisper. "If we shine a big enough light on places like this ... who knows what will happen. Are you in with me?"

Bill considered for a moment. Then he paused and retrieved his broom.

"No, sir, I don't believe I am in with you," said Bill.

"What?" said Medford, confused by the quick reversal. "Are you afraid?"

"Mr. Evans," Bill said with some irritation, "Mr. Homily didn't send you over to me because he's the boss. He sent you over because I'm the boss."

Medford stared at him, jaw slack as if he was just told a joke with a sour punchline.

"And all that I just told you? That's how it is when you're the boss," Bill said. "You wake up early, do the work nobody wants to do, take your pay after everybody else is paid, and go home tired after you count the till and lock the doors."

"I'm sorry, I didn't know," Medford said. "And I guess I don't understand. If you own the store, then why keep that statue?"

"Mr. Evans," Bill continued, shaking his head, "I knew the moment you drove up in that bus out there that I was looking at a book-smart Yankee dandy, coming to save me and mine. But what you don't understand about the south is that it's complicated. Sure, when you see that statue, you see some wild-eyed reb. But me, I only see my grandfather. And once upon a time, this store and all the land around and behind this store belonged to him. And my name, William Grier, belonged to him too."

Medford shrank at the lesson, glancing over at his wife and son to see if they witnessed his embarrassment. They didn't. Lark was still helping them sort the candy.

"I can't use a racist working in my store," he said. "But because you are related to the Crages and I'm the forgiving sort, I am willing to give you a second chance."

"Sir?"

"I'm going to put in a word for you with Dean Hall," said Bill. "He owns an old blacksmith shop in town. It's probably harder work than you are used to, but you'll learn something about rural America and the people who live here. And if you make a film about that, you'll learn something about yourself too."

"I appreciate it," Medford said.

"Black, white, young, old, sober, drunk," said Bill. "We all find out who we are and how to endure. But more than that, we learn that there ain't but one way to love yourself, and that's to treat everybody as right as you can. That's what we have here in Parlor. It would be good of you to know it."

Medford didn't know what else to say, so he thanked Bill Grier with an extended hand. Bill laughed and said Medford wouldn't thank him for standing over hot metalwork, but he would develop some character, resourcefulness, and fortitude — salt-of-the-earth qualities he could pass on to his son.

When he returned to the counter, he told Lark that Bill had other plans for the position but thanked him anyway. He paid cash for their order and they walked back to the bus.

"We learned a little about the history of the area," June lit up when they got outside. "Did you know Evander Grier was Bill's grandfather?"

"Yes. And I learned something else too," he confessed. "When there is sweeping to be done in the south, somebody's going to get it done."

June didn't have any idea what that meant, but she smiled at him anyway. After picking through the candy with Robert, she was starting to warm up to the south but not in the way she had imagined. Medford was too, but for a different reason.

ALL THE ODDS

North Carolina 2020

Katie Noland sat on the barstool and peered into the depths of her Manhattan, meditating on the amber swirls where the ice met the bourbon. She quietly huffed, laughing at herself over how stupid she must look, like a gypsy reading tea leaves.

She wrecked the pattern with a stir of her swizzle. There were no secrets in there. She tipped it back.

"Another, Chuck," she said, letting the weight of the empty glass add emphasis. "Another."

How many did that make? She couldn't remember.

"Are you sure?" he asked quietly, trying not to attract the attention of another lonely soul sitting a few seats over.

"You've got my keys, anyway," she said. "It's my brother's birthday."

"All right," he said. "Just take it easy."

"You're a sport," she said, before talking to no one in particular. "My baby brother. He almost didn't make it, you know. He failed his first test in the womb — the one that looks for chromosome problems. He failed. Or maybe it was my mother who failed."

Chuck set the drink down in front of her and scooped up the bills that she had set down. He had asked her if she wanted to start a tab earlier. She had said no, never intending to stay as long as she had.

"Yep, it's what they do," she said. "They take a blood test, and if they don't like the results, they stick this giant needle right into the woman's stomach and draw out some fluids. The only problem is that there's a risk of miscarriage."

Neither the man to her right nor Chuck said anything, but they were both listening now. Chuck fished the extra dollar that she had pushed onto the rubber-lined bar gutter on his side of the bar, and he leaned against it.

It was a slow night. Katie was drunk but not unattractive.

"So they give you these odds," she continued, louder. "There was a one-in-fifty chance he had Down syndrome and there was one-in-a-hundred chance of a miscarriage. Our folks got in a fight about it, with my father saying, 'So what, so what?' and my mother crying all night after looking up all sorts of terrible things on the Internet."

Her father was so mad that he refused to go with her mother for the scheduled amniocentesis. Katie had gone instead, holding her mother's hand and looking her in the eyes as they inserted the longest needle she had ever seen into her mother's abdomen. She remembered thinking that maybe her dad was right.

God had a plan. She was eight years old.

"Did he?" said the man.

"Did he what?"

"Did he have Down syndrome?" he asked.

"No," she said. "We thought he was perfectly normal until about the time I moved out of the house. Chuck knows. He's heard me yap about it now and again, haven't you?"

"Only when you order Manhattans," Chuck said.

"That's about right." She laughed at Chuck and cast a serious glance at the man. "He's bipolar."

"I'm sorry," he said.

"Not as sorry as my parents," she said.

Chuck took his weight off the bar. It was a story he didn't want to hear again.

"Did you know a bipolar parent has a fifteen to twenty-five percent chance of having a bipolar child?" she asked. "Probably not. Most bipolar parents don't tell anybody it runs in the family until one of their children has their first manic episode."

"No," he said. "I didn't know that."

"You would think they would warn you," said Katie. "But they don't. They didn't warn me, and they didn't warn Jimmy. Either one of us could have been a ticking time bomb. It was him."

"What happened?"

"Nothing the first time," she said. "And then everything, over time."

He burned the house down. Her parents were sleeping. The arson inspector said they didn't even know. The smoke probably asphyxiated them before they woke up, they said. She didn't believe them but didn't think it mattered. Either way, it was horrible.

Katie had been away at the time, enrolled at Clemson University after sporadically taking a few community college credits while living at home. She knew she would never finish at home, which is why she finally moved out.

"That's why I earned some college debt but not my degree," she said. "I had to move back and get an apartment. It was just him and me for a while."

The man had moved a seat closer, sliding his drink along with him. She could smell the cigarettes on him. He must be desperate, she thought.

"Was it always like that?" he asked.

"With Jimmy? No," she said. "He didn't light anything on fire until I moved out. The first time was to punish me for doing it in the first place. He pulled a box filled with my memories from the garage and torched it on the backyard barbecue."

"Well, that's crazy," he said. "I can't even imagine. I was an only child."

She grimaced. Was he even listening? Usually, men were good listeners on the pickup until they didn't agree with you. Maybe she wasn't trying hard enough. She hadn't asked him for a thing. Then again, she wasn't planning on going home with anyone.

"You missed out," she said. "For all the bad, there were a lot of good memories too. Before all these things happened, we were just kids. I mean, I was a lot older, but we were kids who did kid things. We'd play little pranks on each other, like tossing some cold water over the shower curtain or covering cauliflower with mashed potatoes. Things you hate when it happens, and then you end up missing them when they don't."

He wasn't interested anymore. She didn't blame him. Nobody cared about Jimmy, not then and not now. She was ready to leave, but then Chuck came back to check on her.

"Still good?" Chuck said.

Chuck was more her type than the lonely heart. But she wasn't here for either of them, she reminded herself. She was here for Jimmy, and the Manhattan had always been his drink.

"Did I ever tell you about the last time I talked to him?" she teased. "I'll tell you."

Katie had been working at this crazy inner-city diner with a '50s vibe. Things had picked up at the place when a new owner had bought it, and he offered anyone who wanted extra hours the chance to grab them before he staffed up. She was just finishing one of these double shifts and was ready to leave when her brother called.

"Katie," he said. "Katie, it's me. Jimmy."

Jimmy always sounded like her father when he was drunk. And he was drunk.

"It's me. Jimmy."

She could hear he was at a pub, with a hockey game droning on in the background. There were other noises too. Glasses were clinking together at the bar. Pool balls striking each other from across the room. The occasional shout of jubilance and clapping hands. She could almost smell the stale beer and cigarettes over the line.

"I have to talk to you about something," he said. "It's important."

There was a pause on her end, and then she passed the phone to a coworker.

"Would you take a message for me?" she said. "Just take a message."

She had worked a double shift. She was too exhausted to deal with him.

"Just take a message." She shrugged, taking a step toward the door.

"What about your phone?" Julie asked.

"I'll pick it up tomorrow," Katie said.

"All right," Julie said, taking the phone as Jimmy started shouting at them.

"You know, better yet," Katie said, disconnecting the call with her thumb. "Take a message if he calls back."

Katie stopped talking and stared absently into her drink again, looking into a small whirlpool of chaos she was making with the swizzle stick. The bartender and the man on the neighboring stool were looking at her now, frozen in apprehension.

"That was the last time I ever heard his voice," said Katie. "All he needed was a ride, and I couldn't be bothered. So he tried to drive home on his own. What are the odds?"

It wasn't a question anyone could answer. The Carolinas always came up near the top for alcohol-impaired driving deaths. Around Lenore, where he died, more than 53 percent of all vehicle fatalities were related to alcohol.

"I just wanted him to be somebody else's problem for a change. I've got plenty without him," she said before interrupting herself. "Hey, do you mind turning that up?"

"What?" Chuck said, following her finger to the television. "Oh yeah, right."

Governor Roy Cooper was on the news station. She hadn't voted for him, mainly because he always whined when he spoke. She preferred South Carolina's Henry McMaster who spoke so slow and deliberate. He was a true southern gentleman, she always thought.

"This virus is easy to transmit, so we need prevention," he was saying. "It's the single most important thing you can do right now. It means staying away from each other, washing hands, coughing into the elbow. Those simple things can save lives, including your own. You only have to turn on your TV or your iPhone to see what happens. So we're issuing a 'stay home order' starting tomorrow and until April 30 based on the nature and evolving scope of the pandemic."

There were some gasps of surprise behind her. The few people who had remained in the bar had all stopped to listen, but Katie had already tuned it out. He was talking to them like they were five. It was too much to process, so she finished her drink.

"Yo, Chuck," she said, snapping her fingers to get his attention again. "My keys."

"What? All right," he said, sliding them across the bar. "Are you okay to drive?"

She smiled and nodded, snatching them up with little effort. He wasn't looking; eyes fixed on the television. She stood up and shifted her weight to her right foot to compensate for the room's unexpected tilt.

"Happy birthday, Jimmy," she said to no one. "What are the odds?"

She turned around, shuffled toward the entrance, thankful that there would only be a few cars left in the parking lot. The State Farm office and transmission shop were long closed. And by the news on the television, they might not open tomorrow.

THE THIN BLUE LINE

Ohio 2017

Miranda May hurried down S. Roadway past Jake's Sandwich Shop, and her stomach growled, acknowledging the smell of pizza coming out of the oven and the sign's promise of hot corned beef illuminating the sidewalk. She was hungry but didn't have time to stop tonight. She was running late, and the last train out of Tower City Station would be leaving soon.

She usually didn't have to rush, but cleaning up after the office party in the building where she worked had taken longer than expected. While she didn't begrudge them their fun, she sure wished somebody would have considered the mess they left for the cleaning crew.

She crossed the street and glanced to her left while passing under the canopies of Jack Casino. It was late enough now that the typically lively venue looked pacified, except for three underage boys loitering outside the front door.

She shook her head, wondering if their parents were inside punching slot machines, and pressed ahead, barely noticing how two of the boys were pushing the younger one in her direction. All three were laughing, but the boy being forced was resisting whatever dare the other two had pressed.

"You should be home in bed on a school night," she whispered to herself as she turned inside the building. "If you were my boys, you'd be home already."

Only her boys weren't home. They were grown men, raising families of their own. Del was working as a hydrologist in Columbus, and Franklin lived across the water in Detroit. He was the underachiever in her book, working for 3M as a hand packer. But who knows? Their father did pretty well working his way up from a store clerk to supermarket manager before his heart attack ten years ago.

Miranda frowned as she approached the escalator. It was out of service, so she had to take the stairs. She sidestepped her way down most of them, one step at a time to take some pressure off her knees. Then it was through the turnstile and onto the light rail platform.

The train was already waiting, doors open. She navigated toward the closest car but veered away from it when she spied the vagrant talking to himself in the middle seats. She would never make it to a car in the front so she shuffled into the last car, winded after her two-block flight, and yet relieved that she had made it.

She took a seat in the empty car and waited for the doors to close. She didn't like sitting alone so late at night but knew how to make the best of it. The absence of any other passengers meant being able to massage those tired feet. She started taking her left shoe off as the doors slid closed, until a boy — the younger one she had seen on the street just seconds before — slipped in toward the back of the car.

He was alone but looked over his shoulder onto the platform as if he expected the others to join him. When nobody did, he hung onto the back of a seat, absorbing the jolt of the train with a relaxed sway as it started moving. Then, unexpectedly, he looked in her direction once it did. He smiled at her from the far end of the car like a friend might peer at someone they recognize. He was even smiling as he slowly walked toward her, his hands alternating on the seat backs as he went.

"Can I help you?" she asked as he shortened the distance between them.

"You know." He smiled.

"I know," she huffed, eyebrows pinched as if she whiffed something foul. "I remember when my boys were about your age. They always wanted something every time we went to the grocery store. You know what I told them?"

He wasn't smiling any longer.

"I told them no." She shrugged.

He grimaced, first at her, and then when the train hit a bump. He put his hands on the backs of both seats to steady himself. The lights flickered.

"I don't want to hurt you," he whispered.

She looked at him, her eyes meeting his. They were wide and uncertain. His mouth pursed, lips tight. He raised his right hand back, left hand squeezing the other seat for balance.

The lights flickered again when the train hit a second unexpected bump. This time it was bigger, lifting him off his feet. Miranda unconsciously reached down and grabbed the seat below, her body rising as the car twisted and shifted on the tracks.

They could hear a roar of metal ahead of them, showers of sparks streaming outside the windows. Miranda found herself in the air, strangely disconnected from the seat and falling. She saw the boy was also separated from any boundary or barrier, arms swinging and reaching around like a rag doll. Everything was spinning before the lights blinked out and Miranda with them.

When the car came to a stop, the boy found that the side of their train car had become the floor. Dull emergency lights cut through a blanket of haze. He could taste it, a fine grit accompanying the smell of torn metal and tar, an acrid barbecue that felt heavy in his lungs.

His head hurt, but he felt confident enough to try his footing. He was lucky, luckier than the woman who challenged him. She was partly buried under the seats that she had been sitting on, one hand sticking out and still clutching her handbag. He shuffled over to it.

"Crazy lady," he said, pulling the strap free from her hands.

He slung it over his shoulder and turned to exit the car. As he stepped on a shattered sheet of laminated glass, he heard a dull groan behind him. He looked back and saw her hand moving. She was alive.

He shook his head and took another step out, but stopped when she moaned again. He held still.

"Don't leave me, Del," she whispered after him.

He shook his head and squeezed his eyes shut. He didn't know who Del was, but he also knew he couldn't leave her. He turned around and began working her free of the debris.

Helping her out of the train car was difficult, but they managed it together. He helped her sit down again so she could catch her breath. He joined her, and the pair of them sat that way for several minutes before the operator and a plainclothes officer from the forward cars worked their way back.

"Help is already on its way," said the officer, giving the handbag slung across the boy's shoulder a suspicious look. "Everything all right here?"

"Yes, officer," Miranda said. "This young boy ... what's your name?"

"Derrick," he hesitated.

"Derrick just saved my life," she said.

"Is that so?" asked the officer, eyeing him but then finding reassurance in Miranda's face. "Good for you, son. You're a hero. Well, you two sit tight. There are more injuries up front."

When the two men left, Derrick let out a breath. He looked at Miranda, disbelief creeping across his face, and handed her handbag back.

"I don't understand," he said. "Why did you say I was a hero?"

"Because you are," she smiled softly. "Because you are."

It took more than an hour for emergency personnel to reach them. They sat together patiently, Miranda sharing a few pieces of Starbust candy to pass the time. When she told him she would be fine, and he could go if he wanted, Derrick said it was all right. He'd rather be a hero a little longer.

WHEELS GO ROUND

Tennessee 1977

"**D**o you ever wonder where they are going?" she asked the boy next to her.

"Who?"

"All of them," she said, digging into her light blue Kånken backpack at her feet and coming up with a partially eaten bag of Doritos. "Want some?"

"I'm not a fan," he said, but then remembered he hadn't eaten lunch.

"Suit yourself," she said, slipping a chip into her mouth and crunching down.

"A few, maybe," he said, embarrassed to change his mind.

She didn't look at him, but he could see the smile form on her face, cheese powder decorating one corner. She tilted the bag enough in his direction so he could reach. He pulled out a small handful, more than he intended.

"Like that man over there." She pointed with her chin. "He looks like a drug smuggler, secretly harboring marijuana in a tote bag filled with old women's clothes."

He followed her chin to the man with sun-soaked skin. His black hair was mid-length and curly, partly hidden under a straw hat. His mustache was broad, supported by an anchor beard. The man was reaching in the bag as they watched, rearranging its contents. The boy wasn't exactly sure, but would later swear there was a glimpse of a sea-foam green nightgown with dingy white lace sticking out.

"Y'all a mind reader or something?" he asked with a grin. "How could you know that?"

"Nothing like that. Just open your eyes." She laughed. "See the homeless man sitting on the floor in front of the storage lockers?"

He looked over in the direction toward the older man sitting on the floor despite the coffee stains and cigarette butts. It was hard to look at him, back pressed against the once-light-blue lockers that had now turned dreary and gray with age.

"Yes, I see him," he said.

"He's not a wino or anything," she said. "He's a Vietnam vet who lost himself in the swampy bottomland around the Hatchie River for a few a years. Inside the locker he's resting against is his most valuable possession in the world. It's a letter from his daughter in Wilmington asking, 'When you coming home, Dad?'"

"I don't get it," the boy said. "Why is he sitting on the floor?"

"He met his best friend on the ship going over there. They lived in the same tent together, went into the An-Khê together, and their nine-man squad was pinned down by automatic fire in a field near the Cambodian border a few weeks later. Only three men came out. His best friend took two in the chest. He took one in the leg, which is why he likes sitting on the floor to keep it stretched out."

The boy gave a hoot of disbelief, stiffening in his seat. "Y'all made that up."

"His best friend's name was Daniel Davis," she said, absently. "He didn't die right away."

"Why is he here now?" the boy whispered.

She looked at him. "He's going home."

"Right," he said disbelievingly.

"He's not the only one with a letter," she said, tilting the Doritos in his direction again.

"Pardon?" he said, reflexively touching his front pocket where he kept it.

"It's all right," she said. "I didn't mean to spook you. You only pulled it out a half-dozen times before I came over and sat down."

"You were watching me?"

"I watch everybody," she said matter-of-factly. "This station is filled with stories. Triumphs and tragedies. People coming home. People leaving home. People finding fortune. People tempting fate."

He looked at her more intently now — straight, light brown hair with one braid in the front to keep it in place. Her skin was fair and her eyes pale blue, offset only by a few flecks of gold. She looked out of place in her simple pressed dress, a stark contrast to the older girls in dark eyeshadow and miniskirts who were arguing with the guy at the ticket counter.

"The letter is from a girl I know," he admitted. "Her name is Sheryl, but she went by Sheri. We met about a year ago. She was a runaway."

He had been at a middle school barn party and immediately been taken by a blonde girl in a sleeveless button-down print blouse and short skirt with a zipper riding up the front. He kept shyly and awkwardly circling her most of the night until his classmate Melissa introduced them. She was from somewhere close to Cincinnati, which made sense because nobody wore anything like that in Jackson.

The two of them hit it off and spent most of the night together, but seldom alone. Melissa was always hovering close by, excited that her friend had met someone, but cautious about letting them get too close. He thought that was strange, especially when Melissa asked something that made his head spin more than the hint of whiskey in his Coke.

"Johnny boy," she said. "I can't take Sheri home with me tonight. Do you think she can crash at your place?'

"What do you mean?" he said.

"She's stayed with us a week, and my parents are getting suspicious," she said. "Maybe she can stay with you a few days while things get sorted?"

"Maybe you should take her home," he said.

"She can't go home," Melissa said, socking him in the arm. "She ran away from home. Haven't you been paying attention?"

"I guess not," he said, before turning to Sheri. "Is that what you want?"

Sheri just smiled and shrugged. She must need a place to stay, he thought.

"Yeah, I guess," he said. "I'll have to sneak you in. My folks would never go for it."

The term "folks" was an oversimplification. He was an extra wheel on what would have otherwise been a tricycle: his mother, stepfather, and half-sister. They had grudgingly taken him in when his aunt, his mother's older sister, had died. The transition seemed natural on the front end — they had a big console television, long hair, and considered church on Sunday secondary to sleeping in late. But things took a turn when his mother decided to undo any spoiling by her sister with punishments, imprisonments, and sometimes punches.

"Sneak her in, then," Melissa said. "Just promise me no funny business."

He wasn't sure what she meant, but he understood her perfectly fine once he and Sheri climbed in through his bedroom window, laughing quietly and gently kissing each other in the dark.

She stayed with him four days before she decided to turn herself in and head home. His folks found out on the second day when he tried to take a plate of eggs he had made into his bedroom. They had rules about where food could be consumed.

He was shocked when they let her stay, cautiously warning them away from any "funny business" until she sorted things out. She eventually did sort them out — or, more precisely, Melissa's parents did when they learned Sheri had merely been shuffled to another home. Sheri was on a bus within the hour. And here he was, one year later.

"Your aunt must have loved you very much," she said.

"Why would you say that?"

"I've seen it before," she said. "Boys like you. They find unconditional love from a parent, a grandparent, an aunt. Unconditional love is hard to find, harder to lose, and even harder to lose again."

"Yeah, she loved me," he said, thinking back to the last time he saw her in the hospital. Her skin was gray, her lips blue and cracked. Her eyes were sunken. Her spirit was shrinking away. "And then she was gone."

"Your mom probably loves you too," she said. "But only if you measure up to some idea she has of you."

"Something like that," he said. "What she wants is for me to be anything except some idea she has of my father."

She nodded, slowly rolling the top of the Doritos bag closed.

"And Sheri," she said. "She hasn't asked you to be anything. That's unconditional too."

He shook his head.

"Hey, I have to go," she said, standing up. "Just remember, if you do head up, it would be better for you get off in Richwood, and then hitch rides over to Withamsville. You don't want to take the bus all the way into Cincinnati. They'll be waiting for you there."

"Oh, I can't make it to Withamsville." He frowned. "I don't have enough to get outside Tennessee."

"Learn to look a little harder." She laughed, holding the ticket in her hand up higher.

"What's this?" he asked, running a thumb over the stamp as he read it. "One-way ticket to Cincinnati?"

"I was thinking about running away today, too," she said. "But I like your plan better. You're not running away as much as you're running to someone. I think that's nice."

He stared at the ticket. And then he looked up at her, his eyes glossy over the impossibility of it.

"Go on," she said. "They'll be calling that bus number soon."

He stood up with her, and she hugged him.

"I don't know how to thank you," he said. "Heck, I don't even know your name."

"Go find your fortune, Johnny boy. Go tempt fate." She squeezed him.

She let go and gently pushed him toward the doors, where the buses were waiting. He knew well enough, having talked up to them a half-dozen times throughout the day. The attendant rolled his eyes in recognition as Johnny approached.

"Look, kid, I already told you, this ain't a charity," he said, pointing to other doors. "No fare, no ticket. No ticket, no access. And that means the exit is that-a-way."

Johnny held out the ticket and leaned in. His hand was shaking, which was why the attendant finally looked down.

"All right," he said. "Where'd you get this, anyway?"

Johnny looked over his shoulder. The girl with straight brown hair and a light blue Kånken backpack was gone. She was lost in a sea of strangers, people coming home and leaving home. They were all equals, set adrift to parts unknown.

"See that girl over there, the one clutching her over-sized handbag? She looks desperate, but she's not," he said, picking one of them out in the crowd. "She's on the next bus to New York where she earned a full-ride scholarship to Columbia University. Ever hear of it? It's an Ivy League school."

"What is that supposed to mean?"

"It means you need to look a little harder," Johnny said with a smile. "My bus is boarding."

"All right, don't be a smarty," the attendant said, opening the door. "Nobody likes a smarty."

Johnny didn't say another word. He stepped through into a bright blue of a clear but humid day. People were already stepping up into the big blue-white-and-silver bus that would take them all to Cincinnati. But Johnny couldn't help but to wonder where they were really going.

ABOUT THE AUTHOR

Richard R. Becker is an award-winning American writer. He continues to expand many of these stories for inclusion in another collection, with some evolving into larger works.

When he is not writing fiction, Richard works as a creative strategist for Copywrite, Ink., a 30-year-old strategic communications firm with clients that have included government agencies and Fortune 500 companies.

Aside from work, he enjoys a broad range of activities: travel, hiking, exercise, photography, and illustration. To follow his work, find him @RichBecker on Twitter and Instagram or @byRichardBecker on Facebook.